the fruit of
my lipstick

the fruit of
my lipstick

an All About Us novel

SHELLEY ADINA

NEW YORK
BOSTON
NASHVILLE

Scriptures noted KJV are taken from the King James Version of the Bible.

Scripture quotations marked NIV are taken from the *Holy Bible, New International Version®*. NIV®. Copyright © 1973, 1978, 1984 by International Bible Society. Used by permission of Zondervan Publishing House. All rights reserved.

Translation from *Island: Poetry and History of Chinese Immigrants on Angel Island, 1910–1940*, Him Mark Lai et al, University of Washington Press, 1999. ISBN 0-295-97109-6. Used with permission.

FaithWords
Hachette Book Group USA
237 Park Avenue
New York, NY 10017

Visit our Web site at www.faithwords.com.

FaithWords is a division of Hachette Book Group USA, Inc.
The FaithWords name and logo are trademarks of Hachette Book Group USA.

Printed in the United States of America

First Edition: August 2008
10 9 8 7 6 5 4 3 2 1

Library of Congress Cataloging-in-Publication Data

Adina, Shelley.
    The fruit of my lipstick : an all about us novel / Shelley Adina. —1st ed.
       p. cm.
    Summary: Brilliant student and devout Christian Gillian Chang gets her first boyfriend during her junior year at Spencer Academy in San Francisco, but her friends think he may not be good for her.
    ISBN-13: 978-0-446-17797-9
    ISBN-10: 0-446-17797-0
    [1. Interpersonal relations—Fiction. 2. Cheating—Fiction. 3. High schools—Fiction.
4. Schools—Fiction. 5. Chinese Americans—Fiction. 6. Christian life—Fiction.] I. Title.
    PZ7.A261147Fr 2008
    [Fic] —dc22   2007041318

For Camy Tang, Jackie Yau, and Nancy Kato—
When you laugh, I hear Gillian.

acknowledgments

My thanks go to Jim Birdsong, science teacher at Monta Vista High School, who gave me so much help by answering my questions about high school physics and the Physics Olympiad.

To Karina Hou and Gen Wei Zhuo, longtime friends who give me just the right Mandarin words when I need them, no matter how weird the questions are. *Xie-xie!*

To the Looney Bin (Catherine Mulvany, Tina Ferraro, Cindy Procter-King, Susan Gable, Anita Staley, and Diana Duncan), thank you for brainstorming, endless inspiration and support, and the Top Five list.

To my team at FaithWords—Anne Goldsmith Horch and Katie Moore for editorial; Jody Waldrup and his team in the art department for the covers; Lori Quinn, Preston Cannon, and Heather Stevens in Marketing; and Bob Castillo in production—you're amazing. Thanks so much for all the work behind the scenes.

To my agent, Jennifer Jackson, who is as good at pulling me down off the chandelier as she is at handing me virtual roses. Thanks aren't enough.

To Jeff, who gives me grilled salmon on a cedar plank, a brand-new chicken chateau, and excellent proofreading. A man of parts. *Wo ai ni.*

the fruit of
my lipstick

"By him therefore let us offer the sacrifice of praise to God continually, that is, the fruit of our lips giving thanks to his name. But to do good and to communicate forget not: for with such sacrifices God is well pleased."
—*Hebrews 13:15–16 (KJV)*

chapter 1

Top Five Clues That He's the One

1. He's smart, which is why he's dating you and not the queen of the snob mob.
2. He knows he's hot, but he thinks you're hotter.
3. He'd rather listen to you than to himself.
4. You're in on his jokes—not the butt of them.
5. He always gives you the last cookie in the box.

THE NEW YEAR . . . when a young girl's heart turns to new beginnings, weight loss, and a new term of *chemistry!* Whew! Got that little squee out of my system. But you may as well know right now that science and music are what I do, and they tend to come up a lot in conversation. Sometimes my friends think this is good, like when I'm helping them cram for an exam. Sometimes they just think I'm a geek. But that's okay. My name is Gillian Frances Jiao-Lan Chang, and since Lissa was brave enough to fall on her sword and spill what happened last fall, I guess I can't do anything less.

I'm kidding about the sword. You know that, right?

Term was set to start on the first Wednesday in January, so I flew into SFO first class from JFK on Monday. I thought I'd packed pretty efficiently, but I still exceeded the weight limit by fifty pounds. It took some doing to get me and my bags into the limo, let me tell you. But I'd found last term that I couldn't live without certain things, so they came with me. Like my sheet music and some more of my books. And warmer clothes.

You say *California* and everyone thinks *L.A.* The reality of San Francisco in the winter is that it's cold, whether the sun is shining or the fog is stealing in through the Golden Gate and blanketing the bay. A perfect excuse for a trip to Barney's to get Vera Wang's tulip-hem black wool coat, right?

I thought so, too.

Dorm, sweet dorm. I staggered through the door of the room I share with Lissa Mansfield. It's up to us to get our stuff into our rooms, so here's where it pays to be on the rowing team, I guess. Biceps are good for hauling bulging Louis Vuittons up marble staircases. But I am *so* not the athletic type. I leave that to John, the youngest of my three older brothers. He's been into gymnastics since he was, like, four, and he's training hard to make the U.S. Olympic team. I haven't seen him since I was fourteen—he trains with a coach out in Arizona.

My oldest brother, Richard, is twenty-six and works for my dad at the bank, and the second oldest, Darren—the one I'm closest to—is graduating next spring from Harvard and going straight into medical school after that.

Yeah, we're a family of overachievers. Don't hate me, okay?

I heard a thump in the hall outside and got the door open just in time to come face-to-face with a huge piece of striped fiberglass with three fins.

I stood aside to let Lissa into the room with her surfboard. She was practically bowed at the knees with the weight of the duffel slung over her shoulder, and another duffel with a big O'Neill logo waited outside. I grabbed it and swung it onto her bed.

"Welcome back, girlfriend!"

She stood the board against the wall, let the duffel drop to the floor with a thud that probably shook the chandelier in the room below us, and pulled me into a hug.

"I am so glad to see you!" Her perfect Nordic face lit up with happiness. "How was your Christmas—the parts you didn't tell me about on e-mail?"

"The usual. Too many family parties. Mom and Nai-Nai made way too much food, two of my brothers fought over the remote like they were ten years old, my dad and oldest brother bailed to go back to work early, and, oh, Nai-Nai wanted to know at least twice a day why I didn't have a boyfriend." I considered the chaos we'd just made of our pristine room. "The typical Chang holiday. What about you? Did Scotland improve after the first couple of days?"

"It was fre-e-e-zing." She slipped off her coat and tam. "And I don't just mean rainy-freezing. I mean sleet-and-icicles freezing. The first time I wore my high-heeled Louboutin boots, I nearly broke my ankle. As it was, I landed flat on my butt in the middle of the Royal Mile. Totally embarrassing."

"What's a Royal Mile? Princesses by the square foot?"

"This big broad avenue that goes through the old part of Edinburgh toward the queen's castle. Good shopping. Restaurants. Tourists. Ice." She unzipped the duffel and began pulling things out of it. "Dad was away a lot at the locations for this movie. Sometimes I went with him, and sometimes I hung out with this really adorable guy who was supposed to be somebody's production assistant but who wound up being my guide the whole time."

"It's a tough job, but someone's gotta do it."

"I made it worth his while." She flashed me a wicked grin,

but behind it I saw something else. Pain, and memory. "So." She spread her hands. "What's new around here?"

I shrugged. "I just walked in myself a few minutes ago. You probably passed the limo leaving. But if what you really want to know is whether the webcam incident is over and done with, I don't know yet."

She turned away, but not before I saw her flush pink and then blink really fast, like her contacts had just been flooded. "Let's hope so."

"You made it through last term." I tried to be encouraging. "What doesn't kill you makes you stronger, right?"

"It made one thing stronger." She pulled a cashmere scarf out of the duffel and stroked it as though it were a kitten. "I never prayed so hard in my life. Especially during finals week, remember? When those two idiots seriously thought they could force me into that storage closet and get away with it?"

"Before we left, I heard the short one was going to be on crutches for six weeks." I grinned at her. Fact of the day: Surfers are pretty good athletes. Don't mess with them. "Maybe it should be, 'What doesn't kill you makes your relationship with God stronger.'"

"That I'll agree with. Do you know if Carly's here yet?"

"Her dad was driving her up in time for supper, so she should be calling any second."

Sure enough, within a few minutes, someone knocked. "That's gotta be her." I jumped for the door and swung it open.

"Hey, *chicas!*" Carly hugged me and then Lissa. "Did you miss me?"

"Like chips miss guacamole." Lissa grinned at her. "Good break?"

She grimaced, her soft brown eyes a little sad. Clearly Christmas break isn't what it's cracked up to be in *anybody's* world.

"Dad had to go straighten out some computer chip thing in

Singapore, so Antony and I got shipped off to Veracruz. It was great to see my mom and the grandparents, but you know . . ." Her voice trailed away.

"What?" I asked. "Did you have a fight?" That's what happens at our house.

"No." She sighed, then lifted her head to look at both of us. "I think my mom has a boyfriend."

"Ewww," Lissa and I said together, with identical grimaces.

"I always kind of hoped my mom and dad would figure it out, you know? And get back together. But it looks like that's not going to happen."

I hugged her again. "I'm sorry, Carly. That stinks."

"Yeah." She straightened up, and my arm slid from her shoulders. "So, enough about me. What about you guys?"

With a quick recap, we put her in the picture. "So do you have something going with this Scottish guy?" Carly asked Lissa.

Lissa shook her head, a curtain of blonde hair falling to partially hide her face—a trick I've never quite been able to master, even though my hair hangs past my shoulders. But it's so thick and coarse, it never does what I want on the best of days. It has to be beaten into submission by a professional.

"I think I liked his accent most of all," she said. "I could just sit there and listen to him talk all day. In fact, I did. What he doesn't know about murders and wars and Edinburgh Castle and Lord This and Earl That would probably fit in my lip gloss tube."

I contrasted walking the cold streets of Edinburgh, listening to some guy drone on about history, with fighting with my brothers. Do we girls know how to have fun, or what? "Better you than me."

"I'd have loved it," Carly said. "Can you imagine walking through a castle with your own private tour guide? Especially if he's cute. It doesn't get better than that."

"Um, okay." Lissa gave her a sideways glance. "Miss A-plus in History."

"Really?" I had A-pluses in AP Chem and Math, but with anything less in those subjects, I wouldn't have been able to face my father at Christmas. As it was, he had a fit over my B in History, and the only reason I managed to achieve an A-minus in English was because of a certain person with the initials L. M.

Carly shrugged. "I like history. I like knowing what happened where, and who it happened to, and what they were wearing. Not that I've ever been anywhere very much, except Texas and Mexico."

"You'd definitely have liked Alasdair, then," Lissa said. "He knows all about what happened to whom. But the worst was having to go for tea at some freezing old stone castle that Dad was using for a set. I thought I'd lose my toes from frostbite."

"Somebody lives in the castle?" Carly looked fascinated. "Who?"

"Some earl." Lissa looked into the distance as she flipped through the PDA in her head. Then she blinked. "The Earl and Countess of Strathcairn."

"Cool!"

"Very. Forty degrees, tops. He said he had a daughter about our age, but I never met her. She heard we were coming and took off on her horse."

"*Mo guai nuer*," I said. "Rude much?"

Lissa shrugged. "Alasdair knew the family. He said Lady Lindsay does what she wants, and clearly she didn't want to meet us. Not that I cared. I was too busy having hypothermia. I've never been so glad to see the inside of a hotel room in my life. I'd have put my feet in my mug of tea if I could have."

"Well, cold or not, I still think it's cool that you met an earl," Carly said. "And I can't wait to see your dad's movie."

"Filming starts in February, so Dad won't be around much.

But Mom's big charity gig for the Babies of Somalia went off just before Christmas and was a huge success, so she'll be around a bit more." She paused. "Until she finds something else to get involved in."

"Did you meet Angelina?" I asked. Lissa's life fascinated me. To her, movie stars are her dad's coworkers, like the brokers and venture capitalists who come to the bank are my dad's coworkers. But Dad doesn't work with people who look like Orlando and Angelina, that's for sure.

"Yes, I met her. She apologized for flaking on me for the Benefactors' Day Ball. Not that I blame her. It all turned out okay in the end."

"Except for your career as Vanessa Talbot's BFF."

Lissa snorted. "Yeah. Except that."

None of us mentioned what else had crashed and burned in flames after the infamous webcam incident—her relationship with the most popular guy in school, Callum McCloud. I had a feeling that that was a scab we just didn't need to pick at.

"You don't need Vanessa Talbot," Carly said firmly. "You have us."

We exchanged a grin. "She's right," I said. "This term, it's totally all about us."

"Thank goodness for that," she said. "Come on. Let's go eat. I'm starving."

RStapleton	I heard from a mutual friend that you take care of people at midterm time.
Source10	What friend?
RStapleton	Loyola.
Source10	Been known to happen.
RStapleton	How much?
Source10	1K. Math, sciences, geography only.
RStapleton	I hate numbers.

Source10   IM me the day before to confirm.
RStapleton OK. Who are you?
RStapleton You there?

©

BY NOON THE next day, I'd hustled down to the student print shop in the basement and printed the notices I'd laid out on my Mac. I tacked them on the bulletin boards in the common rooms and classroom corridors on all four floors.

> *Christian prayer circle every Tuesday night*
> *7:00 p.m., Room 216*
> *Bring your Bible and a friend!*

"Nice work," Lissa told me when I found her and Carly in the dining room. "Love the salmon pink paper. But school hasn't officially started yet. We probably won't get a very good turnout if the first one's tonight."

"Maybe not." I bit into a succulent California roll and savored the tart, thin seaweed wrapper around the rice, avocado, and shrimp. I had to hand it to Dining Services. Their food was amazing. "But even if it's just the three of us, I can't think of a better way to start off the term, can you?"

Lissa didn't reply. The color faded from her face and she concentrated on her square ceramic plate of sushi as though it were her last meal. Carly swallowed a bite of *makizushi* with an audible gulp as it went down whole. Slowly, casually, I reached for the pepper shaker and glanced over my shoulder.

"If it isn't the holy trinity," Vanessa drawled, plastered against Brett Loyola's arm and standing so close behind us, neither Carly nor I could move. "Going to multiply the rice and fish for us?"

"Nice to see you, too, Vanessa," Lissa said coolly. "Been reading your Bible, I see."

"Hi, Brett," Carly managed, her voice about six notes higher than usual as she craned to look up at him.

He looked at her, puzzled, as if he'd seen her before somewhere but couldn't place where, and gave her a vague smile. "Hey."

I rolled my eyes. Like we hadn't spent an entire term in History together. Like Carly didn't light up like a Christmas tree every time she passed a paper to him, or maneuvered her way into a study group that had him in it. Honestly. I don't know how that guy got past the entrance requirements.

Oh, wait. Silly me. Daddy probably made a nice big donation to the athletics department, and they waved Brett through Admissions with a grateful smile.

"Have any of you seen Callum?" Vanessa inquired sweetly. "I'm dying to see him. I hear he spent Christmas skiing at their place in Vail with his sisters and his new girlfriend. No parents."

"He's a day student." I glanced at Lissa to see how she was taking this, but she'd leaned over to the table behind her to snag a bunch of napkins. "Why would he be eating here?"

"To see all his friends, of course. I guess that's why *you* haven't seen him."

"Neither have you, if you're asking where he is." Poor Vanessa. I hope she's never on a debating team. It could get humiliating.

But what she lacked in logic she made up for in venom. She ignored me and gushed, "I love your outfit, Lissa. I'm sure Callum would, too. That is, if he were still speaking to you."

I barely restrained myself from giving Vanessa an elbow in the stomach. But Lissa had come a long way since her ugly breakup with a guy who didn't deserve her. Vanessa had no idea who she was dealing with—Lissa with an army of angels at her back was a scary thing.

She pinned Vanessa with a stare as cold as fresh snow.

"You mean you haven't told him yet that *you* made that video?" She shook her head. "Naughty Vanessa, lying to your friends like that." A big smile and a meaningful glance at Brett. "But then, they're probably used to it."

Vanessa opened her mouth to say something scathing, when a tall, lanky guy elbowed past her to put his sushi dishes on the table next to mine. Six feet of sheer brilliance, with blue eyes and brown hair cropped short so he didn't have to deal with it. A mind so sharp, he put even the overachievers here in the shade—but in spite of that, a guy who'd started coming to prayer circle last term. Who could fluster me with a look, and wipe my brain completely blank with just a smile.

Lucas Hayes.

"Hey, Vanessa, Brett."

My jaw sagged in surprise, and I snapped it shut on my mouthful of rice, hoping he hadn't seen. Since when was the king of the science geeks on speaking terms with the popular crowd?

To add to the astonishment, the two of them stepped back, as if to give him some space. "Yo, Einstein." Brett grinned and they shook hands.

"Hi, Lucas." Vanessa glanced from him to me to our dishes sitting next to each other. "I didn't know you were friends with these people."

He shrugged. "There's a lot you don't know about me."

"That could change. Why don't you come and sit with us?" she asked. Brett looked longingly at the sushi bar and tugged on her arm. She ignored him. "We're much more fun. We don't sing hymns and save souls."

"So I've heard. Did you make it into Trig?"

"Of course." She tossed her gleaming sheet of hair over one shoulder. "Thanks to you."

I couldn't keep quiet another second. "You *tutored* her?" I asked him, trying not to squeak.

He picked up a piece of California roll and popped it in his mouth, nodding. "All last term." He glanced at Vanessa. "Contrary to popular opinion, she isn't all looks."

Oh, gack. Way TMI. Vanessa smiled as though she'd won this and all other possible arguments now and in the future, world without end, amen. "Come on, Lucas. Hold our table for us while Brett and I get our food. I want to talk to you about something anyway."

He shrugged and picked up his dishes while she and Brett swanned away. "See you at prayer circle," he said to me. "I saw the signs. Same time and place, right?"

I could only nod as he headed for the table in the middle of the big window looking out on the quad. The one no one else dared to sit at, in case they risked the derision and social ostracism that would follow.

The empty seat on my right seemed even emptier. How could he do that? How could he just dump us and then say he'd see us at prayer circle? Shouldn't he want to eat with the people he prayed with?

"It's okay, Gillian," Carly whispered. "At least he's coming."

"And Vanessa isn't," Lissa put in with satisfaction.

"I'm not so sure I want him to, now," I said. I looked at my sushi and my stomach sort of lurched. Ugh. I pushed it away.

And here I'd been feeling so superior to Carly and her unrequited yen for Brett. I was just as bad, and this proved it. What else could explain this sick feeling in my middle?

Two hours later, while Lissa, Carly, and I shoved aside the canvases and whatnot that had accumulated in Room 216 over the break, making enough room for half a dozen people to sit, I'd almost talked myself into not caring whether Lucas came or not.

And then he stepped through the door and I realized my body was more honest than my brain. I sucked in a breath and my heart began to pound.

Oh, yeah. You so don't care.

Travis, who must have arrived during dinner, trickled in behind him, and then Shani Hanna, who moved with the confidence of an Arabian queen, arrived with a couple of sophomores I didn't know. Her hair, tinted bronze and caught up at the crown of her head, tumbled to her shoulders in corkscrew curls. I fingered my own arrow-straight mop that wouldn't hold a curl if you threatened it with death.

Okay, stop feeling sorry for yourself, would you? Enough is enough.

"Hey, everyone, thanks for coming," I said brightly, getting to my feet. "I'm Gillian Chang. Why don't the newbies introduce themselves, and then we'll get started?"

The sophomores told us their names, and I found out Travis's last name was Fanshaw. And the dots connected. Of course he'd been assigned as Lucas's roommate—he's like this Chemistry genius. If it weren't for Lucas, *he'd* be the king of the science geeks. Sometimes science people have a hard time reconciling scientific method with faith. If they were here at prayer circle, maybe Travis and Lucas were among the lucky few who figured science was a form of worship, of marveling at the amazement that is creation. I mean, if Lucas was one of those guys who got a kick out of arguing with the Earth Sciences prof, I wouldn't even be able to date him.

Not that there was any possibility of that.

As our prayers went up one by one, quietly from people like Carly and brash and uncomfortably from people like Travis and the sophomores, I wished that dating was the kind of thing I could pray about.

But I don't think God has my social life on His to-do list.

chapter 2

THE FIRST TWO WEEKS of school are always a big schmozzle of adjusting to new instructors' expectations, figuring out what they want, seeing who's in your classes, making schedules . . . you know the drill. I kind of like it. I like a lot of things going on—comes from growing up in New York, I guess. The city that never sleeps.

By the end of January, our first set of midterms was over—or thirdterms, I suppose you could call them, since we got two sets of them before finals. When you're in your second term of AP Chem, one more set of exams is no laughing matter. Getting A's in Chemistry is like running a marathon. You have to pace yourself, and you have to have rest stops.

For me, music is rest. I can pound the stuffing out of the antique Steinway in the deserted assembly hall late at night and come out of there feeling like my neurons have been given a shot of electricity, making them fire the way they should.

My mother tells me I should just eat my vegetables, get some rest, and stop drinking coffee. Moms have to say stuff like that. The reality is, if I didn't have the piano, I think I'd go nuts from everything my family expects from me. They're on the other side of the country, and yet I can feel the cloud of expectation from here, the way you can see the fog hovering on the hills west of San Francisco before it rolls over them and blots them out.

It's just there, waiting. Like my parents.

It scares me sometimes.

I mean, getting top grades and winning music prizes has been my focus since I was old enough to span an octave with my hand. Side note: my brothers have short fingers, thanks to my dad, so much to their disgust, I turned out to be better at piano than they are. Before they started their careers, they played things like violin and oboe, and I had the keyboard to myself. No competition.

My parents always told me that boys could wait—that while I was in school I had to get the grades so I could get into a good college.

Right. Like the family really cares what I do, when my brothers are out there being insanely successful. I, after all, am just a girl, and the youngest at that. According to Nai-Nai—my grandmother—my job is to find a man like them, get married as soon as possible, and start popping out insanely successful children.

I don't think Nai-Nai understands that I'm only a high school junior. It's not like she was married the minute she hit puberty, but she was born in the old country and she's pretty set in her beliefs about how things should be. My mom says I'm just like her. Which I totally don't get.

My only focus certainly isn't to land a man. Cone of silence, okay? If any of my family learns about my hopeless thing for Lucas, I will never, ever hear the end of it. Between my dad's demands that I think about nothing but chemistry and numbers and getting into an Ivy League college, and my grandmother's nagging about getting married, I'm being pulled from both ends as it is. One of these days I'll wind up snapping in the middle.

This term my free period was still on Tuesdays and Thursdays,

right after breakfast. I snagged a table in the library, which is this
huge, wood-paneled room that reaches up for two stories. It has
heavy wood tables and study carrels and big windows that let in
the light, and it's a lot quieter than the common room or the dining room, but the librarian doesn't let you bring any liquids in,
unfortunately. Lissa had Spanish and Carly had her core class—
History of the Ancient World, right up her alley—so I was on my
own with fifty minutes to look over my thirdterm results and see
where I could have done better.

Math and Chem were okay. I'd missed a couple of things that
were worthy of a smack on the forehead, but on the whole, not
bad. History—ow. Eighty-two percent, and I had no idea why I'd
gotten a bunch of the questions wrong. Maybe Carly would look
it over with me if I bribed her. She probably would even if I didn't.
That kid hasn't got a malicious or unkind bone in her body.

Which kind of makes her a target for people like Brett, who
has the gall to ask her to fetch and carry for him, but doesn't have
the guts to give her more than a smile in return. I guess a smile is
enough for some people.

That's about all she's going to get, since Vanessa Talbot has a
lock on the rest of him.

Contemplating the test printout unhappily, I slowly became
aware that someone was standing on the other side of my table.

"Okay if I sit here?" Lucas Hayes asked when I looked up.

My heart jumped so hard it practically bounced off my chin. I
straightened and wondered frantically if there was residual foam
on my upper lip from the cappuccino I'd knocked back to finish it
before I came in. Or if he'd get up and go sit with Vanessa in the
unlikely event she darkened the library doorway.

"Sure, help yourself," I mumbled. He swung his silver-and-
black backpack into the chair next to him, and I licked my upper
lip as unobtrusively as possible.

"How'd you do?" He indicated my printouts with a lift of his chin.

I spread them like a hand of cards. "Okay. Not so great in History, though."

He nodded. "Me, too—only in my case it's English. The first thing the instructor told us was that there's no right or wrong answer in literary analysis. I'm thinking, what am I doing here, then?"

I laughed. We were having an actual conversation. Maybe he wouldn't get up and leave. "I know. If anyone can say anything they want, what's the point? Other than holding together a logical argument, which you could do regardless."

He shook his head. "If you can just make stuff up and get a grade for it, we all might as well be writing fiction."

"I'm lucky at least that my roomie is good at English. We have a deal. She helps me with my papers and I help her with Biology."

"Your roomie's Surfing Barbie, right?"

I blinked. Was he cracking a joke? "What?"

"You know. Mansfield. I saw her dragging a surfboard up the stairs at the beginning of term. That must be rough."

Not following. "Rough?"

"Yeah. No wonder you have to help her with Bio. Vanessa says you should get community service credits for assisting the disabled."

Whoa. A little too much time spent at the window table, buddy boy.

"Lissa's not like that. She may not be great at Biology, but she's going for the Hearst Prize in English this year." The Hearst was a scholarship open to sophomores and juniors in San Francisco, given to the student with the highest scoring essay in the competition. I picked up steam. "Not only that, she's my friend, and she's in prayer circle with you. Two good reasons you shouldn't let Vanessa do your thinking for you."

He blinked like phosphorus had reacted with air and hit flash point under his nose.

I was on a roll now. "I think you're a nice guy and all, but if you're talking about Lissa like that behind her back, you've obviously been spending too much time with the wrong people. Not to mention you owe her an apology."

"I'm not," he finally got out. "Don't talk to me like that. Don't talk to me at all."

He yanked his backpack off the chair and stalked out, leaving me sitting there churning with a combination of anger and confusion—and a healthy dose of regret.

Maybe Dad was right. At this rate, I'd do better sticking to chemistry.

RStapleton   Thanks, man. 80%—best ever.
Source10   No prob. One large to PayPal.
RStapleton   Already done.

⊚

I HAD THREE periods before lunch in which to contemplate the sorry state of my love life.

By the end of first period, I'd cycled through annoyance and had arrived at that glum place where I concluded I was just a dork where guys were concerned. Halfway through Global Studies, I was beginning to wonder if Lucas had really meant it about never talking to him again.

Because I liked talking to him (today notwithstanding). He was interesting and funny, and, most important, he didn't feel as though he had to compete with me. The guy's brain is a force of nature all on its own—the people here who were competing for the Physics Olympiad had taken their scores with a gulp and as much grace as they could muster when he walked off with a near-perfect qualifying score.

This place is no slouch in the academics department to start with. The competition for openings is fierce, what with all the Silicon Valley moguls wanting their kids to get a leg up, and the old money here in Pacific Heights reserving their children's places the moment they're conceived. It's part of the reason I'm here—that, and because Spencer is as far as you can get from Manhattan without falling off the continent.

So when I say Lucas can beat the best brains on the left coast, I'm not exaggerating. And even after he aced the entrance exam, he was completely cool about it.

"It's something to put on my application to Stanford," he explained the other day, when I stopped in at the physics lab on my way to class. "Placing in all these state competitions isn't enough. Even making the Olympiad semifinals in March won't be enough. It would just be me in a field of two hundred. Big deal. But if I make the top five and get a place on the U.S. team, go to Mexico, and win against competitors from all over the world, that's going to stand out, both in university and when I take on the job market."

Snort. Like Stanford or any business after he graduated wouldn't be lucky to have him, with or without a medal.

And this is the guy I had just alienated by standing up for my friend.

Headdesk. Gillian, Gillian. You don't need another chemistry class; you need to go to charm school.

Needless to say, I was feeling pretty droopy by the time I got my salad and joined Lissa and Carly at our table for lunch. I was all ready to tell my tale of woe when both Carly and I got a good look at Lissa's face. She looked like she'd gotten a mouthful of lemon juice when she'd been expecting a nice Odwalla pomegranate cooler.

"The weirdest thing just happened," she said, lowering her voice so we had to lean in to hear. Not that anyone could pick out her words in the noisy dining room. "You know Lucas Hayes? The one who tutored Vanessa?"

I leaned in a little more.

"He stopped me in the hall on my way here."

"And?" Carly prompted since I'd temporarily lost my power of speech. Yeah, I know. Hard to believe.

"And he apologized to me."

My mouth fell open. "What for?" Like I didn't know.

She shook her head and shrugged, picking up her Odwalla. "No idea. He said he'd done something wrong and he wanted to apologize."

"What'd you say?" Carly wanted to know.

"I said okay. I mean, what do you say to a random thing like that?"

"But what did he do that needed an apology?"

Another shrug. "I don't know. I don't have any classes with the guy. I only see him across the room here and at prayer circle—and he doesn't really talk there."

"He called you Surfing Barbie," I said.

Lissa put her drink down, and she and Carly stared at me. Then Lissa started to laugh. "Surfing Barbie? Now I've heard everything."

"I heard it, and I didn't like it much." I didn't know whether to feel sour about losing Lucas's friendship over something that just made her laugh, or to be amazed he'd taken me at my word.

Even if it was the last word he'd let me say to him.

"What do you mean?" Lissa asked.

"I called him on it. He said a few other things too—" which I was not going to repeat "—and I told him he owed you an apology."

"He apologized to me because you told him to?" Lissa's eyes rounded. "Wow. You must've been scary."

"Or he really likes you," Carly put in. "A guy would never do something like that unless what a girl thought mattered to him."

"Trust me, it's not that," I said. "He basically told me I couldn't talk to him like that and to never speak to him again." My shoulders slumped and I bit into my forkful of mixed greens and cranberries without enthusiasm. What I needed here was comfort food, not rabbit food. A whole panful of my grandmother's *shui jao* with rice vinegar, to start.

"But he did it," Carly said. "And you've got to believe it wasn't easy for him."

"Apologizing to Surfing Barbie," Lissa said, acid tinging the edges of her smile. "That had to be tough."

"He doesn't know you at all, even though he prays with us," I said. "I told him you were going for the Hearst Prize, but I don't think he believed me. I feel stupid now for . . ." I stopped.

"For what?" Carly's eyes sparkled. "Liking him?"

"Aha!" Lissa leaned in and pointed her sun-dried tomato panini at me. "I knew something was going on with you two. Why else do I keep seeing you when I walk by the physics lab?"

"There is nothing going on." There, that sounded convincing. "Especially now."

But I had to wonder.

chapter 3

WHEN YOUR EMOTIONS are all stirred up, there's only one thing to do.

I found an empty practice room and stretched my hands into the opening chords of Harris's "Introduction and Fugato." It wasn't very challenging—I'd memorized it when I was twelve—but it was emotional, which made it the perfect frustration piece. I pounded out its chords and runs, warming up and zoning out.

Which is why I freaked out of my skin when I slammed out the finale and someone said my name from the doorway.

"Lucas!" I clapped a hand to my throat. "You scared me."

"Sorry." He moved a step into the room, which is big enough to let the sound out of the piano, but not big enough to hold more than a couple of people. "I thought you were done."

"I was. I just didn't see you."

He smiled. "I could tell. You were pretty focused."

Silence fell as I took my foot off the pedal and the final chord died away. Were we talking again? What was he doing here? Should I say something? What?

He cleared his throat and jammed his hands into his pockets. "You were right."

About what? His badmouthing Lissa? Or something else?

"I shouldn't have said what I said about your friend. I apologized to her."

"She told me. She didn't know what your reason was, though."

"Did you tell her?"

"Yes. She thought it was funny, you calling her Surfing Barbie."

His eyebrows rose above the tortoiseshell frames of his glasses. "Funny?"

"Yes, Lucas," I said. "Someone thought your opinion of them was funny. But I appreciate what you did. It took guts."

Either there was something really interesting on the carpet, or he couldn't look me in the eye. "I didn't want you to be mad at me."

This was news. "Oh. That must be why you told me never to speak to you again."

"That was stupid, too. I was sorry as soon as I said it."

A happy little spiral of warmth started up in my chest. "So we're cool, then?"

He nodded, and tried on a tentative smile, as if he didn't do it much. It changed his whole face—softening its angles and making you realize he had a very nice mouth. Not that I make it a habit to notice stuff like that. I respect a guy for his brain, not his looks. But still.

"Are you finished?" he asked. "Do you . . . want to walk down Fillmore and get something to drink?"

I glanced at the clock over the door. "What, now?"

"Sure. If you want."

"But it's half an hour to lights out."

"So?"

"So when our dorm mistress checks, I'll get a demerit." For such a smart guy, he really had a problem with the small stuff.

He shrugged. "It's just a demerit. Something for the staff in the office to count. Meaningless."

"Maybe to you, but with enough of them, they'll call my parents. And believe me, that's grief I don't need." I got up and closed the piano lid. "Come on."

The music rooms, which rang with people practicing from seven in the morning until after dinner, were all silent and dark as we walked down the hall toward the dorm wing. The happy glow in my chest was still there. He'd asked me out! So it was only a coffee or a soda or something, and I couldn't go, but it was the thought that counted, right? Maybe I wasn't such a loser after all.

"Is your family pretty hard-nosed about rules?" He held open the double door that led into the main hall with its parquet floors and giant chandelier, and the common rooms for each of the dorms. Wow. I couldn't remember the last time anyone had held a door for me. In New York, a man is more likely to get a stiletto through his foot than a "thank you" for trying it.

"It's not so much the rules as it is excelling in everything. A demerit means you're not doing that. And explaining why to my dad is not much fun."

"I know what you mean," he said. "When I won the mathematics medal in eighth grade, all my dad could say was, 'You got a C-plus in gym.'"

"Some people aren't happy with themselves, and they can't be happy for other people." I wasn't sure if that was my dad's problem, or if I was just one more Chang with performance issues in a family of type-A personalities.

"Oh, he was happy," Lucas said. "He just would have been happier if I'd been more—as they say—well rounded."

"I'm not well rounded, either, then. Phys. Ed. is something to endure. Though I have to say, it's more interesting out here than on the East Coast. No more stupid field hockey. I took sailing last term and got an A."

An accomplishment I was pretty proud of, if you want the truth. It's not everyone who can capsize a sailboat on purpose, get it right way up again, climb into it, and sail it back to the dock. But, working together, Lissa and I got it done.

"Yeah?" Was that admiration in his eyes? I hoped so. "I'm a landlubber, I guess. Give me a track and let me run on it, and I'm good."

By now we'd reached our common room, which was as far as anyone with a Y chromosome could go in the girls' dorm wing. I passed it and headed for the stairs.

"See you tomorrow, Lucas."

He nodded. "Maybe we can still go out sometime. When's your free period?"

"Tuesdays and Thursdays after breakfast."

Call me smitten, but that disappointed look made me feel good. "Mine's in the middle of the afternoon."

"We'll work something out." I pulled a piece of paper out of my pocket, borrowed his pen, and wrote my cell number on it. "Call me. Good night."

"'Night, Gillian." And he stood there, watching me walk up the stairs.

Good thing he couldn't see me walking down the hall to my room. Because I'm sure I was floating at least two inches off the ground.

I couldn't wait to tell Lissa and Carly that Lucas and I were friends again. I found the two of them in Carly's room, surfing fashion Web sites.

"What's that?" I squinted at the screen, which was smaller than mine. "*Entertainment Weekly*?"

Carly shook her head. "Fashionista.com. And guess who's front and center, as usual?"

"Don't tell me." I sat on the edge of the bed to look. "Talbot and Miller light up San Francisco Fashion Week," trilled the headline.

Sienna Miller, in town to promote her Twenty8Twelve spring line of frocks, gives teenage socialite Vanessa Talbot some closet advice in the front row at the Rodarte show. Talbot, who attends the elite Spencer Academy in Pacific Heights, is the daughter of former U.N. Secretary-General Victor Talbot and the globetrotting Principessa di Firenze, now married to London financier Bernard Cook.

"Look at that dress." Carly sighed. "Where did she get the Rodarte watercolor chiffon before the show?"

"She's connected," Lissa retorted. "A walking billboard. Look, here it is on SeenOn.com, too. The designers probably sent it to her so she'd be photographed in it. I wish I'd seen the courier coming up the drive. I'd have hijacked it."

"Guys. Can we talk about real life here for a minute?" I asked.

Lissa laughed and turned to me. "What's up?"

I moved the Mac out of the way and got comfortable on the empty bed. "I was practicing downstairs, and guess who came and found me?"

Carly looked at Lissa. "One guess."

A finger to her chin, Lissa tilted her head and said in a blonde voice, "Oh, please, can I have two guesses?"

"Everyone's a comedian," I said to Carly's Chingon poster above the headboard, but I couldn't keep the smile off my face. "Lucas asked me out."

"Whoa!" Lissa sat back on her hands.

"Well, not on a real date or anything," I said hastily. "Just on a walk down the hill to get something to drink. But seeing as he's only ever talked about planetary volume and the properties of light with me before, this is real progress."

"How romantic." Carly sighed.

I gave her a narrow glance and she giggled, then leaned across the space between the beds to give me a hug.

I hope I hid my surprise. I mean, mine is not a family of huggers, as you can probably imagine. I don't go around greeting people that way, and I'm not used to it when others do. But I guess Carly's family is different. She hugs Lissa and me when she sees us on Mondays, after the weekends she spends with her dad. She hugs stray dogs on the street if they wag their tails at her. And you can bet your lunch money she'd hug Brett Loyola for no reason at all, if she got the chance.

So I hugged her back. After all, being asked out by the most brilliant guy in school is worth celebrating, right?

"So when are you going?" Lissa asked.

Good question. "I don't know. I mean, just the fact that he asked me at all is pretty amazing. I didn't want to scare him off by getting out my iPhone and calendaring it on the spot, you know?"

"Don't let him think about it too long," Lissa warned. "If you let it lie for more than a day, he'll get cold feet and think maybe it was a fluke. Or that you're not really interested—you were just being nice."

Uh-oh. I hadn't thought of that. "I'm such a dork," I moaned, dropping my head into both hands. "What if he thinks I'm pushy?"

"You?" Carly asked in faux amazement.

"Okay, he probably already knows I am," I admitted. "But I don't want to be, with him."

I know I come off all loud and confident with people. Maybe I should have listened to my mother and Nai-Nai, who were always telling me I was too noisy, that I talked back too much, that I wasn't respectful enough. I tried to be what they wanted me to be at home, but once I got out here, words and noise all came spilling out as if they had been penned up inside me for weeks.

I mean, other than when they're telling me to be quiet, my dad and my brothers don't really notice me at home. I guess that's why I make up for it when I'm out on my own. But it's one thing to put on a secure front. It's another thing to be secure behind the front. I think that's where the Lord has His work cut out for Him.

Lissa reached over and patted my knee. "Be yourself. That's what he likes, right? Don't try to be something you're not, because, take it from me, you'll screw up, and usually at the exact wrong time."

"Sounds like the voice of experience," I said.

"It is. I dated this guy in Santa Barbara for months. I tried to be everything he wanted in a girl. The problem was, he didn't want who I really was. He wanted the fake. Then when I relaxed one day, thinking, hey, we're a couple now, and didn't act in character, it was over." She paused for a second. "Of course, what I didn't know was that he had the homecoming queen on autodial, too. And she was really what he wanted. Not me."

I thought about that as they clicked through the rest of the pictures from Fashion Week on the Web sites. I tuned their voices out and leaned against Carly's colorful folk-art appliqué pillows, wondering if I should dial it down a little. After all, Lucas wasn't a noisy person. He was studious, intellectual. When we talked, it was conversation he liked, not smart-mouth remarks. I could still be myself, couldn't I . . . while I acted more like the girl I was at home?

On the other hand, this could just be a whole bunch of speculation on my part. I hardly knew the guy—but what I knew of him, I liked, even if he ate lunch once in a while with Vanessa's crowd. That was probably just politics, anyway. And he'd put himself out

there by apologizing to Lissa for me, hadn't he? This wasn't something just anyone would do. Carly was right. He'd done it because
my opinion mattered to him.

And if my opinion mattered, maybe I mattered to him, too.

I hugged my knees, seeing the gorgeous clothes on the screen
and yet not seeing them at all.

*Father God, help me know what to do. If it's Your will that Lucas
and I get together, help me listen to Your voice. Help me get it right.
And thank You, Father. I've never had a serious boyfriend before. I don't
know why it's happening now, but I'm glad it's Lucas.*

GChang   Friday tomorrow. Half day. How about that walk?

LHayes   OK. Have experiment running. Say 3pm?

GChang   Meet you on the front steps.

LHayes   Look forward to it.

chapter 4

....

✉

To: GChang@spenceracad.edu
From: IsabelCZhuo@gmail.com
Date: January 22, 2009
Re: New Year

Hey Gillian,

Give me a call at work tomorrow as soon as you can. We're
coming up to the City for the big New Year's parade (24th) and you
absolutely must join us. It will be a wonderful family time, especially
since Michael is an Ox (stubborn little guy) and this is his year! There
might even be a red envelope in it for you :) Call me!

Love, Aunt Isabel
....

⑥

PENCER DOESN'T OFFER sailing and rowing in the winter, mostly because no one would go to class. Who wants to freeze their rears off in the water in the middle of January? So for my Phys. Ed. elective, I was stuck with the choice of an individual program with a personal trainer, or team sports—soccer, volleyball, or the cross-country running team. Being allergic to mud and rain, I opted for volleyball, where I could at least make up for size with my defensive skills.

Not to mention a really deceptive bump that fools them every time.

Lissa might look like she belongs on the cover of *Glamour*, but she's not afraid of weather. She came into the shower room splashed with mud to the knees as I was changing to go out on the court.

With a quick look to make sure no one was listening, I whispered, "It's today. Lucas wants to go at three."

Lissa grinned. "Excellent. Did you bring it up, or did he?"

"I did. It was a risk, but it worked."

She began to strip out of her muddy soccer uniform. "Nah, it wasn't. He's got a thing for you. No risk involved."

I hoped she was right. Thinking about it played havoc with my game, and the coach had to remind me twice to get back behind the line when I served the ball. But, hey, who cares about where the line is, when you have Lucas Hayes in your future?

After lunch, when the day students left for home and the ones who had weekend plans took off in everything from rented Hummers to their own BMWs, Lissa and Carly decided they'd be practical and do their Spanish homework until I got back. Carly's dad always sent a car to take her down to San Jose, but it wouldn't be here until six. She was so jazzed about my date that she'd probably stall the car until midnight if she had to, long enough to hear all about it.

Nothing like a little performance anxiety, huh?

I didn't know what was worse—waiting for three o'clock to get here, or waiting for it all to be over.

Chill, Gillian, I told myself as I waited on the front steps. *You're walking down the hill and back. Big deal. It's not like you're going to the opera or meeting his parents or something huge like that. It's a latte or a smoothie, not an eternal commitment.*

I decided to call my aunt, so I'd at least look as though I was doing something productive.

"Gillian, hi!" Isabel greeted me and took me off speakerphone. "I was hoping you'd gotten my e-mail in time."

"I'm OCD about mail. But with classes and everything, I haven't had a chance to call until now."

"I'm so looking forward to tomorrow. We're going to have dinner at the Slanted Door—we've had reservations for months—and then go to some friends' to watch the parade from their balcony."

"It sounds great!" I'd heard that San Francisco's Chinese community really went all out for New Year's—and the parade was bigger even than New York's. It got televised on all the networks and everything. And I had to admit, the big street dragons were always my favorite part. When I was little, we were in Taipei one winter, and the whole city just exploded with fireworks and parades and craziness. A big dragon pretended to bite me as I stood with my parents on the sidewalk, and my mother told people proudly that, instead of screaming, I tried to grab its glittery streamer beard.

"We'll pick you up at the school at six," Isabel said.

"Perfect! I'll be on the front steps. In fact, that's where I am right now, waiting for a friend."

"Ooh, hot date?"

"No. Just a smoothie with someone from class." No way was I saying a word about Lucas. The news would blast to New York, bounce off my mom's ear, and she'd be on the phone to me in five minutes.

"Well, have fun, and we'll see you tomorrow."

I disconnected and, a second later, heard running shoes slap on the steps behind me. "Hey." Dressed in jeans and a yellow anorak, Lucas loped over.

"Hey." I gave him a big smile.

"Ready?"

It was on the tip of my tongue to say, "And waiting," but that might have sounded critical. "Yes."

He had a long stride, and I found myself having to make the occasional hop and skip to keep up. Finally, halfway down the hill, I said, "Slow down, Lucas. Where's the fire?"

"Sorry." He cut his stride in half and I was able to match my steps to his. "You have such a big personality, I forget how small you are."

I fought the urge to press my palms to my cheeks. Was that me? Blushing? "Five-two isn't that small," I finally said. "My friend Carly is the same."

"Is she the Mexican girl with all the curly hair?"

"She's about as Mexican as I am Chinese," I said dryly. "It's not like we're fresh off the boat, you know."

"So do you have a Chinese name?"

Come on, Gillian. Open up. This guy could be your boyfriend. You don't need to be shy with him.

"Jiao-Lan. It means 'fragrant orchid.'"

"Jiao-Lan." The syllables sounded odd on his tongue. "So are you?" He stopped outside a black lacquered door and held it open for me. I breathed in the fragrance of oranges and fresh-cut grass and realized he'd brought me to a juice bar. And not your standard chain, either.

"Am I what?"

"A fragrant orchid?"

"Only after a hard game of volleyball," I cracked, and he laughed.

I kept it simple and ordered an apricot colada. He went for

carrot juice with ginger. What an adventurous pair. The point, though, was that he paid for both of them, putting a hand on my arm when I went to dig my wallet out of my little Stella McCartney satchel.

I can't even tell you the last time a guy other than my father paid for something on my behalf. Try never.

He led the way to a skinny black table whose chairs had extra-long legs, and then my brain proceeded to seize up. I could not think of a single thing to say. Me—the one my brothers call a magpie on amphetamines. If I prayed for something to talk about, would the Lord take me seriously?

And then I had it.

"Have you found a church to go to around here?"

"A church?"

Why did he sound so surprised? "Yes. You come to prayer circle, so . . ." Oh, help. Had I just made a great big incorrect assumption? "You're a believer, right?"

"Oh, sure," he said, and I felt my spine wilt with relief. "You just took me by surprise. Most girls want to talk about other girls and clothes and stuff."

"With you? I don't think so. Quantum theory, maybe. Definitely not Theory jeans."

"Whatever those are. But to answer you, yeah, I go to Pacific Heights Community Church, about three blocks that way." He pointed east. "Have you been there?"

I shook my head. "I kind of got into the habit of going out to Marin with Lissa and her mom. We go to this funky little clapboard church and then to their place for lunch."

"Lissa's parents live here and she's in boarding school?" He looked puzzled.

I explained about the movie and the two-year stint. "Where's your family?"

"Phoenix, mostly. But my dad is scientist-in-residence at a think tank in Palo Alto, so we figured it would be good exposure for me if I were closer. Sometimes on the weekends, if he's running models on the mainframe, he lets me assist. That way I get to know the scientists unofficially, and it will pay off later, when I graduate."

"You mean you might get a summer job?"

"No. When I graduate from Stanford. I'll be doing a double major—physics and computer science—and I plan to get my doctorate in eight years, max. I want to do computer modeling in astrophysics."

"Wow. And here I thought I was ambitious, taking AP classes so I'd get into . . . somewhere that isn't Harvard."

"What's the matter with Harvard? It's a great school."

"There's nothing the matter with it. Except that my brother went there."

"Is he some kind of troublemaker? Will he harm your chances?"

The thought of Darren doing anything like that made me smile. "Of course not. But I'd be competing with him, see. So I'm not going anywhere near the place."

The light from overhead fell into his eyes. A deep sky blue. Loved the color. "I don't get it," he said.

"Because I'd have to meet or beat every one of his grades. That's just the way my family is. I have to work twice as hard to be equal to or better than the boys. At least in my dad's eyes."

"Oh." Understanding dawned. "Why bother? I mean, I'm pretty competitive myself, but that's extreme. Why don't they let you do what you want?"

Why indeed. "It's kind of hard to explain." Again, I thought of the fog, out there waiting. "My parents' expectations are pretty high."

He made a face and took a sip of his carrot juice. "I know how that is. My dad thinks I'll be stepping into his chair when he's ready to retire."

"Is that what you want?" Lucas was talking retirement, and he wasn't even out of high school. Good grief. At least my parents hadn't mapped out my whole life for me. Just the beginning of it.

"It's a place to start," he said. "Maybe not his chair, but if they want me bad enough they'll make a position for me."

"Lucky you. I'll be on my own. But that's a long way out there. I'm just glad thirdterms are over."

He got my made-up word right away. We were so on the same wavelength. "Me, too. Not that they were a problem. Except English for me and History for you."

"They were enough of a problem. Chemistry isn't easy for me. I have to work hard at it."

He gave me a quizzical glance. "Yeah? I thought you were a natural at science. And music."

Was he using the personal *you* or the collective? Maybe I'd give him a little test. "Like most Asians?"

"Huh?" He stared at me. Then, "Oh," he said. "Do you get that a lot?"

I remembered recitals and music festival performances where the blue-eyed, blond girls would stand in the wings and whisper about how unfair it was that the Asians were so good at music. Like it was some genetic thing and not the result of being chained to the piano every afternoon for two hours. "I try not to let it bug me. Lissa honestly thinks I'm brilliant at science. It never occurs to her that the reason she always sees me studying is because I'm not. Going over concepts with her actually helps me."

"But you are brilliant at music," he offered. "Even I can see that, and I'm a complete loss at anything to do with the arts. As Mr. Caldwell implied when he saw my still-life project this week."

"Music is fun." I flexed my fingers—my non-stubby, agile fingers. Heh. "That part is natural. My mom plays, too—just when no one's around." I picked up my colada. "The problem is, I'm not going to get to be a doctor or a scientist playing the piano, am I?

Or goofing off in the art department. So I have to work at what
I'm good at, not what I really like."

"Who says? Your family?"

"Yep."

"What's in the art department?" His tone had a definite "Can
anything good come out of Nazareth?" ring to it.

I looked around as if someone might be eavesdropping. The
place was crowded, but nobody was paying any attention to us.
"Graphic art."

He frowned. "Like what? Pen and ink?"

"Kind of. This friend of Lissa's draws graphic novels, and I
talked to him about it a bit before Christmas. Then when the winter schedule came out, I saw there was a class on graphic storytelling. It sounded fun so I signed up. And it's really cool."

"You? Drawing comic books?"

"Not comic books—but I did make up an action hero, just to
see if I could do it. We're learning how to draw people doing stuff.
Telling a story visually, instead of with words. You know."

He shook his head. "I guess I don't. My brain must be completely one-sided. I mean, I'm drawing apples in Visual Media
because we have to have the Arts credit, but mostly I don't get
art at all, except as something to look at on people's walls besides
paint."

But his words triggered something in my head, so that his voice
faded a little as I thought about it. What if I actually wasn't a
science-and-music geek at all, like my brothers? What if I was only
good at those things because I was pushed into them? After all, I
was the girl practicing scales by the hour when all the other kids
in our building were at the pool or playing in the park. I was the
one missing out on track and the drama club because I had to go
home for practice and study. I was the girl who had to show my
report card to my dad and feel the sag of disappointment when he
wasn't satisfied with my grades.

Had I really overlooked what I could love in favor of doing what I was good at?

There was a scary thought. Because if I changed the status quo and started to find out what kinds of things I could love instead of doing what my parents expected, I'd disappoint them like I never had before. And my whole future would go from being a path that I could see and depend on from here to fifty, to a cloud where I couldn't see the next step.

The only one who might know what lay beyond that cloud was God. What I really needed to do here was ask Him what He wanted me to do.

"Gillian? Are you okay?" Lucas leaned in, looking concerned.

I blinked. "What? Yeah. Sure. I was just thinking."

"That's scary." He smiled.

"It sure is." I saw that his tall glass was empty. So was mine. "Well . . . should we head back?"

But as he held the door for me again—how long would it take me to get used to this?—I wondered if I'd ever be able to head back from this moment. To do what my folks wanted without question. Or, if I was honest with myself, if I really wanted to.

....

✉

To:	kazg@hotmail.com
From:	GChang@spenceracad.edu
Date:	January 23, 2009
Re:	Graphic art

Hey, I have a question for you. When/how did you know that graphic novels were what you wanted to do?

The reason I ask is I had this lightbulb moment about the whole science and music thing, and how maybe I'm good at something, but it might not be the thing I love. Did you ever see that movie *Center Stage*, where the one ballerina isn't so good, but she dances because she loves it, and that shows onstage? The other ballerina is technically perfect, but she only does it because her mother wants her to. Eh, you probably didn't see it. Chick flick. Anyway, how does a person tell?

Lissa says to say hi. Hi!!!

Also, I'm attaching a thing I did in class. My first try at a panel. Tell me what you think, but be kind. :)

Gillian

chapter 5

ON WEEKENDS, the last thing you want to think about is homework, but during winter term, going out and doing something in the pouring rain is even less appealing. So we do indoor things: shopping or going to an exhibition or a movie.

Lissa, Shani Hanna, and I got to talking about movies over lunch, and afterward we all came back to our room to scan the theater schedules online. If Carly were here instead of in San Jose, she'd have voted for the latest Jane Austen adaptation so she could drool over the costumes. As it was, Lissa and Shani couldn't decide between that and the new Johnny Depp movie (which Lissa, who has JDOCD, had already seen once anyway). I didn't care—I was just antsy and wanted to do something that would make me stop thinking and kill some time until my relatives picked me up at six.

When my iPhone chimed, I welcomed the diversion and left the girls to their decision. I'd go with the majority.

"What are you up to?" Lucas asked, and in spite of myself, my spirits lifted.

"I'm just hanging in the room. I thought you'd be going to see your dad."

"No, he's busy today, and it's some confidential thing so I can't observe."

I made a sympathetic noise.

"I was wondering. . . . There's a high-tech exhibit opening down at the Moscone Center this afternoon, and Steve Jobs and James Cameron are giving joint keynotes tonight. Dad got tickets but he can't go, so I wondered if you'd be interested?"

It could be an exhibit about old phone books, but if it meant going with Lucas, I was interested. *Do not squee. Be cool.* "What kind of high tech?"

"Mostly gaming, I think, but there's supposed to be some cool VR as well. A whole environment you can step into and interact with, not just a booth."

Virtual reality wasn't really my thing, with the eye visors and automated gloves and all, but, hey, I'd be going with him. *Wait a minute, girl. What about your cousins? The parade? The Slanted Door?*

"Um, it sounds really fun, but I had something planned with my aunt and uncle and their kids. Will it still be going on Sunday afternoon?"

"No, the tickets are for tonight only, because it's the opening. But they'll get us into the exhibits in the afternoon."

Oh, boy. I thought fast. Jack and Isabel and the kids would go watch the parade anyway. They'd probably only invited me because they figured I was all alone out here, and they wanted to be kind. We kept in touch pretty often, but it wouldn't be like ditching immediate family, which would be impossible.

Things came up. Aunt Isabel would understand. This would be my first real date. How could I say no to that?

"Let me see if I can cancel with my relatives, okay? I'll call you back."

"I need to know pretty soon. If you can't go, I can always ask someone from the Science Club."

There were girls in the Science Club. No way was *that* going to happen.

Aunt Isabel answered her cell so fast she must have had it in her pocket. "I'm out in the garden, trimming ferns," she said. "How are you? I can't wait to see you tonight. It's going to be so much fun!"

"Um, Aunt Isabel, about that. Something's come up." Silence. "Are you there?"

"Sure I'm here. Is everything all right, Gillian? Did you get sick? Do you need me to come? Jack can stay with the kids if—"

Meaning only sickness or death would pre-empt a family get-together. "No, no. I'm fine. It's just that I've had a one-of-a-kind invite to a big science show tonight and I hoped you guys wouldn't mind going to dinner and the parade without me."

More silence. In the background on her end, I heard a bird trill. "Oh, Gillian," she said softly. "A science show? Like a school thing?"

I saw the way out. "I'm going with people from school," I said, giving the truth the tiniest twist. "And it's related to what we're doing in Physics." Even though I was taking Chemistry. There would be computer modeling there, and that was what Lucas did, right?

Aunt Isabel let out a long breath. "Well, I suppose school isn't going to stop just because it's a holiday for some of us. I'm so sorry, Gillian. I was really looking forward to seeing you. The kids will be so disappointed."

"I can take the train over there one of these weekends," I said eagerly. "I'll bring them their red envelopes—it'll just be a little late, that's all. I really want to see you guys, too."

"I'll look forward to that. We'll be thinking of you tonight."

"Me, too. Thanks, Aunt Isabel. I'll see you soon."

With a deep breath of relief, I disconnected. That had been easier than I expected. The hard part would come when she told Mom all about it. Maybe I could use the whole "connected to schoolwork" scenario with her, too. If there were two things my parents held sacred, they were work and school. Nothing was allowed to interfere—even family holidays, as my dad had proven time and again.

I called Lucas back and we agreed to meet in the common room at two. I tapped the phone off and found the others looking at me. "What?"

"You ditched Chinese New Year for Lucas?" Lissa asked.

"Yes." I felt the smile warming my face. Or maybe it was a flush. "He asked me to go to a thing at the Moscone Center, so we're taking off at two."

"What about the movie?" Shani asked. "That's when the matinee is."

"I guess I'm not going." Maybe there'd be dinner involved. A real date. My first one. How exciting was that?

"But, Gillian . . ." Lissa's voice trailed away.

"What? You guys can still go. Or wait 'til Carly comes back and we can all go tomorrow night. Come on—if I can't go see the parade with my family, I for sure can't go to a movie with you."

"I guess not."

"You guys, Lucas just asked me out again. You should be happy for me."

"We are," Lissa assured me, but there was something else in her eyes. Had I hurt their feelings? How could something great happening to me hurt them? We were friends. We supported each other. We celebrated the good things. And going to an exhibit downtown with Lucas certainly qualified as a good thing.

I slid off the bed. "Come on. Help me figure out what to wear. I only have an hour."

Lissa and Shani exchanged a look. Any other time I'd have

called them on it and gotten them to spit out what they were thinking. But I didn't have much time. An exhibition wasn't exactly a walk to the juice bar.

"Come on, Lissa," I begged. "I helped you out, remember? You owe me. And it's a Chinese tradition that you have to pay off all your debts before New Year's."

Uh . . . possibly not the best thing to say, as I realized moments too late. I'd helped her pick an outfit for a special date with Callum McCloud last term, and look how *that* had turned out.

But Lissa wasn't made of sponge cake. "You did," she said gamely. "Exhibition. Right. That means a lot of walking. This is the opening, right?"

"Yup."

"So jeans and sneaks are out." She opened my wardrobe door. "But you still want to do fancy science stuff?"

"Virtual reality, gaming, that kind of thing." I'd have fun watching Lucas have a good time. Maybe then he wouldn't notice I didn't have a goofy helmet on my head. I'd leave the droid soldiers and killer monsters to him. Not to mention the swordplay and the inevitable death throes. Blech.

"Okay." Lissa pulled a couple of things off their hangers. "You want to be dressy but still be able to experiment and move. So, flats."

She tossed the D&G slouchy boots over in front of the mirror, so I kissed the thought of my Report buckled booties with their four-inch heels good-bye. Then she handed me a black Miu Miu jersey mini. "With tights." She reached into the closet again. "And this."

"Ooh, I like it," Shani said. "Where'd you get that?"

"Trunk show in Manhattan." I pulled a black tank over my head and dropped the crimson angora tunic on top of it. It felt like a cloud landing, soft and easy. "An Italian designer, but I forget his name."

"I like how the angles woven into it look almost 3-D," Shani said. "Can I borrow it sometime? I'd be really careful."

"Sure." I pulled on some tights and stepped into the boots. "But you're, like, a foot taller than me."

"Try six inches. I might be able to carry it off."

I did my makeup carefully, trying out a new shade of lipstick that wouldn't clash with the sweater. Makeup isn't a priority for me on school days or at home, but for special occasions like this, it's a must. I have a pretty reliable complexion, but all the same, it's kind of sallow, and a little help goes a long way.

"You look great," Shani said when I came out of the bathroom.

"He won't be able to take his eyes off you," Lissa agreed.

"Which kind of negates the whole exhibition experience," I said with a grin. "But thanks."

I tossed a few necessities into my dressy little Prada leather backpack, and hesitated. "Coat? Or no?"

"It's not that bad outside," Shani reported, swinging the window open. "The rain stopped. And you'll be inside most of the time."

True. You don't wear a red this rich just to hide it, do you?

With a final check in the mirror on the inside of my wardrobe door, I was good to go.

Even though I was five minutes early, Lucas still beat me. He pushed himself off the passenger door of a blue Mini Cooper with a white stripe as I came down the front steps.

"Hey." His eyes held warmth and approval, and I felt an answering warmth deep inside. Usually he looked at me as though I were a fellow scientist. I like to be admired for my mind, don't get me wrong. Lissa has this *Top Five Clues That He's the One* list pinned to her bulletin board—and I'm the first to agree that looks don't need to be number one.

But being looked at like a girl instead of a scientist can be really nice. Especially since I'm not the most experienced person on the block when it comes to being on the receiving end, you know?

"Nice car," I said. "Is it yours?"

He nodded. "Gets great gas mileage and has lots of leg room."

"And it's cute."

He looked from me to the car. "If you say so."

It was so clear he'd never thought about its looks that I had to laugh as I got in. "Most guys go for macho or sporty. Like they have something to prove."

We rolled past the photographer hanging around at the gate, but since neither of us is a celebrity or the progeny of one, he slumped back over to his ratty car again and leaned on it, watching the building.

Lucas didn't have anything to prove in the driving department. There's something to be said for leaving the theatrics to the stuntmen and simply getting a girl to where she's going in one piece. Yeah, call me boring, but don't forget I grew up on the mean streets of Manhattan, where venturing into the crosswalk can mean your life.

"People with something to prove are a bore," he said as we dove down a scary hill. "If you've got it, you don't have to prove it. And if you don't have it, don't bother with the pose."

He sneezed.

"Bless you," I said. "I think so, too. People worry too much about what other people think they should be. Especially at this school. Look at Vanessa Talbot. She's always saying how much she hates photographers, but I bet if you'd been taking her out, she would have made sure that guy got her best side on the way past."

With a snort, Lucas glanced at me and back to the street. "The likelihood of me taking Vanessa Talbot out is approximately one billion to one."

"Approximately?" I teased.

"Give or take a few million, depending on whether I had—" he hesitated "—something she wanted besides solutions to equations. Also a very remote possibility."

Which was probably true for 99.9% of the school's guys.

The exhibition itself is a blur now. I remember some things— the mess of traffic because of the New Year's parade I was missing. A silver tunic on a Japanese girl that I'd swear came from Prada's winter collection. How the VR visor made Lucas look like a star pilot straight out of one of Lissa's *Firefly* DVDs (much to his delight). The welcome by James Cameron, whose new SF movie was set to open the next night.

But mostly what I remember is the way Lucas took my hand almost without thinking as we wove through the crowd. How he saved me a seat and craned his neck to look for me when we got separated in the crush before Cameron's talk. And how he sneezed.

Sneezed? I can hear you thinking. *What?*

After about the fifteenth time, I stopped saying "bless you" and took a good look at his face. It was flushed, and his eyes watered and had kind of a gummy look, and he was squinting. He looked miserable.

"Lucas, are you okay?"

"I don't doh." Even his voice had changed. He sounded like that time someone stuffed cotton gym socks in Curtis Paretski's tuba in seventh-grade orchestra.

"Are you getting a cold?" Couldn't be. It had come on too fast. "Or maybe you're allergic to perfume. That woman beside you at the Cameron thing must have showered in Opium."

One of the more unfortunate by-products of the eighties, if you want my opinion.

"I'b dod allergic do perfube."

Oh, boy. This was getting bad. "Come on. Let's go. Once you're outside, it'll probably clear up—who knows what's circulating in the ventilation?"

We abandoned the buffet and headed for the main doors—but not before I snagged a cupcake for each of us from Citizen Cupcake. I get *Daily Candy SF* every day in my e-mail inbox, and the reviewer raved so much that the name stuck in my head, like tons of other useful and not-so-useful trivia.

I wish I'd retained what to do in the case of a major allergic reaction. Fresh air? The hospital? An EpiPen?

We emerged onto the wide sidewalk and Lucas stood a few steps away from me, breathing deeply. "This helps," he said. "Buch better."

"If you say so." I stepped closer, looking into his face. "Your eyes are still really swo—"

He sneezed violently, and a tear ran down his cheek. "Ged away!" he choked. "Id's you!"

What? I skittered away about six feet. "Lucas, I'm not wearing perfume."

"Id's dot perfume. Id's your swedder. Whad's it bade of?"

I hugged myself, as if protecting it. "Angora. It cost a fortune."

He lifted his hands. "Clearly I'b allergic to angora. Take id off."

I pulled the tunic off over my head, rolled it up, and stuffed it into my leather backpack. It didn't take up as much room as you'd think, the yarn was so fine and soft. But it left me standing on the street with nothing between me and the damp, fifty-degree air but my black cotton tank top. Thank goodness I'd thought to throw it on, or the consequences could have been embarrassing.

Lucas stalked back and forth, throwing his head back and breathing long, cleansing breaths. "Wow," he said at last. "I'm allergic to penicillin and mold. Didn't know about angora."

"Sorry." I sounded so lame, but there wasn't much I could add. *Way to ruin your first date, Gillian.*

He tried to smile, and wiped the heel of his hand against his eyes. "I'll get over it."

The damp air lay on my skin, cold and clammy, and I began to shiver.

"Can we go get the car?"

"Is that thing in captivity?" He peered around me at my back-pack to make sure I'd closed the zipper all the way.

"I promise. There'll be no escape this time."

The *Star Wars* line went right over his head. "Okay. I'm done here."

I had no problem keeping up with his long stride now—in fact, I was happy to head back to the parking structure at the next thing to a run. By the time we reached it and I fell into the pas-senger seat, I was sure I had early-onset hypothermia. I cranked up the heat as we zoomed out of there, but it couldn't get warm enough for me.

"Whew," Lucas said. "Sure you need it up that high?"

"I can't get warm."

"Here, take the wheel."

I hung on for dear life, steering up the side of what seemed like a sheer cliff, while he shrugged out of his herringbone tweed blazer and pushed it over to me. I huddled inside it, smelling the faint echo of his cologne and appreciating the way it had retained his body heat like I'd never appreciated anything before.

"I could go for a coffee," he said as we turned left and headed along the crest of the hill on which Spencer sat. "What about you?"

"You don't have to ask me twice," I said fervently. "I think my core is five degrees below 'still living.'"

So much for glamour and high tech. Lucas and I wound up our first real date much like we'd wound up our practice one—facing each other across a tiny table, with hands wrapped around our drinks.

Which, when you think about it, wasn't a bad thing. Lissa can do glamour with one hand tied behind her back. Me, I'm pretty down to earth. And an extra-hot latte and Lucas Hayes were about as good as it could get.

I've been wrong about a lot of stuff. But I turned out to be right about that.

⸽⸽⸽

⬚

To: GChang@spenceracad.edu
From: MarionChang@hotmail.com
Date: January 25, 2009
Re: Call asap

Gillian,

What is wrong with your phone? I've left three messages for you to call me.

How could you be so disrespectful to your aunt and uncle? Isabel called me this morning and told me you couldn't go to the New Year's celebration because you had to do something on a school project. But, Gillian, this is your family. Your father's sister. School is very important, but they went out of their way to include you in something special and you treated them like it didn't matter. Your father and I are so embarrassed. You need to call your aunt and apologize. And then call me to tell me you did so.

Mom
⸽⸽⸽

chapter 6

FTER WHAT *COSMO* would call a "dating disaster" with no known cure, and then having my mother yell at me on top of it, my expectations sank to a new low. Lissa couldn't help me with my family, but she tried to help with the Lucas situation.

"The fact that he's allergic to something is not your fault," she told me for the eleventh time two weeks later. Contrary to what adults think, it is possible to study and do relationship therapy at the same time. "How were you supposed to know?"

"I could have asked."

With a snort, she said, "Right. That would be number five on the questionnaire you handed him at the beginning of the evening."

Carly snickered and kept her eyes on her Chem notes. I was prepping both of them for our second set of thirdterms, which were at the end of February. Yep. Exams every three weeks or so during a ten-week term. It wouldn't surprise me if we were the smartest student body on the planet, statistically.

"Lots of people are allergic to angora and fur and stuff," I went on. "I should have thought of that and gone with natural fibers."

"Fur is a natural fiber," Carly observed, not looking up.

"You know what I mean."

"The point is, you guys just need to communicate," Lissa said.

"How can we do that when he isn't talking to me?" Honestly, sometimes Lissa really is blond. "He hardly said a thing to me at prayer circle this week."

"Have you gone up to him and tried to talk? Thanked him for the evening?" she asked. "Or have you been hiding out in here with us, making us do more homework than we need to?"

"Do you want to pass Bio or not?"

"Not at the expense of your love life."

"You have a better chance of getting an A on that exam than I do of getting another date with Lucas." Once you nearly send a guy into anaphylactic shock, you may as well cut your losses and move on.

"You could always buy an A," Carly said.

Both of us stared at her.

"I can buy a pair of shoes. I can't buy a grade," Lissa said. "Or did I not hear you properly?"

"You heard it right. At least, that's the word around the halls."

"Back up," I said. "What's this?"

"Rumor has it that someone's selling exam answers," Carly said. "For a thousand bucks, you can get a whole Chemistry exam with the answers all marked."

A thousand. The neurons in my brain lined up and fired. "The week before last, I heard Rory Stapleton telling Brett that he got eighty percent on his Trig test."

"And if you believe he got that without help, I have a bridge to sell you." Lissa made a wry mouth.

"But why would you buy an answer sheet that gave you wrong answers?" I wanted to know. "How stupid."

"What would be stupid is any teacher believing Rory could get a perfect score," Carly said. "That would tip them off right away. With eighty percent, he could say he's been working with a tutor."

"That's some tutor," Lissa put in. "He probably doubled his grade."

The three of us cracked up. Rory Stapleton's dad may own some sports team or other, but his son and heir isn't the brightest bulb in the box.

"Speaking of smart people, I went and saw that Jodie Foster movie last weekend with one of the girls in Dad's condo complex," Carly said. "Have you seen it?"

"I have." Lissa grinned. "Didn't you love the part where she—"

"Spoiler!" I warned, threatening to clap a hand over her mouth. "Don't say a word."

"But it was so cool when she and the guy who was pretending to be a—"

"Lissa!"

"All right, all right," she grumped. "You'd better go see it soon, then, so we can talk about it."

"Ask Lucas if he wants to go with you," Carly suggested. "You can casually bring it up in conversation and then pop the question."

"Ooh, good plan." Lissa sat back and tossed her pen onto her notebook. "The hook 'em and reel 'em in scenario."

"Spare me the marine metaphors," I groaned. "On top of everything else, that's all I need."

It was still a good plan, though—one that ran through my head the next day as I passed the physics lab and remembered that Lucas's free period fell on Thursday afternoons. And where would a guy whose life was physics be during his free period?

Not in the gym or the common room, that's for sure.

I found him at the back of the lab, gazing at the high-resolution, widescreen computer monitor as though it were the window into an alternate universe.

For him, maybe it was.

He didn't even hear me until I was practically next to him, and only then because I made my heels clack just a bit harder than usual.

"Oh," he said. "Hey."

"I haven't seen you around much." I shifted my backpack on my shoulder, trying to be casual. "Thought I'd stop in and make sure my sweater didn't send you to the hospital after all."

He flushed, and I kicked myself. Maybe pointing out a guy's weaknesses was a faux pas. *Mouth, Gillian. Watch the mouth. Nai-Nai is right. You never stop talking.*

"You don't have it around someplace, do you?" He pretended to look behind me. "Talk about a secret weapon guaranteed to bring a man to his knees."

"His sneeze?" Puns are the lowest form of humor, but I can't help it. Sometimes they beg to be said.

"That, too."

Well, this didn't sound like a guy who'd been avoiding me on purpose for almost two weeks. He'd even skipped prayer circle last week. Maybe he was busy with his experiments and studying for the Olympiad. "What do you have there?" I nodded at the screen.

"Oh, this." He leaned back. "Two scientists my dad introduced me to at Stanford discovered a new star. I was just reading the paper on it."

And some people think I'm a geek for doing chemical equations during my free period. At least that's homework. This was recreational reading.

"I'll leave you to it, then," I said. "I'm just on my way to Mandarin and thought I'd look in on you."

"I'm glad you did." He swiveled in the chair and smiled, and my heart did this strange sideways beat in my chest. "IM me or something, okay?"

"Sure." I smiled back and reluctantly got myself out of the lab, managing not to knock anything over with my backpack on the way. Maybe it wasn't me after all, or my deadly tunic. Maybe it was just as simple as a guy being busy with his life.

You'd think Mandarin would be a no-brainer for me, since we speak it at home with Nai-Nai. But no. Is English class easy for you? Uh-huh. With Mandarin you still have to nail down grammar and vocab and remember inflections and tones, with the added pain of learning to write characters. Gracefully. With brushes. Kind of like learning Chaucer's Middle English and then writing it out in perfect calligraphy with a feather quill.

So, bottom line, Mandarin isn't the easiest thing to master on the best of days, never mind when your head is filled with a guy and the what-ifs and if-onlys. If Dad and Nai-Nai knew how I was messing up on the translation exercises Dr. Leung had just handed out, they'd be ashamed of me. Was this the result of going out with someone? Your brain turned to oatmeal as thick as what they served in the dining room, and you were unable to think about anything else but him? Did it work this way for guys, too?

Somehow I doubted it.

After classes were over, and before Lissa and I went down for supper, I opened my Mac notebook and checked my mail. Another note from Mom. One from each of my three brothers. Wow. One each from Kylie Omimura, my best friend from school in New York, and my cousin Kate Fong, who went to Choate. Both of whom I adored, but who were such perfect examples of talented Asian girls making their families proud that I always felt like the rude, noisy bumpkin Nai-Nai accuses me of being when she's annoyed.

Nai-Nai has a hair-trigger temper, which means she's annoyed a lot. One of the reasons I'm out here instead of staying at Brearley, or even going to Choate with Kate.

Don't tell anyone I said that, okay?

....

✉

To: kate.fong@choate.edu
From: GChang@spenceracad.edu
Date: February 12, 2009
Re: Re: winter blah

Hey, cuz, thanks for the note. Things are pretty busy around here—
I'm taking AP Chem, Mandarin, English, and a bunch of other
stuff, along with an advanced piano class, chamber ensemble, and
composition, which is kinda interesting. Also taking a graphic arts
class, can you believe it? And volleyball. Gotta exercise all parts of
the brain, huh?

Congrats on the social coup! I knew all those dance classes would
pay off. So he's the captain of the fencing team AND does social
dance in competition? Geesh. How do you find these guys? All there
are out here are trust-fund babies and scions of old families—oh
wait, that's all there is out there, too! ::snicker::

There might be something interesting developing along that line for
me. Too new to say anything yet, but he's brilliant in physics and
plans to bag his Ph.D. in eight years. Not to mention, tall, dorky, and
cute. ☺ Which is OK, since I'm short, dorky, and cute. LOL

TTYL,
Gill

....

   I hit Send and popped off a similar note to Kylie, then brief
ones to my family telling each of them what they wanted to hear.
Only with Darren did I get really honest, but only about classes
and stuff.

None of them needed to know about Lucas. While it might have delighted Nai-Nai if she heard I was dating an Asian guy, I couldn't have stood the barrage of phone calls and general freaked-out nosiness that would ensue if they found out I was seeing a white boy. No matter what he looked like, a person's first boyfriend was private, at least in the beginning stages. My family would overwhelm a relationship like a tidal wave and drown it before it even got off the ground.

Another marine metaphor. What was with me today? Was my subconscious telling me I needed a day out on the Bay in a sailboat or something?

I'd been sitting so long staring at the e-mail screen that my computer had gone to sleep. I poked a key and opened a note. *IM me*, he'd said. So, confession time: I'd been sitting here doing e-mail while I worked up some courage.

GChang　　Up for seeing a movie? Maybe tomorrow night?

LHayes　　Which one?

GChang　　I've been trying to get to *Seeing Double* since it opened.

LHayes　　What's it about?

GChang　　Jodie Foster goes to Africa and saves her dead best friend's child. Political mayhem ensues.

LHayes　　Chick flick.

GChang　　I like Jodie Foster.

LHayes　　Nothing wrong with that. Have you seen the new *Silver Surfer*?

GChang　　No.

LHayes　　Want to go? It's playing at the Cineplex at the bottom of the hill. Maybe dinner first at TouTou's and then the 9:00 show?

GChang　　Great! Front steps at 6:30?

LHayes　　Me and my cute car will be there.

Smiling, I closed his note and enjoyed the sweetness of the moment. First an exhibition opening, now dinner and a movie! If this didn't mean "be my girlfriend," I was a Ming empress. And so what if I didn't get to see Jodie. It would be out on DVD in a couple months, or I'd download it off iTunes.

And Saturday was Valentine's Day. I'd never paid much attention to it before, but now the timing seemed cosmically perfect. Who knew what might happen on a day meant to commemorate love?

New mail came in while I was gloating—er, sitting there being thoroughly happy.

✉

To: All Students
From: NCurzon@spenceracad.edu
Date: February 12, 2009
Re: Exams

Ladies and gentlemen, a serious breach of the qualities our school colors stand for—loyalty, purity, and intellect—has come to my attention and I need your help.

I have been informed that some of the grades you achieved during our last set of midterms were attained by fraudulent means. In other words, they were bought. Someone has accessed the school server illegally and downloaded some professors' examination materials. These were subsequently marked with answers and sold to students.

If you know of someone who has obtained answers in this manner, please inform your core class instructor or come to me directly. Your identity will be kept confidential. I don't need to tell you how sorry

this makes me. I had thought that the students of Spencer Academy
held themselves and their achievements in higher regard.

Thank you for any assistance you can give us in finding the persons
responsible.

Natalie Curzon, Ph.D., M.Ed.
Principal, Spencer Academy

....

Wow. So Carly's ear for the word on the street was sharp. I
could only imagine what would happen to the person caught selling exam answers. Expulsion, of course. Even though I knew—
thanks to Lissa's experience last term—that Spencer gave people
three chances before they were kicked out, there were still cir-
cumstances under which they'd boot first and ask questions
later. Fire, blood, and drugs being three of them. Fraud probably
ranked right up there, too—especially when it involved something
as serious as grades.

Well, knowing the grapevine in this place, sooner or later the
guilty people would surface, whether they wanted to or not.

Meanwhile, I had a date to think about.

chapter 7

YOU KNOW HOW when you were a kid, Christmas and your birthday seemed to take an eon to arrive? How every day seemed like a week, and all you could think about was that moment when you could throw the covers off and run to where the presents were?

That's kind of how it was for me, waiting for Friday night.

"You are totally crushing on him, aren't you?" Shani said to me as Carly joined us on the volleyball court on the upper level of the field house, after Life Skills and before Phys. Ed. class got started. Idly, we set up the ball for each other while we waited for Ms. Stockton, the gym instructor, to come out of her office and start drills.

"No," I said with dignity. "I like him, that's all. And I think he likes me."

"He must." Shani served the ball in my direction. "TouTou's costs a fortune. Nothing says true love like a hundred and fifty a plate."

"It doesn't cost that." Carly looked shocked. "Does it?"

"Appie, dinner, dessert, and coffee?" Shani got under my return and bumped it to Carly. "Three hundred for two, easy."

"Maybe I should suggest something else." This was making me nervous. "I mean, we could just eat here and walk down to the theater afterward."

"Gillian, let the man take you out." Carly caught the ball and hung onto it. "If he said TouTou's, he had to know it would mean shelling out. And it's not like he can't afford it."

"Or that I can't, if we went Dutch." I didn't come armed with a platinum AmEx for nothing. "It's just that—"

"What?" She tossed the ball, and I bumped it to Shani to give myself time to find the right words.

"I don't want him to think I'm like—" I jerked my head in the direction of Emily Overton and Dani "I'm cashing in on my cousin's fame" Lavigne, who were setting their ball back and forth, dropping it every third time. "I don't care about going to expensive places just because celebrities go there. I don't want him to think he has to impress me that way."

"He won't," Carly assured me. "Any guy who can survive an angora sweater attack has to know better than that."

They both cracked up. I was *so* not going to live this down. Thank goodness nobody else knew I'd nearly sent the school's leading prospective Physics Olympian to the hospital.

"Would you stop overthinking?" Shani tossed the ball to Carly as Ms. Stockton finally appeared. "Just go have a good time. And tell us if you like that movie."

I tried to stop overthinking. Really. But even just thinking about it on the most superficial level (what was I going to *wear?*) made me nervous. By six-thirty, though, I was on the front steps, immaculately dressed in a Tori Wu velvet minidress with a vintage jean jacket over it. Style, comfort, and a little edge, all in one package. All of which I needed badly to shore up my jittery self-confidence.

I know Lissa thinks I have more confidence than is good for me—and in some ways, I do. I have total confidence in God, for instance. Or give me an equation or a chemical formula, and I'm good to go. But with personal stuff? Not so much. You try being a girl in a houseful of boys and demanding mother types, and see how far off the ground your self-esteem gets. It certainly hadn't prepared me to handle a boyfriend. Thank goodness for my friends here at school. If it weren't for them, I don't know what I would have done.

By 6:35 I'd managed to find a little calm by listening to Vienna Teng on my iPhone and watching the branches of the pepper trees on either side of the steps wave in the early February breeze. When I glanced at my watch the next time, it was 6:45.

Well, traffic could happen to anyone, but the school garage was under the field house, and that was only a block away. Maybe Lucas had had car trouble.

I shut off the music and scrolled to his number.

"Yeah?"

"Lucas?" The greeting sounded so abrupt, I couldn't be sure it was actually him. Maybe Travis, his roomie, had answered his cell.

"Yeah."

"It's Gillian. Are you okay?"

A pause, as if to decipher what this meant. "Sure. What's going on?"

Honestly. Guys. Living in a universe where time has no meaning. He was probably sitting in front of his computer, reading another fascinating monograph.

"I'm on the front steps. You know, six-thirty? Dinner at Tou-Tou's and the nine o'clock show?"

He sucked in a breath. "Oh, no." A cold breeze swirled up the hill, blowing my velvet skirt flat against my legs. "Gillian, how stupid can I be? I forgot. I'm in Palo Alto at my dad's apartment. He called right after lunch and said they'd had a breakthrough and would I come down for a celebration dinner. We're just getting ready to leave."

"Oh." My tone held a combination of "wow, great for them" and "gee, I've just been stood up."

"I'm really sorry. My brain is full of work for the Olympiad and I forgot to put the time in my BlackBerry. Can we do it when I get back?"

"Sure." I tried to sound stress-free, like I wasn't really standing out here in full view of the entire school—not to mention two photographers—being stood up. "No biggie. Call me whenever and we'll figure out a time."

It was Valentine's Day weekend. I hung onto that thought like a lifeline. Surely he'd make up for it with something special tomorrow.

"You know, you're really something," he said in a soft tone I'd never heard before. "Most girls would be throwing a fit. But you're cool, even if I am the dumbest rock on the planet."

"You're not dumb," I said with a smile. "You're just overextended right now. I completely understand. Where are you going for dinner?" Like I would know if he told me, but I could look it up.

"El Capitan. That's where the really big deals go down in Silicon Valley," he explained. "All the VCs go there to do their deals, so if I was to go with a startup when I graduate, it helps to be seen."

It had never occurred to me that Lucas Hayes would care about being seen. Which showed me that he had political smarts and I . . . didn't. "Speaking of being seen, want me to cancel the reservation?"

"Reservation?"

"At TouTou's. We had a seven o'clock, and it's nearly that now."

"Nah, don't worry about it. They won't have any trouble filling the table. Thanks, Gillian. I really appreciate it. You have every right to be upset."

"I'm not upset." Not now. Not after hearing that note in his voice that might just have opened a new door in our relationship.

"I'll call you tomorrow."

"Put it in your BlackBerry," I teased.

"Already done. Good night."

"'Night, Lucas."

I turned and pushed open the front doors, welcoming the warmth of the huge entry hall. The potted palms in pairs on either side of the windows looking out onto the quad made it seem a little tropical, too. Just to be on the safe side, I called TouTou's as I climbed the stairs. No point in getting on their black list.

"I'd like to cancel a seven o'clock reservation, please," I told the cool female voice that answered. "A business matter came up. It's under Hayes."

A pause, during which I heard chatter and laughter in the background. "I'm sorry, miss. We don't have a reservation under that name within half an hour on either side."

"Oh. Try Chang."

Another pause. "Not Chang, either."

That was weird. "Okay, not to worry. I guess if it's not there, I don't need to cancel."

She hung up on me without another word. Sheesh. Someone wasn't going to get their Michelin stars at this rate.

I hesitated outside our room. *Oh, come on. You don't seriously think Lissa's going to laugh at you, do you?*

I let myself in and Lissa looked up from her laptop in astonishment. "Did you forget something?"

I nodded and shrugged out of my jean jacket. "My date. Actually, my date forgot me."

Her hands dropped from the keyboard. "No way."

"He's been in Palo Alto since this afternoon. Some big

breakthrough at the brain bank. He forgot to put our thing in his BlackBerry, so when his dad called to say come celebrate, he went."

She gazed at me, brows raised. "So aren't you, like, furious?"

"What's to be furious about? Disappointed, maybe. He has a lot on his mind. People only have so many neurons." I lifted a shoulder. "Not a big deal. On the bright side, I don't have to go see *Silver Surfer*. The reviews were, um, mixed."

She snickered. "Why don't we go see your Jodie movie instead?" A glance at the time clock on her monitor. "We can just make it to the seven-thirty show if we hurry."

I shook my head. I wasn't really in the mood to take the consolation prize, even if it was offered by a caring friend. "I think I'll see what's left in the dining room and then practice for a while."

"Okay." She glanced at her screen again. "I've got a note here from Kaz. He says to tell you to read your mail."

Ooh. I hoped he liked the panel I'd sent, and that he had an opinion about the "do what you're good at" versus "do what you love" question. I wasn't quite ready to share that with Lissa, though. I didn't know why.

Well, yes, I did know why. Because she tended to bubble over with things, especially happy things. And if one of my parents happened to call our room instead of my cell, I didn't want her burbling about my newfound interest in graphic art. That would really start a war, and I just couldn't face it.

"Tell him I will, as soon as I get back."

Dining Services kept cold stuff in a case for people like me who didn't make it to supper between five and six-thirty. But even there I was too late. There was nothing left but egg-salad sandwiches. Blech.

People say that the devil is in the details, but I've always believed that it's really God who cares about every little thing in His children's lives.

On a day like today, though, you'd really have to work to convince me.

....

✉

To: GChang@spenceracad.edu
From: kazg@hotmail.com
Date: February 13, 2009
Re: Re: Graphic art

Hey Gillian,

Thanks for the panel. So yeah, obviously it's your first, but here's what I think. You have talent. Your character is original (*Buffy* meets *Crouching Tiger*? Who knew?) and while you have a long way to go technically, it's just a matter of nailing your craft and getting some practice. The point is, it was only four frames and I could see energy, passion, and storytelling. This is what counts.

As for your question, you have to make the call. Some people would say being a starving artist versus a doctor is a no-brainer. It would be better not to starve. But we can't all be Neil Gaiman. I don't know what to tell you. I'm in the same boat myself. But we can talk about it some more if you want.

Kaz

....

chapter 8

SATURDAY MORNING at a couple of minutes after nine, someone tapped on our door. I opened it to see a girl from my Chem class, but for the life of me, I couldn't remember her name.

"Are you Gillian?" she asked. When I nodded, she said, "Lucas wants you to come down to the common room."

"Uh, okay."

She went on down the corridor, while I closed the door and met Lissa's gaze. "He has my cell number," I said. "Why does he need to use random people as messengers?"

"You could ask him," she suggested. "As soon as you put actual clothes on."

I yanked on some jeans and a T-shirt, then buttoned a soft burgundy velvet vest on over it. I don't know what was with the velvet fetish lately. Maybe because it was cuddly and yet it made me feel elegant. Confident. Or something. I'm not to the point where I'm psychoanalyzing my clothes.

I laced up my sneaks and took the stairs at a rational rate—not so fast he could hear me racing to see him, but not so slow he'd give up on me before I got there. I found him, as promised, in the common room.

And he was holding roses.

Lucas Hayes, the genius. Holding a dozen white roses.

For me.

"Oh, my," I breathed. Wordlessly, he handed them to me and I buried my face in their cool, scented beauty.

"Red and pink seemed kind of boring," he offered. "But these are simple and straightforward, like you. Happy Valentine's Day."

I wasn't about to tell him that to a Chinese person white is the color of mourning, the way black is Stateside. He couldn't possibly know that. And the point was, they were *roses*. My first bouquet from someone I wasn't related to. And it was Valentine's Day.

"I love them. They're gorgeous. You really didn't have to."

"Oh, yes I did. You can throw them in the trash and never speak to me again and I'll understand."

I clutched them between my hands. "Nobody's throwing these in the trash. It was a simple mistake, Lucas. It could happen to anyone."

"Yes, but I made it happen to you. I've been seeing you waiting on the front steps all night. I would have come up to the dorm with these and apologized when I got back last night, but Tobin was on duty patrol and she'd have had me arrested."

I laughed, but only because he was correct. Mr. Milsom and Ms. Tobin between them had everyone in our dorm completely cowed. It was obvious to everyone but them that they were meant to be together. Kind of like two porcupines—they were the only ones who could tolerate each other.

"I'm going to go put these in water," I said. "I'll be back in a second."

"Buy you breakfast?" he asked with a quirky grin. "It ain't El Capitan, but it's the best I can do."

"Who needs El Capitan when we have Spencer Academy oatmeal?" I tossed over my shoulder, laughing, as I climbed the stairs.

"Wow." Lissa's eyes widened as she held the door for me to pass with my prize. "*Lucas* brought you those?"

"He really did. For Valentine's. And he apologized again." I looked around a little desperately. "Do we have anything I can use for a vase?"

Lissa scanned the room, too. "A drinking glass? A test tube? Not one thing." She snapped her fingers. "Wait, I've got it."

She dashed out the door and in less than a minute was back with Carly in tow. Carly carried a clay pitcher—the old-fashioned kind with a fat body and a curved spout. She filled it at our bathroom sink and I put the roses into it. The crackled blue and green glaze set them off perfectly.

"So what's with the white?" Carly asked. "You guys planning on getting married?"

"Of course not." I carried them over to the dresser and adjusted the arrangement. "He said they reminded him of me."

"What—pure and innocent? That's what white roses stand for, you know. In the language of flowers."

"Flowers have a language?" Trust Carly to know this.

"Sure. You know, red roses mean love, yellow ones mean jealousy, pink ones mean . . . I forget. Anyway, that's why they use white ones for weddings. To say the bride's still pure."

"That's way more information than my florist needs to know," Lissa cracked.

Okay, I was *so* getting off this subject. "Where'd you get this?" I asked Carly, touching the pitcher. "It's not exactly on the supplies list."

Color washed into her face and faded again just as quickly. "My mom gave it to me for Christmas. She teaches people to make pottery on the cruise ships. Artist in residence or something."

"Nice work if you can get it," Lissa commented.

"I guess. So. Lucas. Flowers. Things are getting interesting."

I nodded. Now it was her turn to swerve away from something that made her uncomfortable. Carly had told us her parents were divorced but she hardly ever talked about her mom other than to say that she'd gone back to live with Carly's grandparents in Veracruz. And that there was a boyfriend in the picture. I hadn't known she was artistic, but that went a long way toward explaining Carly's love of costume and fabric and history. I mean, she isn't exactly on her way to a computer engineering career like her dad's.

"They're an apology for standing her up last night," Lissa informed her with more relish than necessary. "I hope you're going to torture him a little, Gillian. Make him suffer before you forgive him."

"Too late," I confessed. "We're having breakfast together, so don't you guys even think about crowding our table."

Carly placed her fingertips on her chest. "I'm so hurt."

Lissa gave a slump-shouldered sigh. "Cast aside again."

I rolled my eyes. "Everyone's a comedian. Give me a break, you two. After standing on the stairs for half an hour last night, I deserve flowers. And breakfast. And maybe some more groveling, too."

"You do," Lissa agreed. "Heavy on the groveling. Sure we can't watch? I mean, this has to be a first."

"No." I glared, only half-joking. "No watching, no eavesdropping, no clandestine activity of any kind."

"This from the girl who runs criminal checks on other people's boyfriends." Carly went to the door. "We'll be standing by at the yogurt machine if you need us."

I gave my outfit a final check, swiped on some lip gloss, and headed back down the stairs.

My friends. Even if I didn't need it, it was nice to know that, along with the angels, they had my back.

Don't ask me how it happened, but even with our best efforts at privacy, breakfast wound up being the next thing to a party. Lissa and Carly sat at the other end of the table, as promised, but before long the seats in between were filled by Shani and a couple of kids from prayer circle, plus two or three from the Science Club who seemed to float around Lucas as though they were hoping to absorb more brilliance by osmosis.

Lucas seemed to take it pretty gracefully. I mean, he wasn't completely in Vanessa Talbot's crowd (thank goodness), and at least he knew we were his friends—and we certainly had a lot more fun than Vanessa and Brett and Dani and Todd Runyon ever seemed to.

"What's the definition of popular?" I asked Lucas, glancing at the table in front of the window facing out onto the quad. Dani and Emily took turns trashing people as they went by (my assessment, anyway). Brett was trying to tell Vanessa something, but she seemed to be more interested in her manicure than anything else.

"I've never given it much thought." Lucas's gaze followed mine. "Not relevant."

Shani leaned over. "Do people like you? Do they think you're fun to be around?"

"People like *us*," Carly said from her end of the table. "That means we must be popular."

"Gillian, wasn't it you who asked me once if I wanted to be friends with people who like me just because I get up in the morning, not because there's something in it for them?" Lissa asked. "I know which I'd rather have."

"It's not about people liking you at all," Lucas said. "Popularity is all about who has the most. Looks, money, stuff, whatever. Look at Vanessa."

Our heads swung, just as she looked up. *Oh, you bunch of losers*, her bored expression seemed to say, before she picked up her tray and walked out of the dining room, Brett close behind.

"That was rewarding," Lissa remarked.

"I didn't mean you should actually *look* at her," Lucas said impatiently. "I was using her as an example. She's beautiful, she has a trust fund, and her parents are famous. That's why she's popular."

"Huh," Carly mused, deadpan. "And here I thought it was because of her winning personality."

Next to me, Shani snickered.

I was still recovering from what Lucas had just said. "You really think Vanessa is beautiful?" Guys weren't supposed to say things like that in front of their girlfriends, were they? Or even people they thought might be their girlfriends. Maybe he was just making an observation, along the lines of "Look, the sun came out."

"Oh, yeah." He spooned more Demerara sugar on his oatmeal. "She's pretty bright, too. I had low expectations with the tutoring last term, but it worked out."

"I heard Annie Leibovitz wanted to photograph her when they lived in New York, but she turned her down," Shani put in. Whose side was she on, anyway?

"I find that hard to believe." I'd seen her myself, pretending to dodge photographers while she made sure they got her best side. How else did she show up on places like whowhatweardaily.com?

He shrugged. "Truth is truth, whether you choose to believe it or not."

I sat back, rebuffed and a little hurt. Why were we talking about Vanessa Talbot, anyway? "That isn't truth. It's just something somebody heard."

"Besides," Shani said, "defining what's beautiful is like defining what's popular. It's just people's opinion."

Way to redeem yourself, girl.

"But usually people's opinions form critical mass in a given society. And that's when you get definitions of both," Lucas said. "So for our little society right here, a girl with high cheekbones, puffy lips, big eyes, and a trust fund is defined as beautiful."

I considered my non-cheekbones, wide mouth, Asian eyes, and hair that did whatever it wanted. If he thought Vanessa was so beautiful, what was he doing having breakfast with me? Did he have a crush on her? Was he just using me to fill time until she dumped Brett and left the field open for him?

I pushed my half-eaten oatmeal away.

"Personally," Lissa said, "I define beautiful as a girl with a big heart, a big smile, and a sharp brain. So that makes Gillian a beauty in my book."

Bless you.

Lucas nodded. "Under that definition, she is."

My throat prickled and I blinked back stupid tears. "Sitting right here," I said hoarsely. "Knock it off, you guys."

He smiled at me. "Didn't mean to embarrass you."

Better embarrassed at a compliment than jealous over nothing. My cheeks might be burning, but a happy little warmth blossomed inside me. Time to change the subject. "Do you have any plans today?"

"We should all do something together," Lissa said. "There must be tons of stuff going on around here."

"In February?" Carly asked.

"We could go to the de Young and see the new exhibit," I suggested. "Or to Ghirardelli Square to eat chocolate."

"Or Pier 39," one of the guys said. Jeremy Clay, that was his name. "It's crab season—we could hit Fisherman's Wharf and get one right out of the pot. Eat it on the sidewalk."

"Gross." Shani's whole face scrunched up in distaste. "I'd rather go to Alcatraz and be locked in a jail cell."

"We could do that. Or we could go to Angel Island," Lucas said to me. "Have you ever been there?" I shook my head—I'd never even heard of it. "There's a ferry that runs out there, and you can hike all around it. No cars. "

"The fog's lifted," Lissa said with a glance past the coveted window table, now empty, to the sky above the classroom wing opposite. "I don't know about you guys, but I could really stand to get out of this place."

She wasn't the only one. "Let's do it," I said. "It sounds like fun."

And maybe, while we were busy hiking around, I'd finally get some time alone with the guy who, while he might admire another girl's cheekbones, thought I had a big smile and a big heart.

chapter 9

I F I HADN'T KNOWN it was February, I would have sworn we'd been fast-forwarded to May.

I stood at the rail of the Blue and Gold ferry and let the ocean breeze blow my hair straight back. Fortunately, I'd thought to dig my sunglasses out of the bottom drawer of the dresser, so I wasn't dazzled by the sun sparkling on the Bay as the little ferry churned its way toward the island.

"What a great view." Lissa, Carly, and Shani ranged along the rail on my right, while the boys from the Science Club (probably still congratulating themselves on their luck) tried to talk to them. Shani is the outgoing type, and Lissa will try to make anyone feel comfortable, even a science geek, but Carly didn't know what to say.

That poor girl. If she were going to get Brett Loyola's attention, she'd have to learn to talk to boys in general. Though I suppose a fascinating conversation about knots versus miles per hour wouldn't help much. Still, when you were just practicing, sometimes you had to take what you could get.

Listen to me, running on like I knew it all when the truth was, after the comment about being a beauty, I'd once again lost the ability to say anything at all to Lucas. Either he was going to think I wasn't having fun, or he'd think I was still mad about last night.

Where was my magpie mouth when I needed it?

Leaning on the rail to my left, Lucas pointed at the city skyline. "Nice, huh?"

I nodded. "I've never seen it from here before. Only from the air, flying in."

"There's the Golden Gate Bridge." He pointed off the stern. "I wonder why they call it that when it's painted orange?"

"My Aunt Isabel says that the old folks call San Francisco 'Old Gold Mountain,'" I offered. "Maybe it has something to do with finding your fortune."

"Maybe." He pointed at the bridge ahead of us, the more ordinary one that stitched Oakland and San Francisco together. "It's more interesting than 'Bay Bridge,' anyway."

So much for the history and geography lesson. What was the matter with me today? It wasn't like this was a real Valentine's date. It was more like a group adventure—something to get us all out of our rooms and blow the winter cobwebs away. No pressure, no need to impress, just a bunch of friends out for fun.

So why had my brain locked up?

"You're awfully quiet," Lucas said, and I felt like sliding under the rail and dribbling into the Bay, never to be seen again.

"You just read my mind," I said. "I guess I'm kind of nervous."

"What about?"

You. Me. Whether you think I'm pretty. If we're really going out. If you like me as more than a friend. If today's the day I might actually get my first real kiss. "I don't know."

"I was hoping it would be just you and me out here," he said in a tone so low that only I could hear it.

Gulp. "Sorry," I murmured back. Lissa leaned on the rail about two feet away from me. "I didn't know. I just sort of blurted it out and then everybody at the table invited themselves along."

"That's okay." He moved his elbow on the rail a little, so that his shoulder bumped against mine. "It's a big island. Maybe we'll get lucky and get lost."

I nearly pinched myself. Was this really me, dorky Gillian Chang, standing beside a gorgeous genius who wanted to be alone with me?

"Maybe we will," I agreed. I hardly dared to say any more in case he changed his mind or I woke up.

When the ferry docked, I discovered that Lissa had done a little advance research. "We're going to do a one-hour tour," she told us as the deck shuddered under our feet with the gentle impact. "On Segways."

"What?" Carly's voice spiked. "Those rolling wheelie things? I thought those died."

"Those personal mobile machines, you mean. And they never died," Jeremy corrected her. "They use them at Pixar to get around the campus. Cool!"

A Vespa I might be able to handle. But a platform between two wheels? Was she kidding?

A college student named Megan met us at the dock. "This way, people. We'll run through the features of your Segway, get you helmeted up, and we'll be on our way in half an hour."

The breeze on my face felt cool, but the sun made up for it as I pulled my helmet on and tried to listen to Megan's instructions. If she thought we'd be driving these things in half an hour, she was pretty optimistic. With the eight of us lined up in a row, she ran through the controls and safety features. Then it was time to get on.

I stepped onto the platform and waited for it to do something.

"Turn it on with the key, then lean forward to go ahead, and lean back to reverse," Megan told us for the third time. "Easy does it. Everybody go forward five or six feet, then back."

"Yikes!" I said as the thing rolled forward. Instinctively I jerked back, and it reversed under me, picking up speed.

"Gillian, straighten up and it'll stop," Lucas called.

Easy for him. He rolled forward and back like he'd been doing it since birth. Lissa jerked one way, then the other, as incompetent as me. Ha. Misery loves company.

"Take a few minutes to practice, and then we'll go over the basics of turning," Megan called, rolling smartly out of Jeremy's way as he tried to avoid a collision with Shani.

"Whose idea was this, anyway?" I heard Lissa mumble as she rolled past at a snail's pace. At least she was rolling. I still couldn't get it to go forward without jerking. Learning to drive a clutch had been easier than this.

"Gillian," Lucas said, motoring up to me, "don't look at the controls. Look at where you want to go, and lean toward your goal."

Guhhhh. I got off the thing, moved it around so it finally pointed away from people, and tried again. I lifted my gaze to the end of the practice lot and before I could even take a nerve-choked breath, I found myself rolling smoothly toward the road.

"Whoa!"

"Now straighten, and back up to where you were," Lucas suggested.

With a glance over my shoulder to make sure I didn't kill anything, I did it. I actually did it.

After mastering that, learning to make turns with the controls on the left-hand twist grip wasn't so bad. And before fifteen more minutes had passed, even Lissa and Carly had stopped running into things and had made it to the end of the lot and back without injury to themselves or anyone else.

"We're off," Megan called. "Try not to lose sight of me, and stick to the roads only. You've got off-road tires, but no four-wheeling on these things, all right?"

We rolled out of the parking lot at a dizzying pace that some-one doing a fast walk could probably keep up with—but hey, at least we were moving. We strung out along the road in twos and threes, gaining confidence with each minute. Jeremy leaned for-ward and opened it up so that he kept pace with Megan. I thought he looked a little out of control, but I had enough to do with my own machine. Megan would have to rescue him if he wound up flat on his face in the weeds.

Lissa, Carly, and Shani were just ahead of Lucas and me, keep-ing a tight little formation that was probably more fear than de-sign. With a firm grip on the handles, the wind in my face, and Lucas beside me, I began to relax and enjoy myself. The rain of the week before had made fresh green grass come bursting out of the pale soil, covering the hillsides. Madrone trees, with their curly branches and peeling red bark, shaded the road as we sailed over a shoulder of the hillside and headed down a gentle slope toward the water.

"This is a good place to practice a nice, tight turn," Megan called.

"You'd have to keep it nice and tight," I muttered, "or you'd wind up in the Bay." Now that was motivation for you.

Jeremy and Lucas took the curve at what looked like warp speed, and Lissa and I shook our heads. "Show-offs," I said.

"I think Jeremy's trying to impress you, Shani," Lissa teased.

Shani snorted and tossed her sixties-style ponytail. "That boy could use a dip in the drink. Cool him off before he kills himself."

We took the turn at a speed slightly above a crawl, but hey, at least we made it. We rolled up the hill in the hot sun and followed the road back into the trees while over her shoulder, Megan gave us some history of the island. Not that I was really listening. I was too busy wondering where along this road Lucas might drag me away from the others. Would we hike to the summit of this hill? Would he kiss me up there on the top, where we could see everything and be seen by no one? How were we going to lose the group without looking like we'd done it on purpose?

With the speed and the sun and my happy thoughts, our one-hour rental vanished like morning fog. We coasted back into the lot feeling like total Segway pros. In fact, having my own feet under me again made me feel slow and not very efficient. Like a turtle instead of a dolphin.

But despite that, when Lucas suggested a walk up to the summit that would take a couple of hours, I was the first one to second the motion. The two science geeks had had enough of all this fresh air, though. They opted to hang out at the snack bar until the next ferry came, which left Lucas and me, Lissa, Carly, Shani, and the ever-persistent Jeremy (maybe he did have a thing going for Shani) walking up the road in the opposite direction of the one we'd taken on wheels. Before long a sign appeared, pointing out a trail to the summit.

"Looks like a short cut," Lucas said. "Shorter but steeper. Want to try it?"

"Not me." Lissa slugged back some Evian from her backpack. I did the same while I had the chance. "I don't even care about getting to the top. I just want a nice walk in the trees, admiring the view. No sweat. No muscle cramps. Just a nice, even calorie burn."

"Right, like you need that," Shani pointed out.

"She may not, but I do," Carly said. "No short cuts for me, either. We'll take the long way."

Shani decided to go with them, and where Shani went, Jeremy went. I tried not to sound too eager or too delighted. "See you at the top, then."

"If we change our minds and decide to go back down, we'll be on the four o'clock ferry. Meet at the dock."

See? We didn't have to lose them after all. They walked off down the road and Lucas and I started up the trail. I'm not big into fitness, but half an hour of that and I was wishing I'd worked a little harder in Phys. Ed. But Lucas didn't seem to mind. He didn't have anything to prove in the manliness department—in fact, he seemed pretty happy to stop every once in a while so we could take in the view or just breathe the salty air.

"I love that smell," I said. "Salt water mixed with old leaves and something else. What is it? Peppermint?"

"It's like that stuff my mom put on my chest when I had a cold." Lucas got up from the rock he was sitting on and pointed up. "That's it. Eucalyptus."

Sure enough, a stand of them spiced the air with the smell of Vicks VapoRub. In the warm sun, in that place, it just seemed right, you know? Or maybe I have a warped sense of the romantic. You go find your own olfactory memory. This one's mine. Because what happened next pretty much cemented the time, the place, and the scent in my memory forever.

"Gillian?" He sat back down on the rock next to me.

"Mm?" I took another deep breath.

"Come here."

I opened my mouth to say, "I *am* here," and he leaned in and kissed me.

Oh, my.

My first real kiss—on Valentine's Day to boot—just the way I'd been dreaming about it. The view, the sun, the rock . . . well, maybe not the scent of Vicks VapoRub, but that's not exactly the kind of thing you script when you dream, is it?

His mouth was soft and warm, and I had no idea how experienced he was, because I had no experience to judge by. I just let the moment take me, and you know what? Experience didn't matter. Living it did.

And I lived that moment a hundred percent.

He pulled away and I realized the cramped feeling in my chest was from holding my breath. I tried not to gasp as I filled my lungs. As far as I was concerned, they could bottle that smell and I'd buy gallons of it, just so I could return instantly to this moment.

"I've been waiting for that all day," Lucas whispered, his lean face inches from mine.

I nodded, still trying to control my unsteady breathing. You'd think I'd have the hang of it by now—I've been doing it all my life. But one kiss from Lucas and my body's most basic operations forgot how to work.

"Me, too," I finally managed.

"True? You're not just saying that?"

"No." Gathering up my courage, I leaned in to kiss him this time. The secret to mastering anything is practice, right?

I even managed to breathe a little, so that when I pulled back I didn't feel so light-headed. "I was wondering all morning how we were going to ditch the others," I confessed softly. "But I didn't know how you felt, so I couldn't do anything."

"I'm all for ditching." With one finger, he smoothed my hair behind my ear. "Your hair has blue lights in it."

"Yours has gold." I smiled into his eyes. "Not a very well matched pair, unless you count the school colors."

He grinned. "I think we are. You're the smartest girl in school."

"I don't know about that. There are plenty of girls in my classes with SAT scores like mine."

"So modest. When you have every reason not to be."

"The Lord doesn't like pride, remember?"

"Yeah, but at Spencer it's hard to find a girl who doesn't think it's all about her."

"Maybe. Personally, I think it's all about us—my friends. *Our* friends." I smiled at him. "I don't know Shani very well yet, but from what I've seen of her, she's nice. Funny, too."

He kissed me again. "Are you trying to set me up with her or what?"

I smiled. "Of course not. Jeremy would probably give you some competition anyway."

He huffed out a breath in a laugh. "I wondered where he came from."

"He hangs out at our table sometimes. He likes to listen to my stories."

"That's one of the first things I noticed about you."

"What, that I was loud?"

"No, silly. That it was hard to get near you for the crowd. Always entertaining."

Was that a problem? "I like telling stories. Stuff just seems to happen to me, and people like to listen when I tell them about it."

"Do they?"

"Sure." I hesitated. "At least, I think they do."

"It just seems funny, that's all."

Had I done something wrong? "What?"

He slipped an arm around me, and I lost my grip on what we were saying.

"Seeing an Asian girl at the center of attention, you know? Lacey Takamoto and Vi Truong are in my calculus class, and I can barely get a hello out of them. It's like they're pathologically shy or something."

"Or they listen to their grandmothers better than I do." My tone was wry. "She's always telling me I'm too loud, too disrespectful, that I get in people's faces too much." I heard my own words dissolve into the clear air. "Do you think she's right?"

He settled his arm more comfortably around me. "You are not disrespectful."

Uh-oh. He agreed with Nai-Nai on the other points, obviously. Oh, wow. Maybe it was true. Maybe I really was an overbearing loudmouth and people listened to me not because they were interested, but because they couldn't get a word in edgewise.

Hot blood crept into my cheeks, burning as it went. Why hadn't anybody told me? Why did Lissa act like it didn't matter? Why did Carly put up with me? Was that why she was so quiet? Because with me around, nobody else got a chance to talk?

"Hey." He gave me a little squeeze. "Don't beat yourself up. Ready to go?"

I got up. "Sure." More than ready to walk away from myself. I was really going to have to watch it, or I'd find that not only would I lose my friends, I'd chase Lucas away, too.

Father, thank You for using Lucas to show me what a jerk I am. Help me to do better, Lord. I'll pay attention to Nai-Nai from now on, I promise. I want to keep humble in Your sight, so I guess that means not being the center of attention. Help me put other people first, Lord. Amen.

I felt a little better after putting it in God's hands. We climbed up the lower part of the hill and came out on the far side of the island. Below, I could see a pink dot and an orange one: Lissa and Carly. They were headed to some beat-up looking buildings that stood wearily at attention around a little cove.

"What's that?" Lucas asked. "A museum?"

"Maybe." Instead of leading the way to join my friends, I hesitated. Guys liked it when you asked their opinion first, didn't they? "Want to check it out?"

"Sure."

We met up with the two girls at a sign that informed us this was the Quarantine Station and a tour would leave at one o'clock.

"Quarantine for what?" I wondered out loud as we went to find the meeting point. "Malaria? Smallpox?" Maybe this place had been a leper colony or something. Yikes.

"Where's your other friend?" Lucas asked Lissa.

"Who, Shani? We lost her and Jeremy somewhere along the way."

"Or they lost us, more like," Carly put in. "I'm starting to get a complex."

I exchanged a glance with Lissa and something in my expression made her eyes widen. She looked from me to Lucas and raised her brows. When I nodded, she sucked in a breath and gave me a not-very-subtle grin that, thankfully, Lucas didn't see.

At one on the dot, the guide met us and we found out in the first couple of sentences that these buildings weren't for quarantining sick people.

They were for quarantining Asian people.

Immigrants. Families coming to Old Gold Mountain to make their fortune. Men, women, and little kids stuck in these uncomfortable barracks with their iron beds and laundry strung from one to the other, able to look out the windows and see freedom but not have it. Because the government was busy interrogating them, holding their papers, deciding whether or not they could stay.

"After the facility was decommissioned in 1940," the guide explained, leading us over to a wall covered in a piece of Plexiglas, "these barracks were preserved, primarily because of these poems carved into the wall."

I leaned closer and blinked. In the silence, a gull called as it wheeled over the cove below. I felt Lucas's warmth next to me. "Can you read it?"

"*Bright moon*," I said softly, touching the hard plastic over the characters, which had been carved in with a passionate yet careful hand. An educated hand. A hand that maybe had to settle for building a railroad or doing some rich person's laundry to make a living, instead of painting graceful characters on rice paper.

"*The morning breeze and bright moon linger together.*" My translation was as slow and halting as a child's.

"*I think about the native village far away*
Cut off by clouds and mountains.
On the little island,
The wailing of cold, wild geese can be faintly heard."

"Geese?" Lucas's voice broke the silence.

"Maybe it was fall," Carly said. "This is where they go when they fly south."

I read the rest of the poem to myself and murmured the last line. "*Why else do we come to this place to be imprisoned?*"

But they'd already turned to go, and I don't think anybody heard me.

chapter 10

ALL RIGHT, GIRLFRIEND." Lissa grabbed me and swung me around so that I flopped onto my bed next to Carly. Shani pushed a pillow up against Lissa's headboard and settled against it, and Lissa sat at the foot, Indian style. "You hardly said a word all night and we're dying, here. Tell us about the kiss. Every last detail."

"You're worse than my mother."

We'd gone out for supper at a little seafood place in Tiburon, but with half a dozen people yakking it up at the table, it wasn't exactly the place to reveal your innermost secrets. Besides, I'd made up my mind to watch my mouth from here on out, which is probably why everyone else was doing the aforesaid yakking.

What a concept. Lucas was right.

But here, in our dorm room, it was different. These were my friends, and they wanted every word in a bad way.

"We hiked up almost to the top of the hill," I began, "and sat on this flat rock to look at the view."

"The view." Shani nodded at Lissa. "Uh-huh."

"Shut up." I leaned across and whacked her on the knee. "There were these eucalyptus trees that smelled like Vicks VapoRub."

"I *so* don't want to hear about smelly trees," Carly said. "Get to the good part."

I sighed. "That's called setting the scene, you uncouth wenches."

"What Carly said." Lissa made a rolling, get-on-with-it motion with her hand.

"So I was sitting there saying something inane and he said, 'Come here,' and I was all, 'I *am* here,' and he leaned in and kissed me."

"What was it like?" Carly wanted to know.

"I, uh . . ." Okay, did they really need to know it was my first kiss? That I didn't have anything to compare it to?

Lissa leaned forward. "What she means is, can the guy kiss? You never know with these brainy types."

"The guy can kiss," I said firmly. "Intense research proves it beyond any doubt."

"Woohoo!" Shani leaned over and gave me a high five.

They were so honestly happy for me that I figured it was safe enough to confess my dark secret. "To be honest, it's my *only* research."

The laughter died into amazed silence. Oh, great.

"You mean . . ." Carly began.

I nodded. "First time. Except for, like, relatives. Which don't count."

Carly clasped her knees. "That is *so* romantic. I bet he organized the whole day just so he could kiss you up there in that beautiful spot."

"I don't know about that." But what if it was true? What if he had engineered the whole boat trip and hike and everything, just so he could find the perfect moment for our first kiss? "No way. Guys just don't do stuff like that."

"Ninety percent of guys don't bring you roses when they screw up a date, either," Lissa said. "Think about it."

I was. Intensely. "Wow," I said. "This must be the real thing, then. Even if he does think I talk too much."

"You do not." Carly was so sweet.

"Oh, I think I do. Didn't you notice how everyone got a chance to talk at supper because I kept a lid on it for once?"

Lissa eyed me, puzzled. "We talked about as much as always. Even Jeremy, when he wasn't staring at Shani all googly-eyed."

Shani threw a pillow at her. And Lissa threw it at me. I grabbed a couple of silk ones from Thailand off the head of my bed and chucked them back. And then a full-scale pillow fight broke out, with Shani swinging my down-filled one at Carly, who defended herself with a fat one with an elephant beaded on it.

By the time we'd declared a truce, everyone had forgotten about the conversation except me. Because, you know, I'd noticed they didn't try very hard to disagree with me. They were just being nice. Which made me all the more determined to keep a lock on my lips and give other people a chance to speak up.

My lips had more important things to do, anyway, if you get my drift.

VTalbot	Still doing business?
Source10	Yes.
VTalbot	How do I know you won't turn me in?
Source10	I have more to lose.
VTalbot	Why don't you use a school ID?
Source10	See above. What do you want?
VTalbot	Math final.
Source10	$1.5K.
VTalbot	Rory said 1K!
Source10	Don't you listen to Curzon? Risk is greater. So is the price.

VTalbot   :(OK. PayPal?
Source10   Of course. 24 hours in advance.

ON TUESDAY the gorgeous weather still held, so after classes were over, Lucas and I found a table in the sun in the central quad to study. Since the building shielded us from the wind off the Bay, it felt warm, and the lawn had dried out enough for Maintenance to mow it.

I opened my copy of *The Collected Poems of John Donne* and prepared to do battle with my English paper. We had to choose one of three topics. I'd picked the one that seemed the easiest, but all the same, I was looking at two weeks of screaming mental agony trying to write it. And then there were finals to look forward to. What horrors would the instructor come up with for those?

I'd already asked Lissa to trade me some coaching on the mysteries of seventeenth-century metaphor in exchange for help with memorization of biological processes. I also had to compose a one-minute piece for piano in my Comp class, write a research paper on monotheistic religion in ancient Egypt, and produce another paper on the economics of corn in Brazil for Global Studies.

My whole head hurt just thinking about getting it all done before next Friday.

Somehow, sitting here in the sun with Lucas put it into perspective. I watched him methodically work his way through the word problems the Math instructor had assigned us (which I'd already finished during free period that morning). He had terrific powers of concentration. I decided to follow his example and at least come up with an outline for the Donne paper.

Thirty minutes later, the shadow of the building had crept across the grass and was almost touching us. I had a topic sentence and three possible arguments written in my notebook, which is a miracle no matter how you slice it.

"Thank You, Lord," I murmured, raising my face to the sun, which would slip below the roof of the building any second now.

"Hm?"

"Sorry," I said. "Didn't mean to break your concentration."

"You didn't." He stretched. "I need to take a break anyway, before I look at some physics problems my dad sent me."

Everyone in his life was rallying around him to help get him ready for the Olympiad. An idea popped into my head. I slipped my knotted bracelet with its jade bead off my wrist and handed it to him.

"What's this?"

"It's jade," I said. "It's supposed to bring luck. You and I both know God's in charge of that, but my grandpa gave it to me, so it's kind of special. Keep it until you ace the finals, and every time you look at it, you'll know I'm rooting for you."

"Girl stuff," he mumbled, but he slipped the silk cords over his watch anyway. "Thanks."

Maybe it wasn't a promise ring, but if he wanted to wear something that reminded him of me, I was happy.

As he looked up, Vanessa Talbot strolled across the quad in the direction of the dorm wing, looking stunning in an ultrafeminine Nanette Lepore cropped blazer and black jeans. A froth of lace on her camisole just emphasized the fact that she had something to put in it and I didn't.

Lucas tilted his head, his hand still on my bracelet. "I don't think I've ever seen that girl look bad."

I blinked at him. Again with the Vanessa Watch. "So you said the other day."

"Did I? Stuff like that looks good on someone as slim as her. You're all into clothes." He shook his sleeve down. "What do you think?"

I so did not want to talk about her right after I'd given him something that mattered to me. "I think she got that jacket at Macy's," I mused. "I'd pegged her as a Saks girl."

He gave me a droll look over his glasses. "I have no idea what that means." His gaze fell to my books. "You wrapping up?"

I shoved Donne and my papers into my backpack. I needed to get out of there before I did something embarrassing, like cry. Which I never do. "I told Lissa I'd give her a hand with Bio at four."

"Oh, okay. See you at supper."

He slipped a hand around the back of my neck, under my hair, and pulled me toward him. "Thanks for the good-luck charm."

"Lucas!" I squeaked, yanking back. "Tobin is standing right over there."

Had he really intended to kiss me after hurting my feelings like that? In public? Flushed and confused, I swung my backpack to one shoulder and hurried away over the grass.

Obviously he had no idea he'd hurt me. A kiss to say thank you or good-bye was normal. I was the one who was oversensitive and insecure. Everyone knew that guys were visual creatures, and Lucas was a scientist on top of that. He'd just been making an observation, the way he'd done in the dining room on Saturday.

He liked dark-haired girls, that was all. At least I had that going for me. I climbed the stairs, heading for my room, my thoughts building. I dressed as well as Vanessa—when I put my mind to it. So I didn't have the lips and cheekbones he'd talked about—I couldn't do anything about that.

But he liked to look at her because she was slim. Self-consciously, I ran a hand over my belly as I let myself into the room. Here was something I could do something about.

Lissa looked up from the books opened on her desk. "Hey. I thought you forgot me."

I shook my head. "Lucas and I were studying out in the quad. Lissa, do you think I'm fat?"

Her eyes widened. "You? Good grief. Of course not. Why, did someone say you were?"

"The way I eat, I should be." I patted my stomach. Flat, but not toned. "I've got no ab definition. And my butt could probably use some toning, too."

"Uh, Gillian, in case you didn't notice, you *have* no butt. For which Carly hates you."

"But if it was toned, it might make my clothes look better. If I got serious about this, do you think I could lose a size? Maybe two?"

"And do what? Disappear? There's nothing wrong with how you look. What brought all this on, anyway?"

"Lucas likes thin girls," I confessed, a little hesitantly.

"He should be happy, then. You're a thin girl."

"Not as thin as Vanessa."

"And we all know he thinks she's beautiful, despite the fact she's a piranha." She waved a hand. "Guys. Even Physics Olympi-adans have no brains when it comes to looks."

"Olympians."

"Whatever. Don't worry about what he thinks of her. He's with you. And he loves your brain. Which puts you, like, eons ahead of unevolved things like piranhas."

I laughed and got down to business with the drills and the Bio textbook. But in the back of my mind, I wasn't convinced.

Which is why the next day found me over at the field house, where the class schedules were posted. So what if it was the middle of term? Maybe I could still get into one of them. I scanned the pages pinned to the corkboard.

Soccer. Volleyball. Rowing. Yeah, yeah, I knew about all those.

Water polo. Water aerobics. Hmm. That was a possibility.

Track. Cross-country running. Ugh.

Jazz dance. Ballet. Hip-hop. Possible, but I couldn't see getting the results I wanted fast enough.

Personal Training: All Levels. Aha. Now we were talking.

I found the trainer, whose ID tag said Maggie Modano and who was built like a fire hydrant, in her office. She waved me in. "And who might you be?"

"Gillian Chang," I said. "Music scholarship, secondary emphasis in Chemistry and Math."

"Uh-huh. What can I do for you, Miss Chang?"

"I wondered if it was too late to add a Personal Training session with you."

She folded her hands across what was no doubt a six-pack abdomen. Not that I wanted to see. "Since the second set of midterms is next week, it's a little late."

"I really need to get in shape," I said a little desperately.

"Music not doing that for you?"

"No." Then I had a flash of genius. "You're not regular faculty, right? I could pay you double your going rate."

She looked me over from head to foot, no doubt noticing the flab under my plaid skirt and white blouse. I sucked in my stomach and straightened up.

"All my other clients have been working out since New Year's and my Friday schedule's full. Besides, I don't think you're an ideal candidate for what I do, even at twice the price."

"What does it entail, exactly?"

"It's like boot camp for your body. Running, aerobics, core work, strength training."

"I can do that."

"I'm a demanding trainer. I only work with people who are committed, not people who come in a month into term. Sorry, Miss Chang. No can do."

"Please," I begged. "I have to get in shape fast and this is the best way to do it. It's just for a few weeks. And if I die, it's my responsibility. No harm, no foul."

Her gaze didn't waver as she considered me. "It's going to hurt."

"I know."

"No whining; no complaining."

"Not a sound."

"Fine. Mondays and Wednesdays, fifth period. Be ready to work."

Mondays and Wednesdays. Oh no. That was—

"Dismissed."

Too late now. I fished my schedule out of my backpack to confirm what my sinking stomach was already telling me. Why hadn't I looked at it more carefully before I went to find the trainer?

M/W   1:00–1:50   GRAPHIC ARTS

Was I really going to have to give up the one class that made me happiest in order to get thin for Lucas? No, no. There had to be something I could do. Some way around this.

I found Mr. Caldwell, who is young and looks like the Peter Petrelli character in *Heroes*, in the supply room putting the contents of two open UPS boxes on the shelves. Pastels, inks, thick charcoal sticks . . . all the cool stuff I'd never touched before this term because my parents felt anything beyond the barest appreciation of famous dead painters was a waste of learning hours. He looked up as I hesitated in the doorway.

"Gillian. What's up?"

"Can I talk to you?"

"Sure, if you don't mind me finishing up."

"Go ahead." I stalled. How could I put this? "Um, I've got a scheduling conflict for the rest of term, and I'm hoping we can work something out."

"I'm sure we can. What is it?"

I told him. "So I'm wondering if there's another section of the class I could take."

"No, that's the only one."

"Well, if I complete all the assignments and get the notes from one of the other kids, could we do it that way?"

He put the last of the supplies away and tossed one of the empty boxes inside the other one. "I'm at a bit of a loss here, Gillian. Why the big rush to get a personal trainer at this point in the term?"

The temptation to lie and say it was on doctor's orders or something flooded my thinking, but I fought it back. "I'm in terrible shape, and I think fitness training will help."

"That's pretty lame." His glance pinned me like a butterfly on a board. "Fine, if you don't want to tell me, that's up to you. But I'm afraid I'm going to have to say no on the plan you're suggesting. Art isn't a matter of cribbing notes. It's a matter of experiencing what you're taught."

"But I can experience it. What difference does it make if I'm drawing in the classroom or the dorm room? I'm still doing the work."

"You can't telecommute to art class. You have to learn the techniques in a supervised environment. And if you're going to produce a piece for your final at the end of March, you'll need the techniques we'll be going into during these next weeks."

I stared at him, unwilling to admit defeat. "Is there no way we can work this out? You know I love your class."

He nodded. "But for some reason, you love something else more. Which is entirely your business." He paused a moment. "There's one thing I can do. I can give you an Incomplete instead of an F. That way, you can take the class again during spring term and it won't count against your GPA."

An Incomplete! Dad would have a pink furry *fit*.

And yet . . . a vision of Lucas looking at me the way he looked at Vanessa Talbot blotted out the thought of my father's incredulous face.

"Okay," I said. "Let's do it."

VTalbot   I want to know who you are.

Source10   No can do.

VTalbot   A man of mystery.

Source10   Or woman.

VTalbot   Student or staff?

Source10   What do you think?

VTalbot   Student. Junior or senior, no lower.

Source10   Correct.

VTalbot   Ha! I knew it. Blond or dark?

Source10   Both.

VTalbot   Ooh. I like that.

Source10   They told me you were a flirt.

VTalbot   You think I'm flirting?

✉

To: All Students
From: NCurzon@spenceracad.edu
Date: March 2, 2009
Re: Junior class finals

A few weeks ago I notified you that exam answer sheets were being distributed for payment among students. We have investigated several leads, but as yet have been unsuccessful in identifying the student who is behind this fraudulent activity. During this last round of midterms, however, we found several students in possession of purchased answer sheets. They have accepted failing grades for those exams.

I'm sure you can imagine my disappointment, as well as that of our staff. As a result, I very much regret to inform you that if the perpetrator is not brought to light by the time finals begin on March 23, the entire junior class will be held responsible. This means that you will all receive Fs on your examinations. You will repeat your term and be forced to make up the spring term's work during summer session.

I leave it up to you to do the right thing. I am confident that Spencer's values of loyalty and intellect will triumph, and you will force the person responsible out into the light to take the consequences of his or her actions.

Sincerely,
Natalie Curzon, Ph.D., M.Ed.
Principal, Spencer Academy

chapter 11

M Y JAW DROPPED. I glanced over at Lissa, who was at her desk doing e-mail as well. "Did you see this?"

"The message from Ms. Curzon? Oh, yeah. Some of the kids were talking about it in fifth period."

Whereas I had not been talking. I had been under Ms. Modano's critical eye, doing crunches and laps at the gym, and had had no breath for irrelevant activities like talking.

"But how can they do this? It's not fair to punish all of us for the crimes of a few."

"Of course it isn't. It's idiotic."

"My parents would have matching coronaries if I came home with Fs. They'd never get over it, no matter what the reason was."

I tried to imagine my dad at some board meeting and someone asking how I was doing out there in California. He'd have to lie, wouldn't he? He certainly couldn't admit to his Type-A, driven buddies that his Type-A, driven daughter had gotten a full slate of failure.

Even if it wasn't her fault.

And my mom? She and the women on her charity boards—not to mention the mah jongg ladies—would be twittering about their kids and she'd die of shame before she'd admit the truth.

"There's only one thing to do," Lissa said, clicking rapidly through her messages. "Keep our ears to the ground and flush the guy out of the bushes."

At least it wasn't a marine metaphor.

"Easier said than done," I said, a little hopelessly. How could we do that if the administration couldn't? "What if it's a senior? We don't hang out with them much."

"If they thought it was a senior, they'd have threatened the senior class," she pointed out with crystalline logic.

"Good point. I vote we tackle Rory Stapleton and hang him up by the thumbs until he tells us who he got his eighty-two percent from."

We looked at each other. "Ewwwwww," we said together, and laughed.

My iPhone chimed and I fished it out of my bag. A 212 area code flashed on the screen. "Oh, no," I groaned. Just what I *didn't* need.

"Miss Chang?" my dad's executive assistant said. "I have the Chairman of the Formosa-Pacific Bank for you."

I rolled my eyes. Megan Tam had been working for my dad since I was eleven and she'd never called me by my name yet. I knew she knew it, though, because when flowers came from him, they were addressed to "Gillian," and you can bet a term's worth of grades that he didn't toddle down to the florist's to order them himself.

"Thanks, Megan," I said. "Put him through."

"Jiao-Lan?" my father said as soon as the line clicked through. "What's this I hear?"

"I'm fine, Dad," I said cheerfully, despite the fact that my heart had just bounced off my shoelaces. He never called me Jiao-Lan unless he was massively upset. "How about yourself?"

"Don't try to change the subject. I just received an e-mail from your principal. What is this nonsense about your grades?"

Good grief. You get an Incomplete in one class and they notify your parents? What kind of police state was this? "I switched classes at the last minute, Dad. It's no big deal."

"You get an F for switching classes? Are you insane, or is the administration?"

"No, no. I don't get an F, I get an Incomplete. I'm just going to take it again next term and it won't affect my GPA. The instructor told me so last week."

"That's not what this message said. It said you were going to fail all your classes. Not Incomplete. *Fail.* I want an explanation. What's going on out there?"

My neurons, as exhausted as the rest of me, finally got themselves into line. "Did Ms. Curzon send all the parents a note as well? About failing the junior class if these guys who are selling exam answers don't turn themselves in?"

"What?"

I explained, using as few polysyllabic words as possible.

"That's outrageous!" my father exploded. "Giving universal Fs is simply unacceptable. I'm calling that woman right now and pulling you out of there. They'd never try something like this at Brearley."

"Dad. Calm down. All the juniors are in the same boat." Time for a little improv. "All of us are banding together to find out who it is. It'll never get to the point of us all failing. It can't."

"It better not. I'm certainly not going to be explaining it to the family—not after the New Year's debacle. Your Auntie Jen-Mai and Uncle So send their love, by the way. They're visiting New York from Taipei this week."

Nai-Nai's sister and brother-in-law, with whom we stayed when we were in Taiwan. Dad had a palatial corporate apartment there, of course, but it would have caused a couple generations' worth of offense if he came to town and didn't stay and visit at length with his family.

"Give my love back to them. How are Mom and Nai-Nai?"

"They're both fine. Your mother says to call. She wants to know if you want anything from the Shanghai Tang spring collection. I didn't know you were interested in porcelains."

I grinned. She must be ready to speak to me again if she was holding out clothes like an olive branch. "Shanghai Tang's a designer, Dad. Clothes, not china. I'll let you know how this exam thing turns out, okay? I've gotta go."

"I'll be waiting. 'Bye, now."

Lissa eyed me as I tapped the phone off. "He freaked, huh?"

"Oh, yeah. Big time. But he was pretty calm by the end."

"We have to figure out how to find these guys in, what?" She glanced at the calendar hanging over my desk. "Three weeks?"

"I know. I'm open to ideas." I lowered myself slowly into my chair, but in spite of myself, a groan leaked out from between my teeth.

"Are you okay?" Lissa asked, frowning.

"Oh, sure. Just a little stiff from gym class." Thirty laps and a hundred and fifty crunches over the Blue Ball of Brutality. But who's counting?

"A little stiff. You can hardly move. Volleyball can't be that strenuous."

"It's not volleyball. I have a personal trainer now. And she's kicking my rear."

"When did you start being a Phys. Ed. major? Yuck."

"Last week. I dropped Graphic Arts so I could do this instead."

She stared at me. "Did you go off your meds? Or are you trying to get into the military?"

I started to laugh but stopped short when it involved using my aching diaphragm. "Just trying to get in shape."

"So you dropped art to major in pain? I thought you liked that class. Kaz says you're really good."

"I do like it. Caldwell is giving me an Incomplete so I can take it again next term." I nodded at my phone. "That's what I thought Dad was calling to bellow about."

She stared at me for a second. "I don't get you. Most people would just run around the block or go on a watermelon fast, not drop a class they liked to take something that hurts this bad."

"Painful, maybe, but effective." I snapped the waistband of my yoga pants. "These are already getting looser."

"Okay," she said in an it's-your-funeral tone, and turned back to her laptop. "You gotta do what you gotta do, I guess. Let me know if you need some Tylenol."

I'm no dummy. I took her up on it.

Consequently, when Carly sent out a group IM a little later asking if Lissa, Shani, and I wanted to skip dinner and grab a cab over to a new California Mex place she'd heard about down in the Marina, I was feeling almost human again. Well, at least not broken in three or four places. The wonders of modern pharmaceuticals.

But when we got our food (a tortilla salad for me, without the tortilla strips or guacamole, which is really a travesty, but what are you gonna do?), Carly and Shani weren't nearly so generous.

"Are you nuts?" Shani asked bluntly, her dark eyes disbelieving under a new braided 'do. I swear, that girl changes her hair every week.

"Not according to my therapist," I said, deadpan.

"But why would you give up something you really like for Phys. Ed.?" Her face crinkled with distaste. "I mean, blech!"

"I like Phys. Ed.," Carly put in, nibbling on a chip. "I know you hate volleyball, but not all of us do."

"We're not talking about volleyball," Shani retorted. "We're talking about laps around the gym and chin-ups and crunches. Paramilitary torture tactics."

"That's a bit extreme." I forked up my boring salad and tried to keep calm. "You guys are taking this way too seriously."

"It's not the trainer or what she's having you do. It's the reason you're doing it," Lissa said gently.

"And what would that be?"

The three of them looked at each other.

"Lucas," Lissa said.

"You say that like it's a bad thing. So what if I want to look good for him? It's not like you haven't been fixated on exactly the same thing before."

"I do not get fixated on my looks," Lissa protested with dignity.

"Last term you did. All you could think about for weeks was what to wear for Callum McCloud."

She flinched as if I'd reached over and slapped her, and without so much as a comeback, she dropped her gaze to what was left of her shrimp-stuffed chile relleno. I felt like slapping myself. But instead, my mouth kept talking even though my brain said stop.

"I don't get why you guys are making such a big deal of this. It's just a class. Get over it."

"That's not the point." Eyes on her plate like the secrets of the Bio final were written on it, Lissa wasn't letting go. "It's a big deal because you're giving up something you love to look good for a guy."

"And we all know what *Cosmo* would say about that," Shani said, clearly trying to lighten the mood.

"Be honest, Gillian," Carly said. "Is hanging onto Lucas worth this kind of pain?" She held up a hand. "Don't give me that look. I saw how you were walking on the way here."

"Like every muscle hurt." Shani nodded in agreement. "Guys give you enough pain. You don't have to go looking for it, girl."

"Thank you, Dr. Hanna," I said, and now it was her turn to look hurt. "I so appreciate your support."

"Now, just hang on a minute." Lissa grabbed my wrist as I reached for my bag. "Sit down. We need to do something."

"Like what? Tear apart the way I practice piano?"

"No." I had to hand it to her. She hung in there where lots of girls would have let me storm out long ago. "We need to pray about this."

The waiter whisked our plates away. All around us, couples and businesspeople and random college kids chowed down, oblivious to us. Not that it mattered. I'm not afraid to talk to the Lord in public.

"Sure," I said, and got comfy with my elbows on the table. "Let's do that." I closed my eyes. "Father, thank You for Carly's idea to have dinner together in a public place." *So that they can pick me apart politely and I can't do anything that would cause a scene.* "Thank You that everyone is so comfortable about telling me exactly how they feel." *And not listening to my feelings at all.* "I pray You would fill them with grace." *Because they sure don't have any right now.* "And help us all to be better friends. In Jesus' name, amen."

I opened my eyes to find all three of them staring at me. "You call that a prayer?" Shani turned to Carly. "I'm not a Christian or anything, but I always thought there was more to it than that."

"Oh, so you're judging my prayers now?" This was new. Not unexpected, but new.

"We're not judging anything, girl," Shani said. "We're your friends. We're trying to help you."

"If you weren't so crazed about this guy, you'd see that," Lissa pointed out. And she thinks I'm a bulldog. "Since you've started going out with him, you've ditched us, ignored us, and now you're getting hostile at us just for telling you what we're seeing."

"Love is patient, love is kind, and all that," Carly said.

"You'd know," I snapped. Enough was enough. "I guess you'd have to be the most patient person on the planet to wait for Brett Loyola to notice you."

"All right." Lissa ripped her credit card out of her bag and snatched up the check. "Come on, Carly. Shani, you too. If Gillian wants to make herself miserable, that's fine. But she doesn't need to make us that way, too."

And they left me sitting there, in the middle of the noisy restaurant, where I'd never felt so alone.

chapter 12

HERE ARE TIMES when you just need to hear a kind voice, and this was one of them.

I scrolled to Lucas's number, and even the sound of the call ringing through made me feel better.

"Hey," he answered. "I was just thinking about you."

A smile spread all over my face, and I pushed the door of the restaurant open out onto the street. "Likewise. So I called."

"Sounds like you're outside."

"I am. I'm down in the Marina. I just had a fight with my friends so I'm trying to find a cab."

"Sorry to hear that. Want me to come and get you? I have an experiment to finish, but—"

I shrugged even though he couldn't see me. What a sweetie. I waved, and a cab swerved to a stop in front of me. "No biggie. They'll get over it. So what are you up to?" I settled into the back seat and the cabbie took off as though his sedan ran on jet fuel.

"I just got off the phone with my dad. What are you doing Saturday?"

I thought fast. "The usual. Studying. Practicing. And I have to work on my Comp term project sometime. Like, soon."

"Comp? Like, English composition?"

"No, music composition. I have to compose two to four pages of music and perform it, either solo or in ensemble, for the final. If you do it in ensemble you get extra credit because it means writing out however many parts you have instruments for and rehearsing them and stuff."

"Sounds complicated."

"The music part is pretty straightforward. It's finding people who will sit down long enough to rehearse that's the problem. So I'll probably go with straight piano, or maybe a duet with piano and harp. I just don't have time right now to chase down violinists and cellists." Not with Chem and Math and what would no doubt be another horrific English paper to produce.

"You could always record the harp yourself and play it as background when you do the piano part live."

I drew back and stared at the phone, then put it to my ear again. "What a great idea. You *are* a genius."

"I have a T-shirt that says so," he said with endearing modesty. "So now that we've solved that, do you feel like coming to Palo Alto with me on Saturday? The Olympics are three days after finals, during spring break, so my dad's going to coach me. Maybe you could help us."

He wants you to meet his dad! I fought down my rising excitement. The girls could be a bunch of critical sour grapes if they wanted. Lucas really wanted to be with me, to include me in the most important event of his life. And I'd lost half an inch off my waist. I'd make sure I wore something that emphasized it.

"I'd love to," I said. "What time are you heading down there?"

"Usually I go Friday night, but since you can come, I'll go Saturday so you don't have to worry about how an overnight would look."

Oh, he was so considerate. Only a Christian guy would think of things like this.

"I'll get the car and meet you at eight on the front steps, okay?"

"I'll be there," I said, happiness coloring my voice the way an augmented seventh colors a whole chord and makes it different.

My mood had improved about ninety percent by the time the cab dropped me at the school gates. I took care of the other ten percent by walking around the huge rectangle formed by the streets around the school. If any calories had been lingering in my system after that salad, they'd be gone for sure now.

Even though the slope wasn't too bad, the muscles in my thighs felt weak and wobbly as I walked up the drive and then climbed the stone stairs to the second floor. Maybe by the end of next week, they'd have gotten used to the extra work they were being asked to do, and toughen up.

I opened the door of our room, expecting to have to dive into Round Two with Lissa, but it was empty. What a relief. All I wanted was to fall into the shower and stay there, letting the jet of water massage my poor abused self.

The envelope lying on the floor bounced off the toe of my sneaker, so that I felt it before I saw it. I bent to pick it up. My name had been typed neatly on the front.

```
Miss Chang,
If you return before 8:00 p.m., please come by
my office.
Thanks and kind regards,
Natalie Curzon
```

I glanced at my watch, which said seven forty-eight. What on earth could the headmistress want with me? Had Dad gone off the deep end and called her anyway, threatening to pull me out? I didn't feel like getting in the middle of *that* tug of war. Talk about the clash of the Titans. Dad knew I wanted to stay here, and it would have been easy enough for Curzon to explain what that e-mail had been about.

No, she must want me for another reason. Maybe she needed me to tutor somebody. Or . . . *ooh!* I stopped in the middle of throwing my uniform back on.

Maybe someone had fallen off the Physics Olympics team and she wanted me to sub in!

Holy cats. Could you imagine Lucas and me on the same team, dazzling them all? All those hours of coaching time we could spend together? I mean, I'm a pretty supportive girlfriend, I think, but I don't see a whole lot of him. And I don't complain. I know he's holed up in his room, studying like a crazed person (to use Lissa's expression).

I buttoned my blouse as fast as I could, swiped a brush through my hair, and glanced at my watch again. Seven fifty-four. *Move it, girlfriend.*

Ninety seconds, two floors, and three corridors later, I skidded to a halt outside the oak slab that is Ms. Curzon's inner door. It stood open, and she lifted her head from her computer monitor as she heard my graceless arrival.

"Miss Chang," she said pleasantly. "Do come in, and close the door."

Hugging my prospects to myself, I did as she asked and slid into the chair in front of her desk. She took her glasses off and gazed at me.

"I hope I haven't interrupted anything," she said.

"Oh, no. I just got back from dinner."

"I thought you might be studying in the library or with your friends."

Studying. Wow. Maybe I'd guessed right.

"I have been spending a lot of time on Chemistry this term. And in the Physics lab," I said delicately.

"Have you, now?" She glanced at the monitor. "I must say, your grades in AP Chemistry are impressive, as are your efforts in Pre-Calculus. What will you do with yourself next year, I wonder?"

I wasn't sure if she wanted a real answer or not, so I just smiled and waited. This was it, I was sure of it.

"It takes a student with an advanced grasp of both disciplines, not to mention a certain amount of skill with computers, to access the password-protected area of our server and find the examination files." She looked at me.

I sat there, completely at a loss. "Ma'am?"

"Is that what you've been doing, Gillian?"

I stared at her, lost in the horrific crash between expectation and reality. Words refused to form in my brain. "I don't understand the question."

"Goodness me. You don't understand the question. Well, let me rephrase it. Only the most brilliant of the many fine minds at Spencer have the ability to fill out the answers on such a range of examinations. My pool of suspects is, therefore, fairly small. Hence, my request to meet with you."

Finally, I got it. "You think *I'm* doing this? Selling the answers? Me?"

"Not necessarily. I'm asking everyone on my list the same questions."

"It's not me." How inadequate was that? "Ms. Curzon, you have to believe me."

"And why is that?"

"Because—because I didn't do it! I have no idea who did, but we're doing our best to find out."

As of now, the four of us were totally on the case. The only thing worse than punishing the whole junior class for something they didn't do was punishing *me* for something I didn't do. I'd make it up to Lissa, Carly, and Shani as soon as I got out of here. Apologize on my knees if I had to. Then we'd get to work.

"I seem to remember a conversation last term in which you told me how easy it was to hack into the school server," she said. "Not the sort of thing you'd usually confide to the headmistress, is it?"

"I was trying to help Lissa," I said. "That was a completely different conversation. And I don't even take IT classes, except Intro to Programming, like everyone else. I wouldn't know how to start hacking into anything."

Except my brother's password-protected laptop, just for fun one Saturday when I was at home and bored, but there was no way on earth I was going to tell her that.

"Fortunately, I do have proof of that. Your notebook's IP address does not appear on the IT logs as doing anything out of the ordinary. Though I must admit a truly smart hacker wouldn't use his or her own computer."

"They'd use one of the anonymous ones in the lab," I agreed quickly. Maybe a little too quickly. "I promise you, ma'am, I'm not the one you want. But we'll find them. The junior class won't fail. All of us will make sure of that."

"Let's hope you're right. Have a pleasant evening, Miss Chang. Thank you again for coming to see me."

A pleasant evening. Was she kidding?

My insides shook. I tried to hold myself tall and use a normal stride, but between nerves and overworked muscles, it was all I could do to put one shoe in front of the other. The corridors on the return trip stretched into the distance, endless. All the doors looked the same. The pictures of celebrities who had gone to school here, autographed to various principals dating back to the early 1900s, blurred into one another.

She thought I was capable of selling exam answers! Me! What kind of a Christian was I if the headmistress could suspect me of cheating and profiting from it? Not that I think I should be above suspicion just because of what I believe. But it should be taken into account, at least, shouldn't it?

I'd been nothing but honest and nice in dealing with everyone. I didn't play favorites with people—well, except my group of close friends, and you could hardly blame a person for that. But I guess all that didn't count in the face of the simple fact that I was smart—and only really smart people were the suspects.

Which goes to show you just how weird this situation was. Well, there was a cure for weirdness, and I took it.

Father, I know You see everything, including people's hearts. Forgive me for mouthing off to You earlier, and hear me now. Please give Ms. Curzon the confidence that I'm innocent. Help me to be a better vessel for Your love and kindness—and for Your clarity and truth. And Father, please reveal who's really doing this. I can't believe You'd want the whole class to be punished and for this person to get away with it. If I can help, I'm in Your hands.

My muscles still hurt, but my heart felt better as I finally staggered into my own dorm. The water was running in the shower, and Lissa's Marc Jacobs bag lay on the bed.

I took a deep breath. "Lissa?" I called through the shower door.

No answer. A loofah mitt slapped soap energetically. I'd bet a term's worth of *crème brulée* that the three of them had been in Carly's room, ripping me from one side to the other just as energetically.

"Look, Lissa, I'm really sorry. I apologize for hurting your feelings and making a total butt of myself."

"It's not just my feelings you have to worry about." Her voice sounded muffled, as if she was exfoliating her face, a task much more important than listening to me grovel.

"I know. I was horrible to Carly and Shani. I'll apologize to them, too, but it's you I have to live with." I waited for a second. "Lissa? Are we okay?"

The water shut off and she reached out and snagged a towel off the rack. "It's not that simple." Her voice, even though it was quiet, echoed a little in the tile enclosure while she toweled off. Then she wrapped the Egyptian cotton around herself and stepped out. I moved back into the bedroom to give her some privacy.

"Remember last term, when you tried to tell me how wrong things looked between me and Callum?"

"Vividly," I said. There were some things you just didn't forget, and having your friend try to convince herself she could be a technical virgin was one of them.

"Well, this is *déjà vu* all over again."

Technical virgin. Losing weight. Huh? "I don't get the connection."

"The connection is the things we're willing to do for the sake of having a boyfriend." Lissa came out of the bathroom in her Life is Good flannel pajama bottoms with hearts all over them, and a matching pink tank top. "I mean, look what I was almost willing to do, and what happened."

"Lissa, there's a world of difference between being filmed making out on a webcam video and me losing some weight. In fact, they're not even in the same universe."

She waved her hands helplessly. "I'm not explaining this very well. It's not the what. It's the why."

"Uh, to lose a dress size? In my case, the why just isn't that big a deal."

"Are you sure?"

Okay, this was getting a little annoying. "You're all making a mountain out of a mole hill, and getting mad about something that, in the cosmic scheme of things, doesn't matter one bit. Why should you care about what I do with a trainer?"

Her hands didn't wave around this time. She put them up in a stop gesture. "Never mind. Forget I said anything. Do what you want. I'm done."

"Thank goodness for that," I muttered.

"But if you ever want Carly and Shani to talk to you again, you still need to apologize. You made Carly cry in the cab over that crack about Brett Loyola."

"I did?" Ouch.

"Yes. Use that brain of yours, Gillian. The girl is hurting enough over the fact that no matter what she does, she's completely invisible to him. And you had to rub it in just to be mean."

"I didn't—" I stopped. Yes, I did. "I'll go up there right now."

Before I lost my nerve, I marched up to the third floor, to Room 317. Carly opened the door, and the smile froze on her face.

"Can I talk to you?"

She glanced behind her. "I—uh—"

"She can talk to both of us, if she has the guts," came Shani's voice from inside.

Oh, great. Stereo guilt. A two-for-one deal.

Carly went to sit cross-legged on her bed while Shani lounged on the other. All three of us were breaking lights-out, since Shani's room was down the hall, but some things had to be dealt with before you slept on them and they got all hard inside you.

"I wanted to say I was sorry for being such a *mo guai nuer*," I began in as steady a tone as I could manage. "You guys are only trying to help, and I hurt your feelings. Please say you forgive me."

Carly was already up off the bed. She hugged me and said, "Of course I forgive you."

I hugged her back. It was hard not to. There isn't an unkind bone in the girl's body. Some people see this as weakness. I see it as a gift that I really, really want for myself.

Not very likely, at this rate, but there's always hope.

"Thanks." My throat ached, but I didn't tear up. No way. Not in front of Shani, who was looking at us with an expression that told me she wasn't going to make this easy.

She tossed her braids back, and the beads on the ends of them clicked. "If it were just me, I'd say no problem. But I do have a problem with the way you treated Carly."

"It's okay," Carly began, but Shani cut her off.

"No, it's not. It's not okay to rip a person apart and use the thing that means the most to them like a weapon."

"I said I was sorry." Man. How many times did I have to apologize? "If Carly and I are okay, then you and I should be, too." Plus, this didn't have anything to do with her. She'd just been sitting there when I'd lost my temper. That didn't give her the right to decide who forgave who.

"Oh, we should?" Shani asked in a snotty tone that was uncalled for. "Carly's just too nice, is all. Too nice to see that the people she calls her friends really don't care very much about her."

"Shani—" Carly began.

"Let me say this, girlfriend," Shani begged, and turned to me. "Just because you hang around with all the geniuses—"

"Genii," I corrected, feeling a little snotty myself.

"—doesn't mean you're smarter than we are. In fact, you can't be all that smart if you're deliberately mean to other people. We're getting a little tired of being ditched in favor of Mister Physics Olympian Wanna-be, who's in some percentile that doesn't even let him converse with normal people. Who wouldn't know your friends if they fainted on the floor in front of him. Who knows? Maybe you guys are selling exam answers for fun, and the rest of us have to suffer for it."

Holy crisis on a cracker. I pulled my jaw off the floor with some difficulty. "I can see I'll wait a long time for forgiveness from you," I said. "But for that crack, you're going to wait just as long for forgiveness from me."

Enough was enough. I'd come here with humility and good intentions, and she'd spoiled it all. I spun on my heel and walked out the door, leaving my friendships in splinters behind me.

VTalbot   Miss me?

Source10   You're hard to miss.

VTalbot   Is that a compliment, Mr. Source?

Source10   How can I miss you if you won't go away?

VTalbot   :(Most guys aren't so mean to me.

Source10   Variety is good for you.

VTalbot   I could be good for you.

Source10   ??

VTalbot   Are you seeing anyone?

Source10   Does it matter? You are.

VTalbot   Keeping tabs on me?

Source10   <shrug> Common knowledge.

VTalbot   Would it matter to you if I said I broke up with him?

Source10   Did you?

VTalbot   Yes. Interested?

Source10   Don't have time for jokes. Good night.

chapter 13

BELIEVE ME, I'd never seen anything more beautiful than Lucas's grin as he pushed open the passenger door and waited for me to toss my tote bag into the backseat of the Mini Cooper. I slid into my seat and he leaned over and kissed me—which, as far as I was concerned, pretty much set the tone for this beautiful Saturday morning.

Despite my waist-cinching vintage wrap top, he didn't say anything about the fact that there was half an inch less of me than there had been last week. On the other hand, he usually saved his kisses for the ends of dates, not the beginnings. If seeing me at all, no matter what my volume currently measured, put him in a kissing mood, then I was all for it.

"How's it been going?" he asked as he crunched down the drive and through the gates. "I've been buried under Olympics prep. Did you get that composition thing done?"

I laughed. "Not a chance. I've had some tunes in my head, but nailing them down and arranging them is the hard part. I've got that to do tomorrow, and today was supposed to be going over the chapter questions for Chem with Carly, but I guess . . ." My voice trailed off.

"What?" He glanced at me as he headed for Market, which would take us to an on-ramp for Highway 101 and south to Palo Alto. I'd already Mapquested it.

"I kind of had a fight with them all the other night," I confessed. "Carly's my Chemistry partner, but she hardly said a word to me in our last class except, 'You're overfilling that beaker.' So I guess she'll find someone else to study with."

I wasn't sure when I'd get the chapter reviews done myself, but I still had time. Unlike my Comp project, the stuff was all stored in my brain. The chapter reviews just reminded me about what was already there. In reality, I needed to get my piano arrangement done more urgently than I needed to study chemistry, so spending today helping my boyfriend capture a major achievement like a place on the U.S. Physics Olympics team hardly seemed like a sacrifice.

Lucas just shook his head. "Girls. You're all about the drama."

"It's not drama. It's emotion. I think they're a little jealous."

"Of what?" He accelerated up the on-ramp and we flew over the roofs of smaller buildings as the elevated freeway took us south.

"Of you and me. None of them have boyfriends."

"They're jealous of me?" He snorted. "That's a first."

"They'll get over it." I hoped. Time to change the subject to something less boring for a guy. "So, what's the agenda for today?"

"Breakfast with my dad and one of his colleagues at Il Fornaio first; then we'll head back to the apartment for some coaching units."

"You make it sound like a class."

"We are talking about my dad," he said dryly. "He's got the day all divided into major topics, using his old textbooks from Stanford. Then supper, and you and I can take off and do something fun."

"Like a movie." The Jodie Foster movie was closing tomorrow. I still had a chance to see it.

"Maybe," he agreed. "Or we could go down to the Tech Museum in San Jose."

"Or take in a play."

"As long as it's not a musical. I hate those."

"Oh, too bad. I saw *Hairspray* on Broadway last year and loved it. Not to mention *High School Musical 2* and *3*. Call me corny, but I have this terrible weakness for them."

"I have no idea what you're talking about."

"You don't know what you're missing. *Hairspray* has these great sixties clothes and *HSM3* is all about cute. But you know what? I totally learned all the dance moves in junior high when the first one came out." I did the Wildcat claw thing with my hands for emphasis, but he just looked blank. "Never mind," I said. "You had to be there."

It was a little bit much to expect an Olympic-level genius to know the Wildcat celebration song, I had to admit.

"I may not know how to dance," he said a little stiffly, "but I know the difference between kinetic energy and magnetism, which is what's going to be important two weeks from now."

"Oh, I know," I reassured him. "I hope you're ready for today. You're going to need some R&R by the time we get done with you."

He grinned, and before I knew it, we were parking on one of the side streets off University Avenue in Palo Alto, and walking into Il Fornaio. Inside there were lots of people in power suits, even on a Saturday, as well as men in khakis and collared shirts who could have been golfers—or multimillionaires. It was kind of hard to tell. But what I did recognize in a booth near the rear was Lucas—as he might look in thirty years or so.

"Dad, Thomas, this is my friend Gillian Chang. Gillian, my dad, Andrew Hayes, and his colleague Dr. Thomas Barchuk, visiting from M.I.T."

They stood, and I shook hands. "Dr. Hayes. Dr. Barchuk. I'm very happy to meet you."

"How are you?" Lucas's dad indicated a seat next to him, which put me across from Lucas. "I've heard a lot about you."

"Uh-oh," I joked.

"No, nothing bad at all. Lucas tells me you're the second smartest student at Spencer."

"Oh, thanks." I grinned at Lucas. "Because we all know who the smartest one is."

"You've got competition for the Olympics team, I understand, Lucas," Dr. Barchuk put in. "But it's good to know the school will back you up when you make the semifinals."

"It's props to them," I said. "Anything Lucas has done from the moment he applied reflects well on the school, and they know it."

"Props?" Dr. Hayes looked at his son.

"A feather in their cap," he translated.

The waitress came, poured coffee for all of us, and handed out menus. I ran an eye down the selections, but it was hard to focus. I wanted to make a good impression, which of course made me nervous. And when you're meeting your boyfriend's dad for the first time, you really don't want to make a pig of yourself and spend the whole time with your mouth full.

"What do you think?" I said to Lucas. Maybe I should take a cue from him.

"Omelet," he said firmly. "They're really good here."

When the waitress came back, Lucas ordered his and I kept it simple. "Make that two."

"You seem to have a good grasp of school politics, Gillian," Dr.

Hayes said when the waitress had taken our menus and gone. "That'll stand you in good stead in the working world."

I shrugged, trying not to seem too pleased at the compliment. "It probably comes from listening to my dad talk at the dinner table."

"What does he do?"

"He's the chairman of the Formosa-Pacific Bank. They have offices in Taipei and New York."

"So you're Taiwanese?" Dr. Barchuk asked.

I shook my head. "American. My parents were born in Manhattan. My family has owned the bank since the mid-1800s, but in 1970 they opened offices in the States and my grandfather moved to New York permanently."

"Must be one of the last of the family-owned banks," Dr. Hayes observed. "Most of them have been bought out by conglomerates, same as in any industry. Stock exchanges, publishing, high tech, you name it."

"I didn't know your dad was a banker," Lucas said. "How come you didn't tell me?"

"I did tell you. Remember? Type-A personality? Freaks when I don't bring home the A's?"

"That I remember."

"She's not your average China doll," Dr. Hayes said to Lucas with a smile at me. "I guess you don't have to worry she'll marry you for your money."

I blinked at him. "Not that I'm getting married anytime in the next decade, but I don't think any guy has to worry about that. I'm perfectly capable of earning my own living. My parents want me to be a doctor or a scientist. I haven't decided what I'll do yet."

Dr. Barchuk stared at me. "Pretty forthright with your opinions, aren't you? You sure aren't like any Chinese girl I ever met."

"That's probably because I'm as American as you are, Dr. *Barchuk*." I gave an ever-so-slight emphasis to his last name, which was as ethnic as mine. "My grandmother is always telling me I talk too much."

"Maybe you should listen to her."

Maybe Lucas's dad should choose his friends better. Or maybe the guy was just a colleague and he'd brought him along to breakfast because otherwise he'd be all alone in his empty apartment. I felt sorry for the woman who eventually got him.

Dr. Hayes laughed. "Ease up, Tom. She's just a kid."

"Just a kid who could use a little discipline. Talking back like that. The Chinese girls I know have better manners."

I opened my mouth to explain that I was an American girl, and here in America, it wasn't considered bad manners to express an opinion, when the waitress arrived with our meals.

Just as well, I thought as I tucked into my omelet, creamy with cheese and spiced with poblano chiles and cilantro. So California. It just doesn't taste like this in New York. I wanted to make a good impression on Dr. Hayes, and pointing out that his friend was a pompous idiot probably wouldn't help.

In the end, it turned out that Dr. Bigot—er, Barchuk—had just come along for breakfast and wasn't part of the coaching team. Dr. Hayes lifted a hand as the guy drove away from the apartment complex, and turned to us in the living room. Dad's place in Taipei was a palace compared to this. Of course, it's probably a palace compared to most people's houses, but it was all I had to base an opinion on. Everything here was beige—carpets, furniture, kitchen counters. The walls were white. It had about as much personality as, well, Tom Barchuk, which made me apologize mentally to the place.

While Dr. Hayes got his papers organized in the living room, Lucas showed me around.

"How come your dad hangs around with that guy?" I asked Lucas as we stood on the balcony outside his bedroom, admiring the trees of the green belt behind the building.

"Who, Tom? He's the other senior physicist. Dad likes to talk to someone who operates at his level."

"Too bad his social skills aren't operating at the same level. How come you didn't tell him to shut up?"

Lucas stared at me. "He's a colleague of my father's. It's not my place to tell him what to do."

"It is when he's insulting your—" I stopped. "Friend."

It just occurred to me that Lucas hadn't introduced me as his girlfriend. Only as a friend. Would it have made a difference in how the guy had treated me? I considered this briefly.

Nah. Probably not.

"How did he insult you?" Lucas wanted to know, coming a little closer.

"Oh, all that stuff about needing discipline and manners. I wasn't being rude. I just don't like being treated like—mm!"

I forgot what I was going to say as his kiss cut me off.

I felt the urgency in it—as though he was afraid his dad was going to walk through the sliding glass door any second. It felt secret, dangerous. Exciting. Maybe Lucas had never brought a girl to his dad's place before.

A sound from the living room made him pull back and step away from me.

"What was that all about?" I whispered. Maybe his dad wanted him to focus totally on physics and not the physical. I'd heard of kids whose parents were so insane about grades and medals and competition that they put their kids on complete lockdown. No girlfriends, no dates, no extracurriculars. Just how big a risk had Lucas taken in inviting me here? Was his dad just putting a good face on it, and the whole time he was out there wanting to toss me into a cab and send me back to the city?

"Nothing," he said. "I just wanted to kiss you. You're my girlfriend. Your job is to support me. That's why you're here, right? So we can work together and I can win that place on the team.

You didn't come down to mouth off my dad's colleague. Yeah, you have opinions, but you have to pick your time and place."

"You think I was rude?"

"Doesn't matter if I do. He did."

"I'm never going to see him again anyway," I said. Thank goodness.

"Gillian, that's not the point. The point is, he's one of the guys who can make a big difference in my career. If you're going to support me, you have to be careful what you say to people who are important."

There was something massively unfair about this. "So Mr. Important Guy can say racist things to me but I can't call him on it?"

Patches of color burned under both his cheekbones, and he stepped over the threshold of the sliding glass door and back into his room. I followed him in.

"He isn't racist. Both he and Dad have all kinds of gifted Asian scientists in that lab—how can he be racist? I don't get you," he went on. "You say you're a Christian. Ever hear of turning the other cheek?"

"Why should I? I bet he doesn't say stuff like that to his staff."

"Uh—didn't Jesus tell you to?"

"I don't think Jesus meant for people to lie down and be doormats," I retorted. "He said for people to treat each other as they want to be treated, but I don't see Dr. Barchuk doing that."

"He's not a Christian."

"Yeah, I got that," I snapped. "But that doesn't let him off the hook. He doesn't have to be a Christian to be decent."

"We're talking about you, not him. You can't change how he is, but you can change how you are."

Don't lose it. Or this is going to turn into your first fight. "And how would that be?" I said with a pretty good imitation of calm.

"You do this—this thing." He waved his hands, as if trying to pin down words that fluttered around the room. "You suck all the attention to yourself. But today we just don't have time for that. This is not getting me into a mindspace where I can concentrate."

"I do not—"

"Dad's out there waiting, and you're going on and on about what Tom said. Can't you just put that aside and think about me for once?"

"But I *do*—"

"Stop arguing!" In complete frustration, he threw up both hands. I stepped back to avoid getting whacked, and tripped over a running shoe lying on the floor. I lost my balance—staggered—fell—

Clunk.

The lights went out—and so did I.

chapter 14

I CAME TO in the back of Dr. Hayes's BMW, just as he pulled up to the doors of the emergency room at the Stanford Medical Center.

My head hurt like it'd never hurt before. Lucas—both of him—sort of swooped by in a lazy, sickening circle, holding the doors for us as Dr. Hayes carried me in, and then the black swarmed over my vision again. "I think she's concussed," I heard someone say off in the distance, and then time blinked out.

Until a bright light shone in one eye. Then in the other. *Ow.*

"Hello, young lady," a deep voice said. "Decided to join us, did you?"

"Unngh."

"I'm Dr. Matsuda. They tell me you tripped and fell."

"Uh-hunngh."

"Looks like you clipped your temple on the corner of a dresser or bed frame or some other hard object. We stitched you up while you were out."

Gross. Thank you for that.

"How many?" Was I going to be bald on one side?

"Just three. They'll disappear on their own in a week or so."

"Thanks."

"Look up, then down, please." I did. "Your responses are good. I don't think you're concussed, but you definitely need to take it easy for the rest of the day. Maybe even the rest of the weekend."

"I have to study."

"You'll be able to do that tomorrow. But no swim meets or cross-country races."

"No problem." I looked past him. "Did a guy come in with me?"

"A guy?" Dr. Matsuda looked puzzled.

"Tall, thin. Seventeen or so. Brainy-looking."

His face cleared. "Oh, him. He and his dad left a couple of hours ago."

"Left? *Left?*" How could they have left? Didn't they care about me? What was I supposed to do, stuck in the wilds of Palo Alto with a hole in my head? Flag down a cab?

Dr. Matsuda put a hand on my shoulder and pushed me back onto the pillow. "Relax. When you're ready to be released, they left a number for me to call and they'll come get you. Apparently the younger gentleman had to work."

Work. Oh, my gosh. Because I'd been such a klutz, Lucas had lost who knew how many hours of coaching time. Could my timing have been any worse? Could I have spoiled the day any more?

Dr. Matsuda did a couple more tests with my eyes and reflexes and pronounced me fit to leave. While I ground through the boredom of producing my health insurance card and filling out forms, I asked myself when I was going to get a grip.

Lucas, obviously, had been right. I didn't do it on purpose, but my subconscious had to be hard at work, making sure I was at the center of everyone's attention. A ferry crashes into a New York dock? Never mind the old lady squashed underneath her, is

Gillian okay? An elevator gets stuck in the Eiffel Tower? Yup, there's Gillian, hyperventilating and making a scene. A brilliant mind needs a day of coaching so he can be in the Olympics? Sure, as long as we can take time out to get Gillian to the hospital.

For *tripping*. I couldn't crash something, so my subconscious had worked with what it had—a sneaker. Anything to make it all about me.

Sitting in the waiting room while Dr. Matsuda called the Hayes apartment, I rested my forehead on my cold hand.

Father, I need help, here. I am self-centered, thoughtless, and annoying—not to mention rude to the friends of my friends. Please help me learn some humility. Help me consider Your Son and how humble He was, even when people slapped Him and called Him names. Help Lucas forgive me—and give me the guts to ask for forgiveness from him. If I've messed up his chances at the Olympics, I will never forgive myself.

"Gillian?"

I looked up. Lucas shouldered the emergency-room door open.

"Are you okay?"

I slid off the hard chair and went to him, winding my arms around his waist and pressing my cheek to his chest, completely ignoring the other people around us. "Lucas, I'm so sorry."

"What for?"

"For being a self-centered jerk and ruining your coaching day."

"Oh, hey, don't worry about it. Dad and I got some pretty intense work done while you were getting stitched up."

"Yes, but you could have had hours more if it hadn't been for me."

"The question is, are you all right?"

"Oh, sure. All that fuss for three stitches. Big deal."

"It was a big deal. You had blood running down the side of your face like a murder victim in a slasher movie."

"There's a visual." I made a face. "I'm really sorry. I want to make it up to you. Maybe we can study when we get back."

"Back?" Arms looped around my waist, he looked down at me.

"The doc says I'm supposed to take it easy, but he said I could study. I hereby donate my study time tomorrow to you."

"About that." His hold loosened. "Dad says he can give me a couple more hours tomorrow if I stay the night."

I clicked through the ramifications of this at top speed. The alternatives did not look good. "Uh—"

"I know you can't stay."

"I didn't bring any overnight stuff."

"So I'll drive you back to the city and then come back."

"But that'll take an hour each way." I glanced at my watch. "It's already nearly four." And then I had an idea, inspired by my new sense of selflessness. "Tell you what. You drop me at the nearest train station and I'll go back to school that way. I can take a cab once I'm in the city."

He was already shaking his head. "No way. I'm not going to put an injured girl on the train by herself. Nope, I'll drive you, and that's that."

He took my hand, and we headed outside to the parking lot.

"No, I'm serious. I've already sucked up three hours that you could have been using for equations and important stuff. This is the most elegant solution—you know it is."

"Well, yeah, mathematically, but it feels terrible."

"So what? I'm the only one here, and it feels fine to me. I've made up my mind. I'll take the train, and you and your dad will have a whole evening to work."

"Gillian, I don't know. . . ." In the distance, we heard a train whistle. He looked at me. "The station's only a couple of blocks from here."

"And I'll miss it if we don't hurry."

"My dad has your stuff in the car."

"Come on. Move it."

We began to run. I felt a little dizzy at the sudden motion, but that was okay. I'd have all kinds of time to recover once I was on the train. And it's not like I'm not used to it. The first time I was ever on the subway was when I was about three. One of my first memories, in fact, was the big front light of the subway train coming out of the tunnel with a whoosh and a roar.

So a few minutes later I settled back on the seat and allowed myself to relax as the Peninsula slid by. Until my phone chimed.

"Hey, Mom."

"Gillian, are you all right?"

Oh, boy. Here we go. "I'm fine. Why?"

"Because I just got a call from Stanford Medical Center, that's why."

"Why would they call you? Everything's fine."

"You're a minor. Thank goodness *someone* saw fit to call me."

I slid down a little in my seat, though the car was nearly empty. "Mom, it was just a bump on the head. Three stitches. No big deal."

"And what caused this bump on the head?"

"I was at a friend's place and I tripped over a sneaker lying on the floor. Totally dumb. And they overreacted and drove me to Emergency. Honest, Mom. I'm fine. I'm on the train right now, heading back to school."

"They take you to the hospital and then put you on a train to take care of yourself? What kind of friends are these?"

"It was my idea. My friend has to study. The Physics Olympics semifinal exams are in a couple of weeks and he's in major prep mode."

Silence. "He?"

I winced and mentally smacked myself on the forehead. A slip of the pronoun.

"Yes, he. A friend." I took the truth and stretched it just a teensy bit. "I came down this morning to be part of his coaching team. I figured I could use the practice myself."

"But you aren't taking physics this year."

"Not until next year. But it can't hurt, can it? It's pretty advanced stuff."

"In the meantime, your own homework suffers? I thought your exams were coming up. What are you doing riding around on trains when you should be studying?"

Honestly, there is no winning with my mother. "I'm riding this train so I can get back to school so I can study. The doctor said no vigorous activity for a couple of days, so that's what I plan to do."

"But how can you, with this bump on the head? Do you have headaches? A concussion?"

I did have a headache. The anesthetic was wearing off and my scalp hurt, not to mention the bruising on my arms from an unprotected landing. But this is not the kind of thing you can say to my mom. She'd have the train stopped halfway up the Peninsula and a Life Flight chopper waiting on the tracks.

I tucked the phone between my shoulder and ear and rummaged in my backpack. "No and no. Honest, Mom. I'm fine. Everybody is making a big deal about this for nothing." Aha. I found the bottle of Tylenol that Lissa had given me and uncapped my water bottle. While Mom got her feelings about the situation off her chest, I swallowed two Tylenol and waited for the relief.

By the time she wound down, we were already in South San Francisco. "Mom, I've got to go. My station will be coming up soon."

"Call me tomorrow. I want to know that you had a comfortable night."

"I have Tylenol. No problem."

"I'll call the school and let the medical staff know."

"You will not!" Spencer had two nurses onsite, mostly to

bandage up the newbie golfers who didn't know their own strength—or that of their woods.

"If I can't be there to look after you, Jiao-Lan, then I will find someone who can." I closed my eyes. If she'd reached the point of calling me Jiao-Lan, argument was pointless. She could be like a train herself, barreling down a tunnel with only one objective in mind. If you didn't get out of the way, you'd be seeing the big white light before you knew what hit you.

"Fine, Mom. Talk to you tomorrow."

"I love you, Gillian."

I opened my eyes with a snap. "I—I uh—"

"I know I don't say it enough. But I miss you very much. I wish you would decide to stay home for your senior year."

"Mom, I—" I took a breath. "I love you, too."

"Take care of yourself."

"I will. 'Bye, Mom."

I was in the cab and well on the way up the hill to Spencer before I got over the surprise.

DORM, SWEET DORM. Despite the Tylenol, my head had really begun to pound. I pushed the door open, incapable of anything but crawling into bed and pulling my red silk quilt over my head.

Except that Shani sat on it. The very last person on the planet I wanted to see. She and Lissa had clearly been quizzing each other on biological processes, because each of their textbooks was open to the chapter review.

"Gillian?" Lissa said tentatively. "Are you okay?"

I shook my head. Pointed at my left temple. "Three stitches. Excuse me, please," I said to Shani. "I need to shower and lie down."

She scooped her stuff up and went to sit at Lissa's desk. Turning my back on both of them, I stripped to my undies, grabbed my pajamas, and went into the bathroom. I washed away the dust of the train, the smell of the hospital, and the day that had begun so well and had ended in pain and disappointment.

But my head still hurt when I came out.

"Got anything stronger than Tylenol?" I asked Lissa. "I must've clunked my head harder than I thought. Killer headache."

"What happened?" Lissa asked. She shook a couple of Advil into my hand, and I emptied my water bottle washing them down.

I crawled under my quilt. Bliss. Now if they would only go away and shut off the lights behind them.

"I tripped. Fell against a dresser or something. Went to Emergency." There. That about summed it up.

"Where'd you go?" Lissa asked. "I know you took off with Lucas really early."

They were not going to get off my case unless I told them. I sighed and pulled the covers down. "I had breakfast with him and his dad and this other guy, and then we went back to his dad's place so we could coach him for the Olympics." How many people was I going to have to explain my business to? "I tripped over a sneaker in his room, fell, and had to go to Emergency. I came home on the train. Can I sleep now?"

"The *train?*" Shani said in the same tone she'd probably use if I said I'd come home by elephant.

"Didn't Lucas bring you home?" Lissa asked.

"Obviously not." *Okay, losing patience now.* "Can you guys go down to the library or something?"

"Let me get this straight," Shani said. "You had an accident that needed stitches to the head and they sent you home by yourself, like, forty miles on the train?"

I pulled the covers over my head. "You sound like my mother. It was my idea. Now will you go away?"

"She tripped over a sneaker," Lissa said to Shani. "In his room."

"It's not what you think," I said, my voice muffled.

A second or two of silence. "They always say that," Shani said. "They trip, or fall, or run into doors."

"Who is *they*?" I was beginning to feel like I was playing a game of peek-a-boo with this quilt. I gave up and folded my arms on it. The light from the miniature chandelier overhead hurt my eyes. "Look, are you guys done?"

"*They* are girls who are abused." Shani ignored my second question. "They make excuses, you know? Like 'I tripped. He didn't really push me.' Or 'Klutzy me—I walked into a door and now I have this black eye.'"

"Gillian, what's really going on with you and Lucas?" Lissa asked in a soft voice, as if she was afraid to know.

I stared at both of them. "Are you guys crazy?"

Lissa shook her head. "Worried would be a better word."

"No," I contradicted her, "you're crazy. Delusional. Making up stuff to punish me. Well, I apologized once. I'm not doing it again. Now, please leave."

And to my huge surprise, they did.

"*Thank* you," I said to the back of the door as it clicked shut. I yanked the covers back up over my head.

Too bad I couldn't do the sensible thing and go straight to sleep. I sure needed it. But instead, I got monkey-brain: pictures and snippets of conversation and memory bouncing off the walls of my skull and crashing into one another. My mom's voice on the train. Lucas's kiss. Lucas's hands, flying up. Lucas pulling my chair out at the restaurant. That stupid sneaker, growing bigger and bigger every time I tripped. All of it kept me awake until Lissa crept back in a couple of hours later.

Lights-out had already been called. Huh. Once a rule-breaker, always a rule-breaker.

There was no way I was reopening any kind of conversation with her. So I pretended I was asleep.

I didn't move, even when I heard her crying with her face against the wall.

RStapleton	Thought you might like to know something.
Source10	I know a lot of things. You pay me for most of them.
RStapleton	You don't know this. I got hauled into Curzon's office on Friday and grilled like a steak.
Source10	What's that got to do with me?
RStapleton	She wanted to know about the midterm. But I didn't give you up.
Source10	What did you tell her?
RStapleton	That my dad hired a retired Berkeley prof to tutor me.
Source10	She'll call him. Did you think of that?
RStapleton	I'm not stupid. I paid the guy 1K to say he'd been tutoring me all term.
Source10	But did he?
RStapleton	He must have. Curzon sent me a note saying sorry. LOL
Source10	Who else has she talked to?
RStapleton	For a discount on the final I can find out.
Source10	OK. 1K even for the final. Find out what they told her, too.
RStapleton	Cool.

chapter 15

I T WASN'T GOING to be easy telling Lissa I'd go to church on my own on Sunday, so I didn't. Call me chicken, but she was the one going around calling my boyfriend an abuser for no reason at all, so I didn't feel guilty about leaving her a note and going to the early service at Lucas's church.

She wouldn't miss me, anyway. She had her family.

Lucas was miles away in Palo Alto, but somehow, sitting in the church where he said he worshipped, I felt closer to him. The sermon was about the still, small voice of God, and I let it wash over me, cleaning away the sour-lemon feelings I had toward Lissa and Shani.

I hadn't made things up with them. In fact, our relationship just seemed to be getting more prickly, hurting every time we bumped up against each other.

It's their fault, Lord. They're the ones saying a bunch of stuff that isn't true.

The music and the voices of people praying calmed me. Maybe it didn't matter whose fault it was or who was saying what. Maybe if I heard the still, small voice inside saying, "Time to make it up," then my job was to do it. But, true to form, I had to argue.

This really irks me. Why should I be the one to humble myself first? I did that already.

If not me, then who would?

Uh—just a guess. One of them?

But they weren't here, talking to the Lord. It was just me, and I was going to need strength. Luckily God had shown me before that He had plenty of that to go around.

Thanks, Lord. I'll try again.

I shook hands with the pastor on the way out the door and introduced myself. "Thanks for what you said today," I said. "I'm Gillian Chang, a friend of Lucas Hayes."

He had a great handshake—firm and warm. "Nice to have you with us, Gillian. Who did you say your friend was?"

"Lucas Hayes? Tall, really smart? We both go to Spencer and he told me he worships here."

The pastor smiled a little self-consciously. "The name seems familiar, but I can't place the face. Comes of getting old, I suppose. I hope we'll see you again." He turned to the family behind me, and I pushed the wrought-iron gate open. Either there was a really big congregation hidden away somewhere, or the poor guy really did have memory problems.

I turned my iPhone back on when I started the walk home, and got my reward. Lucas.

"Hey," I said happily. "Guess where I am?"

"Judging by the time and the day and your usual habits, I'd say that you're either on your way to or coming back from church."

"Right you are. But which church?"

"That would take more input."

"Okay, so here's some for you. A equals I didn't go to lunch with Lissa. B equals I've just come from the early service. C equals you've only known me to go to three churches here, one of which doesn't have an early service. So A plus B plus C equals—"

"You went to my church."

"Give the man a hundred percent."

"I wish I was there with you."

"So do I. I told your pastor I was a friend of yours, but he didn't remember you."

Lucas laughed. "That guy. He's such a joker. Of course he remembers me. I'm there every week."

"Did you go with your dad today?"

"He's not a believer. So we did differential equations and calculus all morning. I'm going to head out after lunch."

"Maybe we could study together when you get here." I tried to keep the wistfulness out of my voice, but I don't think I succeeded.

"Probably not, Gillian. I really have to concentrate, and you're kind of . . . distracting." I just had time to feel a little glow of happiness when he added, "Especially when hospitals are involved."

Ha. Geek humor. So much for romance.

"I promise to watch for stealth sneakers next time. Though if some people would keep their rooms picked up, I wouldn't have to."

Joke. It was a joke, honest. But something in the quality of the silence told me he hadn't taken it that way.

"Yeah, housekeeping is right there at the top of my list, along with making the semifinals," he said in a tone edged with sarcasm. "You might have time to think about stuff like that, but I don't."

Inferring that I was a girl, and girls think about housekeeping. Which in my case is so not true, as Lissa will tell you. "I'm sorry, Lucas." Could I not say or do one thing right this weekend? "Of course you don't. You need to focus right now, and I want to do everything I can to help you."

"Thanks." His tone softened. "So, I hear they have a suspect in the exam answer case."

I'd just passed through the school gates, and hurried up the driveway, out of earshot of a disappointed photographer who was glaring at me for not being somebody famous. "They do? Who?"

If it wasn't me and it wasn't Lucas, the pool of suspects was pretty small. "It's not Shen Huang, is it? He's so nice. He always helps me clean up my lab station."

"No, it's not a guy. At least, I don't think so. What was the name?" He paused. "It was a chemical. That's what tripped my memory. Titanium? No. Beryllium?" He made a disgusted sound. "Man, I hope this doesn't happen when I take the exam. No, wait. I've got it. Argon."

I stopped walking. "Argon? That's not a name."

"I didn't mean that's their name, I mean it's like that. You know. Mnemonics."

"So, someone with a name like Argon who could actually pull this off. That doesn't leave very many people. Except maybe—" I stopped.

"Who?"

"Oh, no one." My heart began a slow, horrified drubbing in my chest. "Maybe it wasn't Argon. Maybe you're thinking Barium. As in Barry Stockton. Or Francium, like Ernesto Francese. Both those guys are in AP Chem."

"Maybe," he agreed easily. "I thought it was one of the noble gases, though. Not my business, anyway. As long as they figure it out before finals, I'm just going to keep doing what I'm doing. Talk to you later."

"'Bye." I disconnected with fingers that felt cold and clumsy.

Not Barium, or Francium, or anything like that.

Argon. Aragon. As in my friend, Carly.

Who had been very emotional lately. And who was clearly a lot smarter than I gave her credit for.

IT NEARLY KILLED ME to keep my mouth shut Sunday afternoon instead of storming up to Carly's room and screaming at her for putting the entire junior class in danger. But I did it. I locked myself into a practice room and forced my galloping brain onto the composition track, where it slowed down and began to produce measures of music. I guess it's true that passion produces art. I didn't have unrequited love to fall back on, but I sure had a lot of horror and frustration, so I put it to work.

By four o'clock I had the melody and accompaniment hammered out, which is the hard part. The chord arrangements were more mathematical and less creative, so I could do those in pieces throughout the week. The harp part, to be recorded on my Mac and mixed in my GarageBand software, was pretty straightforward once I had the piano melody. I was working on that in our room when the door opened and Lissa, looking very stylish in a Max Azria short jacket and lace blouse, stepped in.

She glanced at me but didn't say a word as she shrugged out of her clothes and pulled on a T-shirt, jeans, and the creamy Arran cableknit sweater she loves.

"Very après ski," I said, laying my hand against the harp's strings to silence them. "Makes me want some hot chocolate with marshmallows in it."

To my surprise, she took the silly image as it was meant—as a hint that I still wanted to be friends. "I underdressed today. The fog was all the way in over Marin and I had to borrow one of my dad's sweaters. I asked Bruno to turn the heat up in the car on the way back and nearly melted him."

Bruno is her dad's driver. To hear Gabe Mansfield tell it, he found the guy on a street corner with a Will Drive For Food sign and hired him. But with Lissa's dad, you never know if he made that up or if some magazine did.

"Mom says hi, and Dad said the same when he called," Lissa added. "We missed you."

My throat closed up with an unexpected ache. I'd been going to church with them and then having lunch at their place since September. It started out with Lissa feeling kind of sorry for me, because except for Aunt Isabel and her family, I'm on my own out here, but since then it had become something we both looked forward to. I love her dad. Her mom is a little harder to warm up to—she and my father would probably get along, though—but I really respect her. They do their best to be home on Sundays for family time, except when Gabe has to be in places like Scotland for filming, like now.

"He called you guys?" I glanced at the clock and counted ahead eight hours. "It must have been late there."

"Just ten at night. He calls every Sunday because he knows we'll all be together. And with the video feed on my computer, it's the next best thing to being there."

Another little silence fell.

"Gillian—"

"Lissa, I—"

We grinned sheepishly at each other. "You go," she said.

I took a deep breath. "I want to apologize for being so hard to deal with lately."

"And I'm sorry we said that about Lucas. We were talking and stuff has been happening with a friend of Shani's and we, um, probably jumped to conclusions because that's been on her mind so much. She's stressed; Carly's stressed; we're all stressed."

I just bet Carly was stressed. "I should have realized you were only trying to help." Delicate pause. "Carly's stressed? More than usual for this point in the term, I mean?"

Lissa nodded. "Finals are horrible. I hate this time of year. Especially when I'm struggling with Bio and she's banging her head on her Chem book. I'm thinking of giving up AP next term and just going with the regular class. Even with your help, I can't take it."

I refused to let myself get sidetracked. "Is that it? Just Chemistry?" I waited for a clue. Was Carly spending more time in the computer lab than studying? Was she looking over her shoulder all the time and getting distracted? Was she nervous and not sleeping?

Lissa dropped her voice, though no one could hear us through these hundred-year-old walls. "I think she and Shani are both struggling with God. It's just harder to tell with Carly."

My jaw dropped and I clutched the soundbox of the harp. "What? You mean Carly's not a Christian? I thought she was. She comes to prayer circle."

"Maybe that's why. I thought she was, too, but Shani says she's not. She's all mixed up. Shani wants to talk to her about it, but Carly just shuts her out. And as for Shani, she feels sure God wants her, but she doesn't think she can be a Christian." Lissa took a deep breath while I tried to sort all this out. "I've been talking with her, but one person's opinion isn't going to change her mind." She glanced at me. "This is more your thing."

"My thing?"

She nodded. "You're so open about your faith. You know how hard it is for me to talk about stuff like that, and if Carly won't even talk to Shani, she sure won't talk to me. But Shani . . ." She searched for the right words. "It's like she's hungry to hear about it, but it makes her mad at the same time."

"Talking with me wouldn't help, then," I said bitterly as I got up to sit on the bed, the better to deal with this. "Everything I say seems to make her mad."

Shani, struggling with becoming a believer. Wow. And how could Carly be the mastermind behind the exam fraud if God was trying to set her straight with Him? The two were mutually incompatible.

Why hadn't I noticed what was going on? I mean, granted, Carly hardly ever talked about herself, but you'd think I'd have noticed *something* in prayer circle. But Carly wasn't like me, putting everything out there for people to see. On the other hand, if she was struggling against surrender, maybe she'd act out in a big way. Do something really spectacular and say, "Here—do You want me now?" Still waters run deep. Maybe she held things in until that kind of a grand gesture was all she had left. Self-destructive and crazy, maybe, but if she thought it would make God love her less, and leave her alone to do her own thing, she might go for it.

But even if that were true, I was still having a hard time getting my mind around it. We were like the Three Musketeers. Friends. Lissa would hardly have made it through last term if it weren't for us—and Carly had been just as loyal in her quiet, loving way as I was when I got into people's faces.

How could she do this? Was it the money? A thousand bucks a paper would mount up pretty fast. Or was there some daredevil aspect hidden in her character that would make her break all the rules and put everyone at risk?

The next question was, how could I bring this up to Lissa without making her mad at me all over again? Because if Lucas was right, I couldn't approach Carly by myself. I'd need backup, not to mention evidence. We'd have to tell one of the instructors, and to do that I'd need proof. For instance: Who had told Lucas? And how had they found out?

Yikes. This could be a major deal, and we only had, like, thirteen days to wrap it up before exams started.

Lissa opened her mouth to say something when someone knocked on the door. "Hello?" a muffled voice said.

"It's open," she called.

Shani stepped in and shut the door behind her, and I sucked in a breath, as if she might catch me thinking bad things about

Carly. "Did you hear?" she said. "I was walking behind Dani La-vigne and I heard her on the phone. Wow. This is amazing."

Oh, my. If everyone was talking about it, maybe I wouldn't have to say anything to Lissa at all. The jungle telegraph would take care of everything—including the evidence and the confes-sion. "Lucas told me this morning after church," I said. "Does everybody know?"

"If they don't now, they will by tomorrow. Isn't it great?"

"Great for us. Not so great for her."

Shani looked at me, puzzled. "Us?"

"Well, sure. The whole junior class."

Her face hardened in a look that was getting all too familiar to me. "You know, I'd think you'd be a little happier for your friend. It's not like she doesn't know about the competition."

"What on earth are you guys talking about?" Lissa sounded ex-asperated. "I lost you at 'hello.'"

"I have no idea what she means about competition," I said, "But by tomorrow everyone will know Carly's the one who's been selling the exam answers."

"What?" Lissa's eyes bugged out.

"Are you insane?" Shani hissed, both hands on her hips.

I stared at them both. "You just said it was great that they found out it was her. And I agreed with you. What are you looking like that for?"

"I have no idea what you're talking about." Shani tried to get her breath back. "I was talking about Brett and Vanessa breaking up. This will totally make Carly's week—until she finds out what you just said."

"What *did* you just say?" Lissa asked, suspicion fighting with confusion in her gaze.

"It's not just me who's saying it. Lucas told me this morning that he heard she was the one selling the answer sheets. Someone with a name like Argon, he said."

"Impossible," Shani said flatly. "He's nuts for passing that on, and you're nuts for believing it."

"Thank you."

"We're even, then."

I let it pass. This was too important. "The point is, we have to ask her if it's true."

"I'm not asking her." Lissa folded her arms and settled her back against the wall next to her bed. "It's not true and I'm not going to dignify it by bringing it up."

"Lissa, someone has to. Do you want to fail your whole term?"

"I'd rather fail than think my friend—*our* friend—could be capable of doing something like that."

"I wish I was as noble as you, then. Because I can't afford those Fs on my transcript."

"Gillian, how can you think about your grades at a time like this?" Shani wanted to know. "I thought Carly was your friend. And Lucas didn't say it was her, did he? He said it was someone with a name like Argon. How vague is that?"

"I already thought of that." I ran them through the possibilities. "She's the only one with a name that close who actually has the brains to pull it off."

"You're forgetting one thing," Lissa said stubbornly. "God's calling her."

"You said yourself she won't talk about it. We didn't even know she wasn't a Christian. What if He isn't calling her? Or if He is, what if she's doing this to make Him go away? To make it impossible to give in?"

"That's pretty extreme," Shani put in. "She could just say no. She doesn't have to get the whole junior class involved."

"We don't know what goes on inside people," I informed her loftily. "Why say no when you could make this grand gesture instead?"

"Uh, because you're normal?" Lissa suggested. "If you're going to think badly of her, go right ahead. But I swear, Gillian, if you rat on her and it turns out that you're wrong, you're going to have to look for a new roomie next term."

I stared at her. That wasn't all.

If Lucas and I were wrong, I was going to be looking for a whole new school.

chapter 16

✉

To: All Students
From: TArnzen@spenceracad.edu
Date: March 12, 2009
Re: Physics Olympiad semifinalist

I'm delighted to announce that a Spencer Academy student will be one of two hundred semifinalists from across the nation competing for the top five spots on the U.S. Physics Olympiad team this spring.

My congratulations and that of the entire administration go to Lucas Hayes, whose outstanding score on the exam placed him among the brightest young stars in the field of science today.

Please take time to congratulate Lucas and to wish him well as he prepares for the last set of exams taking place early next term.

Terence Arnzen, Ph.D.
Dean of Sciences, Spencer Academy

COULDN'T JUST GO to an instructor like Milsom or Tobin on the basis of a rumor. I had to have evidence. The problem was, when was I going to get it and still find time to prep for finals in Math, Chemistry, and Mandarin, write the term papers for English and History, finish up my Composition project, and, last but not least, survive the ongoing agony dished out to me courtesy of my personal trainer?

Gaaaahhh. Why did all this stuff have to happen at once?

But if I didn't do something, none of this would matter. We'd all get Fs and there'd be nothing left to do but cry . . . and resign ourselves to repeating the pain next term.

Talking with Shani and Lissa was pointless. Talking with Carly, impossible.

I needed to talk to Lucas.

The physics lab was empty, the computers at the back deserted. I found the instructor in the supply closet, humming something that sounded like fifties do-wop.

"Dr. Arnzen? Have you seen Lucas Hayes?"

He straightened and gave me a huge grin. "I imagine he's off somewhere, celebrating."

I sucked in a breath. "You mean—"

"Didn't you see my memo? We got the call this morning. He made the semifinals—as if we had any doubt."

"This morning?" And he hadn't shared this tremendous news with me?

"Yes, about an hour ago." He smiled. "He said something about starting in on some extra reading right away. You might find him in the library."

"Thanks."

Beneath my excitement for Lucas at this tremendous news was a little undercurrent of disappointment. So, okay, we'd both been in classes all morning, and now it was lunchtime, but still. He could have sent me a text message when he got out of class, couldn't he? Or was he so new at this business of being a boy-friend that he hadn't even thought of it?

Sure enough, I found him in the library, surrounded by a cel-ebrating crowd of science geeks. They didn't exactly hoist him onto their shoulders and parade him through the stacks, but it was close. With all the congratulations and back-slapping and that man-hug thing that guys do, the poor librarian was freaking about all the noise.

"But, Mrs. Lynn," I said, taking her aside, "how many times has Spencer produced an Olympian before?"

"Several times, if you must know. Just not with such a high score. But—"

"Uh-huh. Let them have their moment, okay?"

"That's all very well for you, Miss Chang. But there are students here trying to study for their finals."

Dani Lavigne and DeLayne Geary lounged at a table near the back, and I'd bet my next allowance deposit they weren't coaching each other on photosynthesis.

"Gentlemen!" Mrs. Lynn called. "You must either respect the rules of this department or take your celebrations elsewhere."

"Hey, Gillian." Lucas had finally seen me. He tossed his books into his backpack and waded through the noisy knot of people so that they turned and began to follow him.

"Congratulations, Lucas!"

Before I could take a breath to say another word, he'd grabbed me around the waist with one arm and laid a big kiss on me, right there in the library in front of God and Mrs. Lynn and the Science Club.

"Mister Hayes. Miss Chang!" the librarian said in such scandal-ized tones you'd think she was a theater major playing a Victorian matron. "This is unacceptable. Detention, both of you! My office, four o'clock today."

"But, Mrs. Lynn—" I began.

Lucas laughed and pulled me away. "Come on, Gillian. Don't let her spoil this. Common room, everybody—sodas are on me."

His arm around me, Lucas and I led the way down the corridor to the common room. So I had detention for, like, the first time in my life. On the bright side, we'd be serving it together. I could think of worse punishments.

Sodas dropped out of the machine one after the other as Lucas went through a week's worth of snack money in five minutes. We only had half an hour before class, so we made the most of it.

And you know what? Somewhere between me arriving in the library and us walking into the common room, something changed. Of course I knew what it was—that kiss. Yes, it got me a detention. But it got me something else: The science guys were looking at me differently.

Not at Gillian Chang, the brain.

Or Gillian Chang, the music prodigy.

But Gillian Chang, the girl. The kissable girl.

Not that I wanted to kiss anybody except Lucas, but you know what I mean. It was like Jeremy and Travis and Michael and the rest were looking at me with new eyes. It made me a little uncomfortable. But part of me liked it.

Was this how Vanessa Talbot and her crowd felt all the time? Like they secretly knew the guys wanted to get together with them? Did this change how they acted toward people? How they dressed? How they thought about themselves?

Whoa. I had enough to think about, just getting through finals. This was too much for me.

But just having a reason to think about it—tasting it—was kind of satisfying. And it was all because Lucas Hayes kissed me in public. Who knew?

Eventually people began to filter out, and with a glance at the clock, I got up as well.

"I need to talk to you," I said to Lucas. "After detention, okay? I doubt she'll let us talk during."

He'd already forgotten about detention. I guess little things like that wouldn't register on such a happy day. "Four o'clock, right?" He pulled out his BlackBerry and made a note. "What do you want to talk about?"

I glanced around, but everyone had moved out of hearing range. "About that thing you said. Argon, the noble gas."

His eyebrows went up. "Yeah? Did they find the person?"

"Later," I said. I had three minutes to climb a couple of sets of stairs and race down a corridor to U.S. History. "After detention."

How weird is it that the whole afternoon dragged while I waited for four o'clock? I'd never have thought I'd be so anxious to get to detention. But finally, my Mandarin teacher tossed her chalk down on the ledge and dismissed us. All those circuits of the track must have been doing me some good, because even after I ran all the way back down to the library, my backpack thumping against my spine, I wasn't even breathing hard.

Mrs. Lynn assigned us to reshelving books until dinnertime— big surprise—but she didn't seem to care if we did it together, as long as we were quiet.

"So what's going on with the exam thing?" Lucas whispered as, with the cart between us, he took the tall shelves and I went with the ones that were lower. "What did you want to tell me?"

"Not tell. Ask," I said. "Where did you hear about this Argon person?"

He stuck a couple of books in their places while he thought. "I can't remember. I think someone was talking in the lab. Or maybe the locker room."

"Who? Do you remember?"

He shook his head. "Brett, maybe? I have a lot on my mind right now. Unless they're talking directly to me, I don't pay attention."

"It couldn't have been Brett." Not a chance.

"Why not? He and I have been training on the four hundred meter track before breakfast the last couple of weeks."

I rolled my eyes and slapped a book into its slot. "Because Brett Loyola doesn't know Carly exists, much less whether she's capable of pulling off something like this."

He practically dropped the book he was holding. "Carly Aragon? The girl who comes to prayer circle? She's the one doing this?"

Two kids rounded the corner of the stacks and I shushed him until they were gone. "That's what I'm trying to find out," I whispered. "I need to know who told you it was a name like Argon. If they know for sure, we have to tell Curzon right away."

His eyes held a faraway look, as though he were running probabilities in his head. "Wow. You know, it could be her."

"Yeah, but *could be* isn't good enough. If it wasn't Brett who told you, who was it?"

"Gillian, honestly, I can't remember. But hey, why not tell Curzon anyway?" His voice had risen, so he lowered it. "She's dragging people into her office just because they're in the ninety-fifth percentile, which is completely illogical. At least you could make a case for this."

It would also be a massive betrayal of my friend. And if she was struggling with giving her life to God, this might be a death blow to her. And to Shani.

But we weren't talking about just me, or Lucas, or Shani. This was about the entire junior class. Like, nearly fifty people. How was I supposed to put that in my imaginary scale and balance it?

"I can't do that," I said finally. "Not without proof. Like an e-mail or something."

"I doubt you'll get that unless you hack into her school account."

I couldn't. But— "Could you?"

His eyes widened. "Are you kidding?" He dropped his voice again. "I mean, half the Science Club could. But I wouldn't. That's a massive invasion of privacy, not to mention I'd probably get expelled."

"Only for blood, drugs, or fire." That's me. Little Miss Helpful.

He stared at me but obviously decided not to ask me how I knew this. "Regardless. There must be some other way."

"Well, when you think of it, let me know."

"You could ask her."

"Uh, no. End of friendship. And other things."

He leaned across the book cart. "Gillian, this means flunking the term. A bunch of Fs on our records. And after we graduate, who's to say you're ever going to see her again? You might not even be friends after summer break. You'll have failed for nothing, knowing you could have stopped it."

"I know, I know," I said miserably. "I just have to pray that God will show us a way to solve this. He won't let us all go down for something we didn't do."

"He let His Son do that, didn't He?"

I stared at him. "Not helping."

Not one bit. Even though it was true.

VTalbot	I want to meet you.
Source10	Why?
VTalbot	It's not fair that you know who I am, but I don't know who you are.
Source10	Not fair, maybe, but safe.
VTalbot	You could call me.
Source10	Sorry. Caller ID.
VTalbot	Call me from a school phone.
Source10	Nope.
VTalbot	You're mean.

Source10   I'm practical. It's dangerous to trust a woman.

VTalbot   Not this woman. I know how to keep my mouth shut.

Source10   I bet you know how to do other things with it, too.

VTalbot   Bad boy. Do you want to kiss me?

Source10   I probably wouldn't survive the experience.

VTalbot   I'd be gentle.

Source10   You don't strike me as the gentle type.

VTalbot   Try me.

VTalbot   I mean it.

chapter 17

MAYBE LUCAS WAS RIGHT.

After dinner Tuesday night, Lissa and I made our way down to prayer circle, which had grown and shrunk over the term to leave a core group, namely me, Lucas, Lissa, Carly, Shani, Jeremy (of course), and Travis. Even though it would mean breaking up our group, I had a decision to make.

Listening to the prayers didn't make it any easier. I led off, and then Lucas spoke.

"Father, thank You for everything You do for us, and for the things You let us do for ourselves. Thank You for helping me make the semifinals. Thank You for all my friends here, and especially for Gillian, who keeps me sane. Amen."

It took all I had not to open my eyes and smile at him. This was a moment between Lucas and God, not Lucas and me. But the glow of it hung over me until everyone else had said their prayer, leaving Carly for last.

Maybe that was a sign.

"Father God, I'm glad the people in this room are my friends, too. Even though we have our problems, we stick together, and I know You're a part of why that happens. Help us all get through finals, and help us to help each other. The Bible talks about the power of discernment, Lord. Help us have that. And the power of honesty, too, especially with ourselves. In Jesus' name, amen."

And didn't *that* make me feel whole bunches better about what I had to do.

To ease us out of prayer time, I sat at the piano at the other end of the room, where we belted out a praise song in passable four-part harmony. I nearly lost the chords in a couple of places when I realized that Lucas had a really sexy bass, the kind that makes your chest and stomach vibrate along with those deep notes. He hadn't used it in quite that way when we'd sung contemporary songs. Talk about bringing the outside world in.

Whoa. Concentrate, girl. This is not the kind of thing you're supposed to notice during a praise moment.

Maybe it was his voice. Maybe it was the music. But somehow, by the end of the third stanza, my mind had made itself up.

"You guys go ahead," I told Lissa and Lucas. "I need to talk to Carly for a second. We'll catch up in a few minutes."

Carly paused as she grabbed her bag—a Juicy from two seasons ago—and coat.

"What can I order for you?" Lucas asked from the doorway.

What a sweetheart. "A half-caf nonfat caramel macchiato."

"I can stick around," Lissa offered. As she glanced from me to Carly, I knew she knew what I had in mind. The problem was, I didn't know if she'd support me or Carly.

"That's okay," I assured her. "We'll be right behind you."

Shani was the last one out of the room, and she shot me a furious glare as she shut the door.

"What's going on?" Carly leaned on the side of the piano while I took my time closing it up. It was only a spinet, so it didn't take long.

"I need to apologize for being so hard to get along with lately. And for the other night."

She nodded, settling into a chair close to the piano. "*De nada.* Don't worry about it."

"Are you sure? I mean, you were pretty upset. Not that you didn't have good reason to be, but . . ."

"I'm sure. Forgive and forget—isn't that what we're supposed to do?" I must have had a funny look on my face because she added, "I've been thinking a lot lately."

"About believing?"

"Yeah."

This just wasn't going to get any easier, was it? But at least she'd brought it up. "I thought you were a Christian already. But Lissa says . . ." I trailed off, leaving it open for her to tell me if she wanted.

"I always thought so, too. But lately . . . with you guys being so up front about what you believe and how you live and every-thing . . . I got to thinking maybe I'm not. So I figure this is giving me some practice, you know? I forgive you; you forgive me. That's how it's supposed to work, right?" She paused for a second. "It feels kind of good." Then she picked up her bag and glanced from me to the door.

"Um, wait a second." I waited for her to relax a little. "I won-dered if . . ." *You'd hacked into the mainframe.* "If . . ." *You'll come clean about selling the exam answers. Oh, gack. Spit it out.* "If you've noticed anyone acting strange."

Which wasn't what I'd meant to say at all.

Her dark brown eyes, which usually held a whimsical smile, filled with confusion. "Strange how?"

"Like hanging around the computer lab late at night, or maybe passing envelopes or money or anything."

"No." A thought struck her. "You mean like in drug deals? When we lived in south San Jose, I saw a few of those."

"Well, not exactly. More like the exam answers."

"Oh." She slouched against the chair back and crossed her ankles, staring at her Report turquoise suede mary janes, also from last year. "No, I haven't seen anything like that. And believe me, most of the junior class is on the lookout. All of us have a lot to lose."

"No kidding." I couldn't do this. I just could not come out and ask her point blank. And look at her. Not a care in the world, as relaxed as if we were talking about the new things in for spring at Neiman-Marcus. If she were guilty, wouldn't she be going all tense and nervous? Or was she so good an actress that she could look me in the eye and lie through her teeth?

Or was it that she was innocent and really cared about forgiving me because that was the right thing to do?

In either case, I wouldn't get an answer. To find out for sure, I had to think of something else. Some way of trapping her into blurting out the truth. In three more days.

But what?

"Come on," I said. "I'm dying for that coffee."

She grabbed her purse and walked beside me as we headed down the corridor toward the front doors.

At least, I consoled myself, we were back to being friends again. Until I could figure out how to get my prime suspect to betray herself.

WHEN WE WENT down to breakfast Wednesday morning, I could feel something in the air. It wasn't just that the fog was sucked up to the windows like big pieces of used cotton batting. It wasn't the hush in the dining room. It was the way people looked at us as we came in.

Jeremy was as white as a blank Scantron as he looked up from his tray. At the table by the window, silhouetted against the emptiness outside, Vanessa and Dani lounged with Rory Stapleton, watching us and whispering.

"Something's wrong," I said to Lissa in a low voice. "What's going on?"

Travis put his tray on our table and slid in beside me. "Did somebody die or what?"

Behind him, the doors opened and Carly walked in alone. She waved at us and got her tray, then headed for the fruit bar, which is the only alternative to oatmeal here. Two juniors ahead of her slid their trays along the rail so fast they crashed into a knot of freshmen. The noise made us all jump.

"Whoa," I heard her say. "Careful, you guys. The oatmeal isn't going anywhere."

"I bet you are, though," the second guy sneered. "Cheater."

Her fingers went loose on the tray, and I thought she'd drop it. The Christian half of me wanted to rush over there and defend her. The suspicious half kept me pinned in my seat, staring.

"I have no idea what you mean, Jake," Carly said, "but please don't call me names. I don't like it."

"I don't like failing because of you," Jake said. "I hope you get what you deserve."

Oh, my stars above. The word was out.

It couldn't be true.

It could if everyone believed it.

I couldn't. Could I?

Carly snatched up a yogurt and a dish of apricots in syrup, and hurried over to us. She dropped her tray so clumsily that her cappuccino slopped foam over into the saucer.

"What was that all about, I'd like to know." She blinked back tears. Travis picked up his tray and went to sit with some of the guys from the Science Club. Staring after him, she asked, "What did I say?"

Lucas stopped dead in the middle of the floor, his carton of milk wobbling next to the bowl of oatmeal. "Gillian," he said carefully, "why don't we sit over there?" With his chin, he indicated an empty table by the wall.

"I—I—why?"

"I think it's obvious," he said in a low voice, but Carly still caught it.

"What's so obvious?" She looked around and slowly got to her feet. "What does everyone seem to know but no one's telling me? What's going on?"

"Don't act so injured, MexiDog," Vanessa called lazily from her table. "We all know it was you."

"What did I do?"

"Gillian," Lucas said urgently. But I couldn't move. Couldn't get out of the way of the train wreck.

Carly turned to me, her eyes huge, begging me to stand up for her, to explain, to do something. "Do you know?"

"They think you're the one selling the exam answers," I whispered. "But, Carly—"

She laughed, a high, abrupt sound. "That's insane. Who would believe that?"

Silence.

"Is this what last night was about?" she asked me, going from hurt to incredulity in a second. "Did I see anyone passing envelopes or money? Are you kidding? Did you think what everyone else thinks?"

"I—"

"Wow." She stared at me, shaking her head. "That was a really nice touch with the apology and everything. Way to soften me up and then go in with the *knife!*" The last word came out more harshly than I'd ever heard Carly speak in all the time I'd known her. She stood back. "And I forgave you. A nice little practice Christian. Well, so much for that. So much for all my friends."

The headmistress appeared in the doorway and they locked eyes. "Miss Aragon? Is there a problem?"

"I'd say so." She tossed her curly hair. "Everyone thinks I'm the one selling the exam answers. Even my friends have put me on trial and decided I'm guilty."

"And are you?" the headmistress asked coolly.

"Does it matter?" Carly walked to the door. "I'll be in your office, ma'am." And she walked out the doors with all the dignity of Anne Boleyn going to the scaffold.

VTalbot	Test.
Source10	What?
VTalbot	OMG. I knew it wasn't you.
Source10	How?
VTalbot	Uh . . . because I don't flirt with girls?
Source10	Glad to hear it.
VTalbot	What's going to happen to her?
Source10	Does it matter? They've got what they want, and we can get on with it.
VTalbot	Do I still get my Math exam?
Source10	You give me what I need, I give you what you need.
VTalbot	You don't really need the money, do you?
Source10	Who's talking about money?

INSTEAD OF the suffocating mood lifting now that the administration had the guilty party, as the week wore on it just got worse. Or maybe it just seemed that way because of the contrast offered by people like Rory, Vanessa, Emily, and even DeLayne. They went around exchanging big grins for no reason at all.

"It's like they all won the lottery," Lissa muttered to me on Monday morning, as we gathered our stuff after breakfast in preparation for the first of the week's load of exams. For me, it was

Math. For Lissa, Bio, and for Shani, History. "When those guys are happy, it creeps me out."

No kidding.

"This is so wrong," I said for about the fortieth time as I made sure I had enough Scantron forms in my backpack. "I know it's not her. I just know it."

"That 'confession' was totally bogus."

"They have to know that by now," Shani agreed. "Do you have an extra one of those?"

I handed her a form. "Has anybody seen her?"

"I heard she got suspended," Shani said, her mouth a thin line.

"Not expelled?"

She lifted her shoulders. "No proof. So they suspended her until they can find some, I guess."

"Again with the wrongness," Lissa said. "How's she going to take her exams?"

Good question. So maybe the junior class wouldn't fail, but Carly sure would. "This is all my fault," I moaned as we headed down the corridor. "If I'd just kept my mouth shut, this wouldn't have happened."

"I don't think it was you," Shani said, the beads on the ends of her braids clicking restlessly. "I heard it in the halls at least the day before."

"But she's so defenseless. I'm louder than both of you combined. I should have defended her when Jake and those guys got on her case."

Since they'd both been listening to variations of this all weekend, there wasn't much they could say. "Remember the verse you found the other day?" Lissa reminded me. "The truth shall set you free. And it'll set Carly free, too."

That was about all I had to go on—the promise in that verse. I don't know what had made all my suspicions of her fall away.

Maybe the fact that she'd been so guilt-free that night after prayer circle. Or the fact that, just before she'd gotten all snotty with Ms. Curzon, the hurt and shock were plain on her face. This didn't wash with the administration, of course, but it had turned my thinking around. And then finding that verse the other morning . . . well, that did it for me.

Which didn't help us now, on our way to write exams that might get thrown in the trash on Friday.

Shani found me in the dining room at lunch, her eyes wide with suppressed excitement.

"What? Is it Carly?"

"It's not Carly," she whispered, dumping her books on the table and pulling a chair up close. "Not directly, anyway. The profs are running the Scantrons right away instead of waiting until spring break to do it and post grades. And guess what?"

"I got a B on the Math test?" My heart sank.

"I don't know what you got. I'm sure your prof will tell you. But I heard Callum McCloud talking to Rory and Emily, and Rory said his tutor was really kicking—he got a ninety-two on his!"

"That's impossible." My voice went flat while my brain whirled with enough exclamation points to fill a book.

"Duh. But don't you see? It means Carly couldn't have done it."

"She could have set it up when she was here. Like a last good-bye." Why was I saying this? I didn't even believe it.

Shani shook her head impatiently. "Milsom told us all the profs weren't going to use the tests they always use anymore. They all juggled the answers around—days after Carly was suspended."

I stared at her. "So someone hacked the mainframe, like, on the weekend?"

She nodded.

I let out a long breath. "We are *so* in trouble now."

chapter 18

IF IT WASN'T CARLY, then who was it?

My friends were as clueless as I was, and none of us were exactly *CSI* material. I hadn't seen Lucas over the weekend, mostly because he was not only studying for finals but also doing extra work prepping for the Olympiad.

If he got into the top five in the country, he'd be off to Mexico this summer. I wondered if Dad would let me go if I could convince him it was science-related. I couldn't imagine anything more exciting than being in the audience when the U.S. team took the gold medal.

But I wouldn't be going anywhere unless we found the exam fraudster. I'd be in summer school, broiling in my own humiliation.

Not going to happen. Nuh-uh.

After classes that day, I sent Lucas a text.

GChang Where RU?
LHayes Library. Table behind astro books.

Figured.

Sure enough, I found him with books spread all over one of the study tables that were interspersed between the stacks. Away at the back, he'd have a little quiet.

"Hiding from your fan club?" I slid into a chair on his left, careful not to disturb the blizzard of papers around him.

He snorted. "I tried staying in the room, but Travis just kept letting people in. I don't think he gets how important this is." Clutching a bunch of his hair in each hand, he hung over the sheet in front of him. "Or how difficult."

"What is it?" I leaned over to look.

"It's a question from last year's exam and I can't get it. It's driving me nuts."

I read it rapidly.

An otherwise uniform disk of radius R has a circular hole of radius R/2 cut out so that the hole touches both the center and the edge of the disk. The disk has a mass M after the hole is cut out. The disk is placed above a wheel so that when the lower wheel rotates, the disk will rotate with a constant angular velocity. The disk is constrained so that it can only move in the up and down direction or rotate freely. If the angular velocity of the disk exceeds a certain value (Ω) the disk will bounce up and down on the lower wheel. Find the total kinetic energy of the disk when the angular velocity is Ω. Express your answer in terms of M, R, and G (the acceleration due to gravity on the earth's surface) but not in terms of Ω.

Guhhhhh. I mean, I'm no dunce in the science department, but face it, when it comes to physics, he's like an Olympic gymnast doing backflips on the balance beam while I'm still trying to find the handle on the gym door. But at the same time, I was his girlfriend. It was my job to try to help. I focused on the problem. "Let me see your work."

He pushed the sheet over. Equations marched down the middle of it and then ended in a tangle and a bunch of irritated question marks. "I'm taking a break. Want to get a soda?"

"Just a sec." Something caught my eye. This was math, and I was good at math. Okay, that looked reasonable. So did that. But . . . hmm. If you replaced M with R there, then that would change this and this and—

I put my finger on one of the equations. "Here. I think you reversed your variables. Try it with M there instead of R."

He shook his head. "Come on, Gillian. This is advanced stuff, and you haven't even had Physics yet."

"No, seriously. I don't know as much as you, but math is logic. And logically it makes sense to swap them."

"Oh, for—" With a sharp sigh of impatience, he pulled a clean sheet toward him. His pen flew as he worked the equation, all the way to the bottom.

And there was the answer: $(13/8)MGR$.

I grinned with delight. "There! Now let's go get that soda."

He tossed the pen on the table, where it bounced off and landed on a computer science book. It wasn't until we got to the soda machine in the cubbyhole under the stairs that I realized he was annoyed.

Really annoyed.

About what, I had no clue. Maybe the best thing would be to share some news. Get him thinking about something else—applying his formidable brain to the problem that plagued all of us.

"So did you hear the news?" I began.

"What now? R instead of M?"

"No, silly." I pretended he'd made a joke. "They'll probably de-suspend Carly now. Apparently our exam answer guy is still at large. The profs juggled the answers and Rory Stapleton still got a 92 on his Math final this morning."

"What does that prove?"

"That Carly couldn't have done it, obviously. The fraudster had to have gotten ahold of the tests sometime over the weekend, but she'd already been gone since last Wednesday."

"Obviously. Gee, Gillian, I don't see why you don't find the person yourself. You're so-o-o smart."

I drew back a little, the soda icy in my hand. "What's wrong with you?"

"Nothing that you can't fix. Obviously."

Okay, that sneering tone was starting to hurt. "Is this about that problem? I was only trying to help."

"Yeah, I know, but did you have to be quite so smug about it? Do you have any idea how much pressure I'm under?"

Smug? "Yeah, of course, but—"

"No, you don't. You can't. In fact, you don't know anything about what I'm going through right now."

I put a hand on his arm. "I know. I know. It must be awful. Come on, let's go back to the library and you can tell me how to help you the most, okay?"

He calmed down a little, and chewed on his lower lip. "I'm sorry. Sometimes I think I'm going nuts."

"I can imagine." Time to change the subject. "So, here's a ques-tion. How can we do some damage control with Carly?"

A puzzled glance. "I don't know. Can't we talk about some-thing else?"

"No, we need to do something. I mean, we were some of the ones spreading her name around, so it's probably up to us to—"

"What?"

"I said, after you told me, we were spreading the rumor about her as much as anyone—"

"I heard you. What I don't get is how you could say I was in on it."

Now it was my turn to stare, puzzled. "But you said yourself that she was the one doing it."

"I don't think so."

"Yes, you did." I pointed back down the corridor toward the library. "We were standing in the stacks during detention, and you said—"

"That's enough!" He threw up his arms, and I stumbled backward again, just like I had in his dad's apartment. This time, thank goodness, there was nothing on the floor. Instead, I banged up against the soda machine, making everything inside it rattle and clink.

"What is it with you, Gillian? Are you some kind of control freak? You always have to be right and everyone else is wrong?"

"Of course n—"

"Would you listen for once? I said I'd heard it might be someone with a name like an element from the periodic table. How did you get from something as vague as that to accusing Carly?"

"I—"

"Because you jumped to conclusions. And that makes you a lousy scientist, *doesn't* it?"

On *doesn't*, he pushed me—a ten-finger chest push that took me by surprise and threw me off balance again. I staggered back into the soda machine a second time and I couldn't help it—tears spurted from my eyes both from landing on its sharp metal corner, and from sheer emotion.

Deep in my chest, it felt like my heart was tearing in half. How could the boy who'd kissed me on the side of a mountain do this? How could that easy grin turn into—into—

"I'm sick of you!" He got in my face, and I'm ashamed to admit

I scrunched up against the soda machine and brought both arms up to defend my chest. "It's always about you, isn't it? I'm just arm candy to you. Just a white boyfriend you can parade in front of your Asian friends and say, Look what I got, like I'm some kind of catch."

Since this had never once occurred to me, I just stared at him, my mouth opening and closing as I tried to drag breath into my lungs.

"Honey, you ain't looking like much of a catch to me."

I gasped, and Lucas spun around.

Shani stood in the corridor, Carly beside her holding a duffel bag and a toile hatbox. Hipshot, a thumb hooked in the front pocket of her cargo pants, Shani stared Lucas down. Disdain curled her generous mouth.

"You make a habit of picking on people who are smaller than you?"

"Butt out," he snarled.

She crossed her arms and settled back on the other foot, clad in an orange D&G stiletto pump. "Not 'til Gillian comes out of there, away from your sorry a—self."

"Gillian's not going anywhere."

Carly's eyes had gone hard and flat. "Oh, yes, she is." She ducked under the arm he had stretched out like a barrier across the cubbyhole's opening and grabbed me. "Come on, Gillian. Here, take this hatbox."

"We're not finished." His voice followed us up the stairs. I did my best not to break into a run, but all the same, his voice goosed me up a couple of steps double time.

"Sunshine," Shani called down to him, "finished is exactly what you are. Once the word gets out, you won't get a date from now 'til graduation."

He called her a name that made my skin go cold, but Shani just tossed her hair—now braidless, and ironed flat and smooth—and sniffed. Like what he'd said was mildly amusing but hardly worth the energy to acknowledge it.

The three of us climbed the next flight of stairs to Carly's third-floor room. "It looks to me," Carly said, "as if you two are over. And I have to say, I'm glad."

I was still in shock. I couldn't process what had just happened, much less talk about it, so I veered away from it altogether.

"What are you doing here?" I managed. Carly unlocked her room and took the hatbox from me, tossing it on the bed without looking at it.

"What do you think?"

I couldn't think if I tried. I just shook my head, and the implacable queen softened into Carly Aragon, history buff and long-lost friend.

"I went to my dad's while I waited for all of you to come to your senses. Ms. Curzon called me at noon to apologize and sent her personal driver to get me."

"Can you do make-ups for what you missed today?"

She nodded. "They're falling all over themselves to make sure my dad doesn't call a lawyer. Like I would do that. But right now, I get pretty much anything I ask for." She paused, looking thoughtful. "Hm. I wonder if I can have *crème brulée* delivered to my room every day?"

I attempted a smile, but it wobbled into something close to tears again. This was crazy. I never cried. I had to get myself under control, even if my chest felt like it was about to explode.

"You guys, about what happened down there. How much did you hear?"

I found myself walking beside them, heading back downstairs again. I had no idea where they were going. I just needed to be with someone, so I stuck to them like Velcro.

"Enough." Shani glanced at me. "We heard a big crash and went to see what was going on—you know how things echo in that entry hall—and there he was, pushing you around. Miserable son of a—"

"But, Carly, did you hear what he said about you?"

"Oh, the rumors? Yes, I heard."

"I'm so sorry. I don't know how you can ever forgive me."

"I'm not sure, either, but we'll have to work on it, okay?" Talk about bone-scraping honesty—how do you reply to that? Carly opened the door to Lissa's and my room and I went in ahead of them.

Lissa looked up from her laptop and with one glance at my face, shoved it aside. "What happened?"

"Mr. Olympics was using Gillian to show off his manly strength," Shani said with withering sarcasm. "You got bruises, girl?"

Something in her eyes told me I'd better check, or she'd be ripping clothes off me until she got an answer. I unbuttoned my uniform blouse and pulled it off. Carly gasped, and it wasn't until I craned around to look at my back in the mirror that I saw why.

A big black bruise on my shoulder blade.

A row of them marching down my ribs.

And a couple of them on my chest, too, just below my collarbone, where his hard fingers had left their mark.

"You should call the cops." Shani's tone was as flat as her gaze. "Press assault charges."

"I can't do that!" I hung up my blouse and pulled on a T-shirt and my thick gray Columbia hoodie. After stripping off my plaid skirt and tights and climbing into my old reliable baggy jeans, I felt better. More myself. Less vulnerable.

"Why not?" Carly asked. "He's shoving you around. Are you going to wait 'til he slugs you for real?"

"He's not like that." I couldn't look at them, so I fiddled with the drawstrings on my hood. "He's under a lot of pressure right now, you guys. I antagonized him when I should have been trying to help him."

"He needs help, all right," Shani said. "Can we say *anger management*?"

"Gillian, maybe this isn't the best time to bring it up—" Lissa stopped.

"Oh, I think this is the perfect time," Carly put in.

"Bring what up?" I looked from one to the other. "Did you get your Bio grade back or something?"

"For once, can you think about yourself instead of your grades or other people?" Lissa asked.

If they only knew. Thinking about myself was my whole problem. "Then what?"

"What's happened to you that you let Lucas walk all over you, do sick stuff to you, and push you around like this?"

"It's not like that."

"He's got you so brainwashed you don't know reality when it—"

"—throws you into a soda machine." Shani finished Lissa's thought grimly.

"Listen to us," Carly begged. "We're your friends. We care about each other."

"Fine. Yes." I sank onto my bed and pulled the quilt up around me like a shawl. "But I think you're overreacting." I glanced at Carly. "I'd rather talk about what we're going to do about you and your situation."

"I don't have a situation. Not now," Carly said. "But you do."

"Here's how we see it," Lissa said. "One." Oh, great. Another one of Lissa's lists. "You go to that technology show or whatever it was, which makes you ditch your family. Much offense ensues."

"And when you're there, he gets angora up his nose," Carly added.

"That wasn't his fault," I protested.

"What *was* his fault was you showing up here in nothing but a tank top," Lissa pointed out.

"He gave me his jacket . . ." My voice faded as I remembered that disaster of a date. "But he didn't give it to me until we were in the car."

"So, what, you walked how many blocks to the parking lot? In a tank top? In February? At night?" Shani ticked off her fingers one by one.

"Two," Lissa said, "he stands you up. The flowers the next day were a nice touch, but still."

"They were white," I said.

"For purity. Or penitence," Carly said.

"Or death." They looked shocked, so I explained about what white flowers mean to someone from my background.

"Ew," was Carly's opinion. "Now, that *is* sick."

"Three." Lissa wasn't finished. "He sends you home alone on the train when you've just been to Emergency, thanks to him."

"He did it again tonight," I said, instant replay getting a real workout in my memory. "He does this thing—" I demonstrated with my hands. "And both times, I stepped back to get out of the way and hurt myself instead."

"Not hurt *yourself*, girl," Shani corrected me. "Indirectly, maybe, but *he* hurt you."

"And then the weirdest thing," Carly said. "Number four. Angel Island."

"What was weird about that?" My voice trembled, and I swallowed. "It was my first kiss. It was perfect. Don't take that away from me."

They exchanged a glance among themselves. Then Lissa said gently, "I'm glad you had that moment, Gillian. At least that part was good."

"Lots of it was good."

Was. When, in the last fifteen minutes, had I started thinking of Lucas in the past tense? And lots of it *had* been good. Stifling our laughter in the library over some stupid joke. Eating oatmeal together, happy that the first thing we'd seen that morning had been each other. Comparing grades. Thinking about the future. At least, I had been.

As of tonight, I had no idea what he'd been thinking.

"Of course it was," Carly said in a soothing tone. "But why Angel Island? Why not the Presidio or John Muir Park or Point Reyes?"

"Um, so we could ride Segways?"

My attempt at flippancy fell flat.

"That was my idea," Lissa told me. "Whose idea was Angel Island? And whose idea was it to go to that creepy detention station so we could all learn about Chinese people getting locked up in what was practically a concentration camp?"

I couldn't say a thing.

But at the same time, there had been something haunting and poignant about that place . . . about those words carved into the wall. Something that had touched me. Something that I might want to go back and experience again because it made me feel thankful. Connected. Part of a bigger community than just the one I'd grown up with and taken for granted my whole life.

But Lucas hadn't given me that. It had been that lonely poet who had filled long, cold hours carving those words to fight off his despair.

"Do you see?" Shani said gently. "He's been messing with your head from the beginning."

From where she sat on her bed, Lissa leaned closer. "I've seen you go from a girl who could own a room to this—this *accessory* who doesn't have an opinion of her own. Who has to check with Lucas first every time she wants to do something."

"I was just being considerate," I said feebly. "He said I was self-ish. Sucking up attention."

"That's a bunch of garbage," Carly said with a snort.

"He just wants all the attention for himself," Shani said. "He's probably loving this whole Olympiad thing, with everybody in the Science Club treating him like he's God and all the teachers patting him on the back and wishing him luck every time he walks by."

"Too bad we can't do anything about that," Lissa said. "If he wins this thing and goes to the finals, it'll just be so wrong."

"Be fair." I could hardly speak, my mind was such a jumble. Memories were rearranging themselves in a new order, like a deck of cards being shuffled in different ways, giving you a whole new hand. "He might be a jerk, but he's still good at physics. His winning has nothing to do with me."

"I'm glad to hear that, at least," Shani said. "I was thinking we'd have to tie you down in here to stop you getting back together with him."

I needed time to think. To figure out what I was going to do. But one thing was clear.

"We won't be getting back together. I have to break up with him."

The sooner the better. Like, before my bruises healed.

chapter 19

TUESDAY AT MIDMORNING break, I was called into the administration office, where a huge bouquet of flowers sat on the counter.

"These are for you, Miss Chang," the receptionist said with a delighted smile. "They're just beautiful. Is it a special occasion?"

Not that I knew of. I breathed deeply. Ginger flower. Bird of paradise. Lilies. Maybe Dad's assistant had actually gotten a date mixed up in her immaculate planner.

I opened the card.

> Dear Gillian,
> I was a jerk. I hope the flowers make up for it a little.
> Can we have dinner Friday night to celebrate finals being over?
> Lucas

As I read each word, my thumb pressed harder into the heavy ivory stock, until with a wet-sounding *crack*, it bent in half. Was he insane? Did he seriously think he could toss me against a soda machine and then ask me out? Did he think I was so desperate for his attention that I'd overlook all these bruises and go on as if life were normal?

I looked up at the receptionist. "Would you like to have these?"

She blinked. "Anyone would. But—"

"Please. Take them and put them on your desk. You'll enjoy them much more than I will."

"But—"

Before she could actually refuse, I ducked out the door and speed-walked down the corridor, so that I'd be out of sight by the time she rounded the counter. I made it to my next class with seconds to spare. U.S. History. With an exam I was in no shape to take. I muddled through it somehow, and then at last it was lunchtime.

I waved a yogurt and fruit salad to go at Lissa and Jeremy, who were already at our usual table, and slipped out the door. I hoped Lissa would understand—I really needed to be alone to think this through. Closing the door of our room on the noise in the corridor, I breathed a long sigh of relief and cracked the yogurt open.

I'd been putting off the breakup speech because—let's face it—I have pretty much zero experience with dating a guy, never mind breaking up with him. How come we aren't all issued a manual when we turn thirteen that tells us how to do this stuff? I mean, you can't just send him a text message that says "Game over," can you? It'd be tacky to call his voice-mail inbox and give the speech to it—but I only knew that from watching movies.

What I did know was that Lucas still thought we were a couple. My friends thought he was a loser and a bully, with a sprinkling of sociopath. The less my parents knew, the better, so I couldn't ask them for help—though I was beginning to think my dad was right about sticking to academics while I was in school. If that History final was any indication, guys could really mess with your mind.

Should I arrange a meeting tonight and just get it over with? Or should I go out with Lucas Friday night and do the deed at the restaurant, where he'd be in a public place, forced to be normal and unlikely to hurt me?

There's your answer right there, girl. How can you put Lucas *and* hurt me *in the same sentence and want to do anything but unload him as fast as possible?*

But what should I say? What would he do? Good grief, this was awful. Too hard. I needed help, right now.

I opened the drawer of my night table and pulled my Bible out of it.

Lord, You're the only one I can turn to. I need strength and wisdom, all in one indestructible package. I need a safe place and the right words. In fact, if the angel Gabriel is just sitting around up there polishing his sword, I could use him for backup, too.

Eyes closed, I ran a finger down the gilt edges of the pages and opened the Bible at random. Then I blinked and focused. Proverbs 2.

> "If you call out for insight and cry aloud for understanding . . . then you will understand the fear of the Lord and find the knowledge of God. . . . Discretion will protect you, and understanding will guard you. Wisdom will save you from the ways of wicked men, from men whose words are perverse."

What had Lissa said? That I'd turned into some kind of silent accessory? I'd lost my voice—my ability to call out for anything—because Lucas didn't like it. Didn't like people listening to me instead of him. I mean, give me a break, here. Asian girls are brought up to be seen and not heard, you know? If Nai-Nai had her way, I'd say nothing but yes and no and please pass the white pepper.

I'd always been wired differently, always used my voice to praise God and tell people about how cool He is. When was the last time I'd done that? When had I stopped talking about the thing that was most important to me—my faith?

I felt the heat burn in my cheeks as it came home to me just what my relationship with Lucas had cost. He was the man whose words were perverse. And that might have cost me my friendship with Carly—the jury was still out—and maybe even her ability to surrender to God.

That was a very scary thought.

I ran my fingers down the pages and flipped to the book of Hebrews.

"Through Jesus, therefore, let us continually offer to God a sacrifice of praise—the fruit of lips that confess his name. And do not forget to do good and to share with others, for with such sacrifices God is pleased."

The sacrifice of praise. But I'd turned it inside out, hadn't I? I'd sacrificed praise. The fruit of my lips was all bottled up inside, afraid to come out because it might make Lucas angry. After the webcam disaster last term, Lissa had told me that the thing she'd learned to love most about me was my honesty. And honesty had to be spoken, didn't it? If that was the fruit the Lord was cultivating in me (despite what Nai-Nai wanted), then who was I to throttle it back and keep quiet?

Slowly, I closed the Bible.

I get it now, Lord. You want me to speak out, don't You? Use this big old mouth of mine to praise You. And that means saying good-bye to the guy who wants to keep me quiet. Thank You, Father. Thanks for showing me what I needed to see. And thanks for sending me friends who are

*willing to tell me the truth—who have the same kind of fruit You want
in me—even when I don't appreciate them.*

I thought of Carly, and all the ground I had to make up with
her. But one thing at a time.

In spite of the flowers—or maybe because of them—I had to
find a time and a place to break up with Lucas ASAP.

GChang I got your flowers.

LHayes Did you like them? You didn't seem very thrilled with the
roses so I got something else.

GChang They were beautiful. Can I see you before Friday? I need
to talk.

LHayes Girls. Send them flowers and they need to talk. :)

GChang About what happened at the soda machine.

LHayes Can't it wait until after finals? I'm under so much pressure
you can't believe it.

GChang So you said.

LHayes Oh OK. After prayer meeting?

GChang You're going?

LHayes I always go. Or didn't you notice? :)

GChang See you then.

"WE NEED A PLAN."

Lissa closed the door of Room 216 after making sure no one
coming to prayer circle was walking down the corridor. Carly and
I pulled chairs over so we could huddle.

"You guys, I have to do this on my own," I said. "I can't bring
my posse to a breakup."

"I don't trust him," Carly said. "What if he gets mad? What if
he hits you?"

"He won't do that. Pushing is one thing. Hauling off and hitting someone is—"

"—grounds for those assault charges Shani was talking about," Lissa finished.

"Well, yeah," I admitted. "But what I was going to say is, it's not his style."

"Abuse has a style?!" Carly's eyebrows shot up along with her voice.

"I get it," Lissa said thoughtfully. "He's like this stealth abuser. Actually hitting someone would be too obvious for him. He likes to be subtle when he's messing you up."

"Yeah. So subtle I didn't even pick up on it while it was happening to me."

"That's not your fault." How could Carly be so nice, even leaving out the fact that I'd accused her with hardly a second thought? How did I deserve a friend like this? Maybe she was like Lissa, who only got mad once a year. Though it looked like Carly was getting there now on my behalf—her eyes were practically snapping with sparks. If Lucas walked in right now, she might take him out at the knees and I wouldn't have to go through with this. "Maybe he won't come," she went on. "I don't see how he can treat you like that and look God in the face."

I didn't either, but that part wasn't up to me. It was something else I had to put in God's hands.

"Anyway. Back to the plan," Lissa reminded us. "We'll probably walk down to Starbucks afterward, so everything looks normal. You could get a private table and do it there."

"Right. In front of you guys and who knows how many other people from school," I said.

"Or on the way," Carly suggested. "It doesn't matter, as long as we're close, right?"

I looked at her. "That's a good idea. I could make sure we tagged behind a little. Then I could catch up with you . . . after."

Lissa nodded. "And then we can—"

The door opened and Jeremy stepped in, followed by Shani,

and a few minutes later, Lucas, who came in with some new kids. At the sight of him, I felt a cold chill dart through my stomach.

Truth? I could go the rest of my life without seeing him ever again. But now, in front of people who didn't need to know my personal business, I had to pretend that everything was fine.

I smiled, like I always did.

He sat beside me, like he always did.

Lissa plunked herself down on my other side, practically hip-checking Jeremy out of the way. He sat next to Shani (no surprise), who proceeded to stare at Lucas like a cat watching a mouse hole.

When prayer began and we joined hands, Lucas squeezed mine. I didn't squeeze back—instead, my hand lay in his like a cold, limp wad of newspaper on a snowy New York street. It was all I could do to leave it there and open my heart to God at the same time.

Playing the piano afterward was a different thing. You try eight- and ten-note chords when your hands are so cold they need gloves. I muddled through it, mostly thanks to Shani, who took the music's gospel roots and made them soar—meaning people listened to her, not me.

We headed out to Starbucks in a straggly group, and when I saw that most of them were out of earshot but still in sight, I dropped Lucas's hand.

"Lucas, I need to tell you something."

"You already told me you liked the flowers. I wasn't looking for a personal thank-you."

"No, it's not that." I took a breath. *Just dive in.* "I didn't keep the flowers. I gave them to the receptionist."

He stopped walking. Out of the corner of my eye, I saw Lissa grab Carly's arm and stop her too. They looked in some random store window, then kept going in double slow time.

"You gave them to the receptionist?" Lucas repeated in astonishment. "Why?"

He even sounded hurt. What an actor. "Because there's no way I could keep them. I can't go out with you anymore, Lucas. This is it."

He stared at me, then walked on. "You are one crazy chick."

"See, this is exactly why." It took me a couple of steps to catch up. "I do something you don't like, and suddenly *I'm* crazy. I don't expect you to apologize for what happened at the soda machine, but—"

"Why should I? If it wasn't for you ragging on me and making everything worse, I wouldn't have lost it."

"Oh, that's right. I threw *myself* into a solid metal object."

"Well, you are naturally clumsy." He smiled at me, clearly aiming for "affectionate," but it didn't look that way to me. It just looked fake. "It could happen to anyone."

"Breakups can happen to anyone, too. I'd like my jade bracelet back, please."

"Sheesh, Gillian, what's the Chinese equivalent of 'Indian giver'?"

"I don't know, nor do I care. I want it back."

"I thought it was a gift."

"It was for luck, until you passed the prelims for the Olympiad. Now that you have, you don't need it anymore."

"I don't think so. It's my lucky talisman. I'm keeping it until I get into the top five."

Now it was my turn to stop. "Lucas, God is your lucky talisman. You don't need that bracelet."

"Who says? Maybe I need all the help I can get."

"And maybe you're just doing this as a power play."

"Paranoid much?"

"You're doing it again. You do something unacceptable, and then you blame the other person for reacting."

"You know what, Gillian? You think too much."

How could I have been so attracted to this guy? "When it comes to you, I didn't think enough. I mean it. I want that bracelet back."

"Sorry, I don't have it." He shot his wrist to show me it was bare. "It's in my room."

"Then you can give it to me tomorrow."

"And if I don't?"

"You sound like a little kid. Grow up, Lucas. This isn't a game."

"Oh, really? But it's all about the property, isn't it? Just like my mother. She dumped my dad and suddenly all she cared about was what she could get out of him. You women are all the same."

Oh, boy. We have now left the world of reality, folks. Fasten your seat belts.

"This isn't about your mother. This is about you and me."

"Not anymore, it's not. You go have a nice cup of coffee, Gillian." He spun on his heel and headed back up the hill. "I hope you enjoy it."

He probably thought he was being all generous and open-minded. But I didn't care.

I ran to catch up with Lissa and Carly, who waited at the corner on my side of the street while everyone else went into Starbucks. And you want to know something?

I'd never been so happy to see my friends waiting for me in my whole life.

chapter 20

WHEN I HADN'T seen so much as a thread of my bracelet by breakfast the next day, I realized I had two choices:

a. I could write it off as a loss and figure it was a fair price to pay for learning how to spot a loser.

b. I could burgle Lucas's room.

"I'd buy a ticket to see that," Carly said around her oatmeal. She always puts half a dozen spoonfuls of brown sugar on it—like that's going to help.

"It just makes me mad." Okay, I was sulking. Can you blame me? "He's already humiliated me and made a fool out of me. How come he needs my bracelet, too?"

"He doesn't need it. I think he just likes the idea that he can still play with you," Lissa said. "And, hello, you're letting him."

"Who's playing with you?" Jeremy slid in next to me, and Carly went back to her oatmeal.

"Never mind," Lissa said. "What exams do you have today?"

But I'd just had an idea. Jeremy was friends with Travis Fanshaw, who was Lucas's roommate.

"That was subtle." Jeremy spooned yogurt over his mound of fruit, then sprinkled granola on top of that. He crowned the whole thing with blueberry syrup that I hadn't even seen in the array of breakfast choices.

"What have you got there?" After seven-grain toast, anything looked good to me. I leaned over to inspect his masterpiece.

"Have some." He indicated the side closest to me, and because it was such a change for a guy to be straightforwardly nice, I did. "So, who's playing with you? Lucas?"

I blinked and my spoon stopped in midair for a full second. A single drop of blueberry syrup fell, and I hastily shoved it into my mouth. "Why do you ask?" I said, not very elegantly, crunching granola. The syrup was the first sugar I'd had other than at Starbucks since I started training with Ms. Modano. It tasted wonderful.

He shrugged. "Travis told me you guys broke up. I guess Lucas is pretty bummed."

"Why?" Lissa's tone dripped acid. "Because now he doesn't have anyone to be his punching bag?"

"Huh?" Jeremy gawked at her, then at me.

I could feel the heat of humiliation burning its way into my face. This was exactly what I didn't want. I shot Lissa a "would you shut up?" look. "Nothing. How about those exams?"

"I thought that was just a rumor."

"What, exams? No, they're very real. Unfortunately." At least there were only three more days to go. Today's big scary one was AP Chem during fourth period. Tomorrow I'd do my Composition performance, turn in my term paper and write an in-class essay for English, and do my Mandarin presentation. And then other than my Chamber Ensemble performance, which would be fun, and the training torture session Friday morning, which I'd undoubtedly fail, I'd be free.

"Tell me about it. No, I meant the rumor about you two break-ing up. Is that why? Did he mess you up?"

"I don't want to talk about it, Jeremy," I managed.

"Oh." He sort of deflated, like I'd hurt his feelings. "Okay. I wasn't being a ghoul. I just wanted to help."

For some reason, my throat got thick and my eyes flooded with tears. I reached for my backpack, slung it over my shoulder, and picked up my half-eaten container of yogurt and empty coffee cup. "See you guys later. I've gotta go."

I got all the way to my core classroom, which, because I was half an hour early, was totally empty, when I heard steps behind me.

"Gillian?"

Jeremy followed me into the room, where I dropped my back-pack and sat slumped in my usual spot by the window. "What?"

"I'm sorry if I said anything that upset you."

I shook my head. "It's not you. I'm just feeling bummed right now, you know?"

"You must have really liked him, huh."

I wrinkled my forehead and gave him a look. "I appreciate the thought, really I do. But that's kind of . . . not your business."

He pulled over a chair opposite me, looked down at his hands drooping between his knees, and the tips of his ears turned red. "I know. I'm sorry. But I hate seeing that guy get away with it."

I just stared at him. Had the entire student body known all this time what Lucas was? Was I the only one who couldn't buy a clue?

"He dated my sister when she was a freshman," he went on. "From some of the things she said, and the way she changed while they were together, I was glad they broke up. It lasted two weeks, but still."

"What did she say about it?"

"Just weird stuff. He made her feel bad about nearly every-thing." He looked up. "So I'm glad you guys broke up, too."

"Thanks, Jeremy." I took a slow, cleansing breath. "You're friends with Travis, right?" He nodded. "Is he still friends with Lucas?"

Jeremy grinned, and for the first time, I noticed he had dimples on either side of his mouth. Shani must be an idiot to treat him the way she did.

"Are you kidding? Travis has a Ph.D. in aggravation. Lucas wants to kill him half the time."

"My kind of guy. Listen, Lucas has a bracelet of mine—knotted silk cords with a jade bead. I gave it to him for luck and he won't give it back. Do you think Travis could look for it?"

Jeremy shrugged. "Sure."

"Good. I'll just hang around in the common room while he finds it. Lucas goes to Palo Alto on weekends, usually. And I bet he will this weekend, too, because finals will be over."

"Okay. Give me your cell number. I've never tossed a room before. This could be fun."

"There'll be no tossing," I warned. "I don't want him to know a thing. I just want my bracelet back."

"You'll get it back, don't worry," Jeremy said as the first of the students began to trickle in. "Score one for the good guys."

AT TWENTY PAST six that evening, when I was practicing my harp piece for Chamber Ensemble, my iPhone chimed.

"Hey," Travis said. "Jeremy told me you wanted to know when Mr. Olympics left the building."

"And?"

"He went to some lame presentation at the university with the Science Club. Won't be back until nine or so."

I grinned even though he couldn't see me. Better to get this over with sooner rather than later. "Thanks, Travis. I owe you." I told him what the bracelet looked like. "Don't disturb anything, so he won't know you were looking. I'll wait in the common room. I hope Mr. Milsom isn't around."

"According to my spy on the janitorial staff, Milsom is in the staff room having after-dinner herbal tea with Tobin. I think something's going on there."

With a snort, I said, "The only people who don't know something is going on are Tobin and Milsom."

"I'll find the bracelet and meet you downstairs."

When my phone chimed again, I sank deep into the easy chair and answered it as if I didn't have a care in the world.

"Hey, it's me," Travis said. "What'd you say it looked like, again?"

"It's made of black silk cords, all knotted in a pattern, with a green jade bead in the middle. Looks Chinese." Duh.

"It's not here, then. I've been over his side twice."

It had to be there. The only other alternative was that Lucas was wearing it. But I didn't want to think about that. "I'm coming up."

Travis laughed. "Your funeral. Meet you at the door."

I'm sure the Lord doesn't condone breaking and entering, but in spite of that, He made sure the corridor was empty. It had to be a God thing. What else could explain the complete absence of students right after dinner? Travis let me in and we ran to his and Lucas's room.

Unlike mine and Lissa's, this room looked like something out of a movie from the forties. They had no chandelier, but on the plus side, their floor was a nifty checkerboard of black and white marble. Lucas probably threw pajama parties where each person got to be a chess piece. Woohoo. Geek fun.

But I couldn't waste time looking at the scenery or I'd lose my nerve. I began my search in a clockwise direction, starting to the left of the door. Dresser. Wardrobe. Desk. Nothing. Bed. I ran my hands under the mattress and found nothing but a magazine. Floor.

Backpack. I searched all the pockets. Nothing. Then I reached into the main part, feeling along the bottom.

Aha!

With a yank, I freed my bracelet from its ignominious prison at the bottom of all his junk, under his heavy textbooks. The cretin. Showed you what he thought of my gift. As I pulled it out, a gray folder came with it, hit the floor, and disgorged Scantrons all over the rug.

"Oh, no." Hastily, I gathered them up. Then I focused on the top one, dated March 26.

Wait a minute. These weren't his old tests. Teachers didn't return them—all we got were printouts. And March 26 was tomorrow.

I flipped through them. Math: bonehead, regular, and AP. Chemistry. Physics. All dated March 26 and 27.

"Travis."

"Yeah?" He leaned in the door from where he'd been keeping an eye on the corridor outside.

"Come and look at this." When he hunkered down beside me, I said, "What do these look like to you?"

He scanned them. "Uh-oh," he said softly. "I have a bad feeling about this."

"Has it been Lucas?" I said in a high voice that didn't sound like me at all. "All this time, has it been him selling these?"

Travis fanned through them. "Why didn't I know?"

"What about me? I was going out with the guy."

"He's smooth, I'll give him that." He got up, leaving me still holding the condemning evidence. "So what now?"

"We have to tell someone. Milsom. Right away."

"Would that be before or after I get you out of the dorm?"

I looked up. "You can tell him when he does the lights-out check. We can't wait. The ones on top are for tomorrow's tests."

"How'm I going to say I found out? That I was rifling through my roommate's stuff?"

"Just say you were looking for a pen," I said impatiently. "Or that I asked you to find the bracelet. Which I did."

"I feel pretty weird about ratting him out."

I stared at him. "Would you rather flunk all your classes?"

"No, duh. But maybe there's some other explanation. Maybe he found them on someone else and was holding them until he could get them to a teacher."

"You're reaching."

"We should at least ask him. What if it wasn't him? I mean, I'm not above giving the guy a hard time because he's such a dweeb, but we'd be accusing the next freaking physics medalist and probably getting ourselves expelled if we're wrong."

I nibbled at my lower lip. There was a chance—okay, a really slim one—that Travis could be right. And with the Carly disaster fresh in my mind, I couldn't afford to go around saying things I didn't have proof of.

I looked at the Scantrons in my hands. Well, more proof, anyway. Some link between these sheets and the people they were going to. Because in my search of this room, I hadn't found anything like—hello?—money. Or e-mail printouts. Or a sticky note saying "I need illegal help."

Either Lucas had something really sophisticated going on here, or he was innocent. And I was in no position to go pointing fingers a second time.

"All right," I said at last. "We'll ask him before we do anything. Rewind—*you'll* ask him. I wasn't here, and you haven't seen me since English class yesterday."

"Deal. Come on. Let's get you out of here."

I stuffed the folder in the backpack and stashed it under the bed, the way it had been. Then I slipped my bracelet on my wrist and tiptoed down the corridor after Travis. Once I was out of the boys' dorm and heading back to my own, innocent and fancy-free, I expected to breathe easier. Instead, my breath came faster and faster until I found myself running for the safety of my room.

Lissa looked up as the door slammed behind my back, and her eyes went wide. "What happened? Couldn't Travis find it?"

"No. It's Lucas."

"Did he come back?"

"No. He's the guy. The one selling the exam answers. I think."

Her jaw dropped. "*What?*"

Breathlessly, I told her about the backpack, the folder, the plan Travis and I had worked out. But even before I finished, she was shaking her head.

"It's not going to work. If you ask Lucas about this, of course he's going to lie. If those answer sheets were in his backpack, he's the one. Open and shut. You have to tell someone right now."

"But there's no . . . what do you call it?" My mind blanked. "Like on *CSI*." Then I had it. "Chain of evidence. No link between him and people like Rory Stapleton."

Slowly, Lissa's gaze swung from me to her laptop, sleeping on the desk. "Rory Stapleton. That's it."

"What are you going to do?" I asked anxiously. "Lissa, focus. You have to help me figure this out."

"I am. Right now."

LMansfield	Question for you.
RStapleton	I heard you might have more than that for me. Shot any videos lately?
LMansfield	Ha ha. Rumor has it you might know where a person can get help with Bio before the exam tomorrow.
RStapleton	Never trust rumor.
LMansfield	So you don't know? Too bad.
RStapleton	I never said that. What's it worth?
LMansfield	Meet me outside after the Bio exam. I'll show you.

RStapleton	Yeah? Can I bring my camera?
LMansfield	Bring your whole computer. Who do I contact?
RStapleton	It's $1.5K a pop and you IM Source10.
LMansfield	Who's that?
RStapleton	Duh. That's the point. No one's supposed to know.
LMansfield	Then who do I pay?
RStapleton	Source10 at PayPal.
LMansfield	Slick.
RStapleton	And you didn't hear it from me. See you tomorrow.
LMansfield	You will. XO

"Not." Lissa hit Send with a vicious poke of her finger.

"Wow," I said on a long breath. "Source10, huh? How'd he get a school ID, I wonder?"

Lissa looked at me over the fashionable black rectangles of her glasses. I was one of the few at school who even knew she wore them. "He hacked the teachers' exam database. How hard would it be to hack the mail server?"

"Good point." I pushed my hair behind my ears. "I'm really out of it. I think I'm in shock. To think that my boyfriend—"

"Ex-boyfriend."

"—could be capable of something like this. It's unbelievable."

"Maybe not so much. Think about it. The guy spends nearly a whole term basically tearing you down to nothing, just for his own amusement. What kind of arrogance does it take to do that? It's not much of a leap from there to selling answers."

Arrogance was right. The kind that had no place in a Christian guy. Had that all been fake, too? Was it all part of a colossal, blind conceit that believed it was too smart to get caught?

I pulled back my sleeve and looked at my bracelet. Caught by my gift. If it hadn't been for me being so stubborn about getting it back, Lucas would probably have gotten away with it and gone on to triumph in the Olympiad. A cheater would be a hero with a medal on his chest.

Lissa was still at the computer. "I'm not done yet."

LMansfield	I hear you can help people.
Source10	You heard wrong.
LMansfield	Rory Stapleton told me you could. And I'm going to flunk Bio if I don't get help.
Source10	Get your roommate to help.
LMansfield	We're not talking right now. She's responsible for what happened to Carly.
Source10	No.
LMansfield	Look, just because we have to room together doesn't mean we're friends anymore. And I have the money.
Source10	No.
LMansfield	Chicken.
Source10	What?
LMansfield	Rinse and repeat.
Source10	You'll squeal like a pig.
LMansfield	If you get caught, I'll get caught. No one's talking. You're safe.
Source10	Fine. $1.5K to me at PayPal. Locker #254 30 min before class.
LMansfield	:)

chapter 21

A FEW MINUTES BEFORE ten o'clock that evening, someone knocked on our door. Lissa had finally calmed down and was studying in bed, wearing her blue flannel pajamas with the flamingoes on them. That girl's sleeping wardrobe is as extensive as her daytime one. I was still dressed, so I got up to answer it.

Ms. Tobin stood there. "Miss Chang, would you please come with me to the headmistress's office?"

At lights-out? Did these people not sleep? "Why?"

"Come with me, please. It's urgent."

And then I knew. Travis had changed his mind and gone to Milsom when he did the lights-out check, and since I was the only other witness, they needed to talk to me.

"I'll be right back," I said to Lissa, touching the jade bead on my bracelet to reassure myself as I followed Tobin down to the first floor. She showed me into Curzon's inner office and closed the door behind me.

"Where's Travis?" I asked Ms. Curzon, who sat behind her huge desk, her fingers steepled in front of her lips.

"In his room, studying, I imagine," she replied. "At least, the optimist in me would like to think so."

I stayed silent, puzzling this out.

"And why would his whereabouts matter to you?"

Man, this lady clearly didn't watch *CSI*. "I thought you'd want to talk to us both together, that's all. Get all the facts at once."

"Was he in on this with you?"

Careful. I didn't want to implicate Travis when he'd put himself at risk to let me into the dorm. "I asked him to help me. But it was all my idea."

"Yes, I'm sure it was." Her gaze dropped to a folder on her desk. A gray folder, not the manila ones everybody used.

"Is that—" I began.

"Let me bring you up to speed, Miss Chang. I've just spent the last forty-five minutes with Lucas Hayes, who is practically beside himself with distress."

"I bet he is."

I don't think she heard me, because she went on, "It took me thirty of those forty-five minutes to get him calmed down, in fact. So I've called you in here to get your side of the story."

"My side?"

"Yes. Start with telling me how you managed to get into the boys' dorm."

Wow. Travis must have spilled everything to Lucas, who had spilled it to her in the course of being interrogated. That meant there probably wasn't any point in trying to protect Travis.

"Lucas had a bracelet of mine and wouldn't give it back," I began. "It was obviously a control thing—we'd just broken up and he was pretty angry about it. So I asked Travis to find it for me, but when he couldn't, he let me into the dorm so I could look myself."

She made a note on the yellow legal pad in front of her. "Go on."

I decided to leave out some details and skip to the bottom line. "I found the bracelet. And I also found that." I nodded at the folder in front of her.

"And what is this?"

"You probably already know it's full of exam answer sheets. Math, Chem, Physics, all levels. Dated for tomorrow and the next day."

She nodded. "And then?"

"Well, it was clear that Lucas is the one who's been selling the sheets, but Travis and I didn't know whether it would be better to confront him about it or to go straight to Mi—Mr. Milsom. In the end Travis decided it would be better to ask Lucas first since I got it wrong with Carly Aragon and we didn't want to risk being wrong twice."

"Commendable."

"And then I went back to my room." I took a breath, getting ready to tell her about Lissa laying the trap for Source10.

"It's a very convincing version of events." She made a couple more notes.

"Version? That's what happened. Travis can back me up."

"Would you like to hear Lucas's story?"

Oh, I'd love to. Complete with pictures at eleven. I sat back and got as comfortable as possible in the old-fashioned slat-backed chair.

She got up and tapped on the outer door. "Lucas, would you come in now, please?"

I shot upright and gripped the wooden arms as he walked in. "Lucas?"

His shoulders were straight, and he wore khakis and his school blazer. He'd obviously come to the headmistress almost immediately after he got back from the presentation at the university. Right after Travis would have confronted him with that folder.

He didn't even look at me as he tugged briskly at his pant legs and sat.

"Lucas, would you mind telling us again what happened this evening?"

He tucked his chin once in a nod. "I went to a science symposium at USF on computer modeling, because that's the area I want to concentrate on at Stanford. It lasted until about eight thirty, and I got back to my room around nine. I found my roommate, Travis Fanshaw, in a very agitated mood. I asked him what was wrong and he said he'd had a girl in there while I was gone."

"That wasn't what—" I began hotly, but Curzon shut me up with a look.

"Go on," she said.

"He apologized, which I thought was weird at the time. So then I went to get my stuff organized for my exams tomorrow, and I found that folder in my backpack." He nodded toward her desk.

You've got to be kidding. "What, it just apparated in there by itself?" I blurted.

"No," he said, as though replying to a very small child. "I imagine someone put it there."

"Uh-huh. Like you."

The headmistress frowned at me. "Miss Chang, please. Go on, Lucas."

I looked from one to the other. Since when did she first-name a student? Girls were always Miss Whomever and guys were addressed by their surnames. Archaic and sexist, yeah, tell me about it. So what was up with the favoritism?

"So I asked Travis and then it all came out. He thought it was mine. I said I'd never seen it before—especially when I opened it and saw what was inside it. And then I got the real story."

For the first time, he looked at me. There was no emotion at all in the blue eyes I thought I'd known so well.

"Travis says she bribed him into letting her into our room. She told him it was to get something of hers, just to get his sympathy, but it turned out it was more than that. She asked him to keep a lookout in the hall, and when there was no one in the room, she slipped that folder into my backpack." His gaze faltered, and his voice hushed. "I'm sorry I hurt you so much, Gillian. But I had to break up with you. I just can't see a girl who says she's a Christian and then does things like this when things don't go the way she wants." He paused. "In fact, you've damaged my faith so much, I've asked myself what's the point of going to church at all if Christians are like this."

My mouth fell open and all the breath in my lungs whooshed out. On top of everything else, he was going to pin his loss of *faith* on me?

And then a memory surfaced. A pastor with a puzzled look on his face as he tried to remember who Lucas Hayes was. "You hypocrite," I breathed. "When did you ever go to church? What was prayer circle, huh? An acting experiment?"

Oh Lord, I see it now. How could I be so dumb? Here I was all over Lissa last term about the power of discernment, when I could have used some myself.

Lucas ignored me and looked up at Ms. Curzon. "I was so upset I couldn't do anything but come straight to you. I apologize for being so out of control before, ma'am."

"That's all right," she said. "Thank you, Lucas, for being willing to repeat all of that. I'm sure it was painful for you."

He dipped his head and swallowed. If looks could kill, then my withering scorn would have at least burned a big black hole in his jacket.

"You may go. Try to get some sleep. You're in the exam home stretch now."

He smiled at her, then made his dignified, Olympian exit without wasting so much as another glance at me.

Ms. Curzon sighed. "Are there any changes you wish to make to your story, Miss Chang?"

"Are there any you'd believe?" Who, me? Bitter?

"Whether I believe them or not is irrelevant," she said. "All I want is the truth."

You and your Olympiad semifinalist, happily lying through your perfect teeth. Oh, I knew what this was about. She wasn't going to risk Spencer Academy's chance of seeing its name in the papers, science mags, and on Web sites all over the world as being the school that had produced the gold medalist. It meant more wealthy students. It meant fatter donations. And it probably meant a few more laurel leaves in her crown, too.

Never mind that the medalist was a liar and a fraud.

"My version *is* the truth, Ms. Curzon," I said as quietly as I could, considering the anger ripping through my veins. "I have to tell you something else. My friend Lissa made a deal with Lucas, who calls himself Source10 online. He's leaving the exam answers she pretended to buy in locker number two fifty-four. It'll be there half an hour before the second-period Biology exam. Put one of the security cameras on it, if you don't believe me."

"I shall. Thank you. In the meantime, you are suspended."

The anger roaring through me froze abruptly and fell into my stomach in a shower of icy shards. "What?"

"Clearly I can't allow you to go on as though nothing had happened. At the very least, you're guilty of being in the boys' dorm and consorting with a boy in his room."

"We did not *consort!*"

"Define it as you will, the fact remains that you, by your own admission, were there."

"That's grounds for detention, not suspension."

"True."

"But I didn't do what Lucas said. He made all that up to cover his own actions. And what about my exams?"

"At the moment I'm in the mood to give you Fs in all of them. But if I feel differently tomorrow morning, you would attend only the classes in which you have exams. At all other times you'll be confined to your room. We'll confiscate your laptop now, to prevent any communication."

"With who?" Losing my laptop would be like losing an arm.

"If you are guilty, I imagine you'd want to warn your customers that you have been discovered."

"And since I'm not guilty?"

"According to our manual, anyone who is suspended has their privileges revoked." She held out her hand. "I'll need your cell phone as well."

I pulled it out of the pocket of my cargo pants and gave it to her. "I'm innocent, Ms. Curzon. When you go to that locker tomorrow, you'll find out it's true."

"I don't like to think that any of our students is capable of this, Miss Chang," she said, and buzzed the intercom. "No matter how it turns out, I shall be most upset."

Ha, I thought as Ms. Tobin appeared. Not half as upset as I was right now. Not by a long shot.

....

✉

To: Faculty@spenceracad.edu
From: NCurzon@spenceracad.edu
Date: March 25, 2009
Re: Urgent: Math and Science Departments

The student who committed the exam-answer fraud has been apprehended. However, in the event that answers for tomorrow's and Friday's exams are already in circulation, I am directing you all to substitute and/or scramble your exam questions and answers fifteen minutes before class time.

I realize this will cause some inconvenience, but the integrity of our school is at stake. I have no doubt that by using this strategy, we will also be able to pinpoint students who have compromised themselves by buying answer sheets in the last day or two.

Thank you for your help, and I look forward to the results of tomorrow's exams.

Natalie Curzon

....

ⓖ

Source10	You awake?
LMansfield	I'd better be. Bio in 2 hours.
Source10	Where's the money?
LMansfield	I pay you when I get the sheet.
Source10	Wrong. In advance.
LMansfield	Thanks for telling me. Not.
Source10	I'm canceling the deal.
LMansfield	Why? I'll pay you!
Source10	Sorry.
LMansfield	But I'll flunk Bio!!
Source10	Not my problem. No tickee, no laundry.
LMansfield	That's not fair!

Lissa turned from her monitor to me, her face white with panic. "He backed out of the deal."

I sucked in a breath. "Why?"

"He says it's because I didn't pay in advance. Now what are we going to do?"

The urge to just give up and cry swamped me, and I fought it back. "There's nothing we can do, I guess. Curzon will go to that locker—if she hasn't already—and it'll be empty. Nothing will show on the cameras. End of story."

"Gillian, I'm so sorry." Lissa's eyes were full of tears. "I should have paid attention. I should have asked if he wanted the money up front."

"I don't think it's that. I think he's spooked and being careful. On the bright side, you won't get whatever punishment they have in store for the people who bought answers."

"But that isn't helping you."

"Hey. Just having you for a friend is helping me." I gave her a hug. "As you reminded me yourself the other day—the truth will set us free. I told the Lord all about it last night and put everything in His hands. It'll be okay. You'll see."

She gave me a watery smile. "I wish that included my Bio final. If I'd gotten that answer sheet, it sure would have been tempting to use it."

"No, you wouldn't."

"My brain is so seized up I don't think I can squeeze a single fact out of it."

"Try to relax," I suggested. "Close your books and don't even think about it. Listen to some music or something, and let your cortexes unclench."

That got a laugh out of her. "Thank you, Dr. Chang. Does that work for the gluteus maximus too?"

And then it was time. We met Shani at the top of the stairs, and Carly joined us. We hadn't even gotten halfway down the stairs when half a dozen juniors I recognized from my various classes stopped us.

"Thanks a lot, Chang," a tall boy sneered. "Thanks for almost making us flunk."

His friend stepped up, getting in my face. "Why are you still here? I heard you got kicked out."

"Get away from her," Lissa snapped.

"Little Miss Christian," the first boy said, not giving an inch. "Read the Ten Commandments lately? Oh, wait. You need the answer sheet!"

"Are you deaf?" Shani swaggered up to him, five feet six inches of girl, four inches of stiletto heel, and ten feet of attitude. "Get away from her and keep your pinheaded comments to yourself." She jerked her face into his and he stepped back, lost his footing on the step, and had to grab the wood and wrought-iron railing to keep from rolling down the stairs like a basketball.

His friends turned to give him a hand, and I grabbed Carly's arm and took the stairs down to the foyer two at a time.

But there was no escape. The word was out, and the word was *Gillian*.

Every ten feet, someone had to tell me what a skank they thought I was. Some people made themselves happy by flipping me off. Two girls from our volleyball team who were way better at bumps than brains pinned me up against a locker and told me their opinion—or would have, if a teacher hadn't passed just then. As it was, I had to detour to the girls' restroom to wipe the spit off my cheek.

Mentally, I kissed any hope of straight A's good-bye. I didn't care anymore whether I even passed my classes. I wouldn't be coming back. I could be thankful for small mercies, though—since Curzon had confiscated my cell phone, I couldn't get any hysterical calls from my parents.

At noon, I trudged down to the dining room to get a tray to take back to the dorm. As I stood at the cooking island waiting for my helping of *goulaschsuppe*, the nasty looks were enough to make me want to skip lunch and run. Maybe that was what house arrest was all about: safety, not punishment. If those two girls from volleyball were any indication, a riot could break out if too many people realized I was in the room.

"It didn't take much figuring out," I heard a voice say from the tables on the other side of the beverage bar. A voice I knew well. "After all," Lucas went on, "the suspect pool is pretty small. And when one person in that pool goes around accusing someone else, you can pretty much guarantee it's guilt talking."

Oh, Lord, help me now.

Lucas had a nice big metaphorical knife, and he wasn't afraid of stabbing me in the back with it. Not after last night. Not when he knew I knew, and the whole school didn't.

"How could you go out with her and not know what she was up to?" someone asked. A girl. With a smoky, unmistakeable voice.

I rounded the beverage bar and saw Vanessa Talbot leaning on the end of the table, her body a lazy, seductive curve.

Vanessa?

Lucas?

I *so* did not want that picture in my head.

Frozen to the spot, I watched him shake his head with fake regret. "I cared about her. And when that happens, sometimes you can be blind to the truth. I wish I'd figured it out sooner."

"You can't blame yourself." Vanessa tossed her glossy hair, and as she did, she saw me standing there. "At least you're rid of her now. We all are. She'll be out of here by the weekend."

Lucas nodded. His back was to me, and the kids at the table were so riveted by all his garbage that they hadn't seen me yet, either. "It took me dumping her to finally send her over the edge and try to get revenge."

"She really broke into your room and planted that stuff?" a blond kid asked. "Wow."

"Such Christian behavior," Vanessa drawled. "But then, considering the people she hangs out with, what can you expect? They're all a bunch of hypocrites."

They could say what they wanted about me, but nobody runs down my friends and gets away with it. I stepped forward, and everyone's gaze swung to me.

Except Lucas's. He glanced over his shoulder and returned his attention to his drink, as if the very sight of me bored him into a coma.

"Watch who you're calling a hypocrite, Vanessa, or someone might find out about your hidden talents with video manipulations," I said. "And both of us know who really sold those answer sheets. I don't need the money. But I hear tuition at Stanford is expensive, and the think tank can't be paying Daddy that much."

"Go to your room, Gillian," Vanessa mocked. "Or don't you know what house arrest means?"

"Oh, I do. And soon Lucas will, too. If he isn't expelled for being the guy who's really behind this, that is. And then what will Stanford do? Or the Olympiad team?"

I spun on my heel and left the dining room.

But it didn't help that the rising tide of noise behind me contained mostly laughter.

chapter 22

RStapleton	Dude. Your sheet was totally bogus.
Source10	What are you talking about?
RStapleton	Math, bonehead. I got a freaking 45! You set me up!
Source10	You must have made a mistake. Took the wrong one.
RStapleton	It was right. The answers were wrong. I want my money back.
Source10	Back off. The sheet was right. You messed up.
RStapleton	You are so going to regret this.
Source10	How? You don't know who I am.

'D EXPECTED MY BRAIN to completely implode while I stared at the English essay questions, but instead, it kicked into gear.

Thanks to Lissa's coaching, here was something I knew. Something I had opinions about. Something I could control. I threw all my brain power into those thousand words and came out on the other side of two hours knowing I'd given it the best I had in me.

And then it was back to the room for ninety minutes until I'd be allowed down to the dining room for supper. After the fiasco at lunch, I was looking forward to it about as much as a root canal.

When Lissa came in, followed by Carly and Shani, it was a welcome relief.

"Hey, girl." Lissa tossed her Kate Spade tote on the bed and flopped down next to it. The others grabbed desk chairs and faced the two of us on our beds. "How'd you do?"

"It went all right," I said. "I don't want to say any more in case I jinx it."

"Which in Gillian-speak means she aced it," Carly told Shani.

"She probably did," Shani allowed.

I looked over at her. This had to be said, and it had to be now. "I want to thank you for what you did earlier. At lunch. On the stairs."

She shrugged. "It was nothing."

"No, it was something." I looked down at my nails, which, I saw, needed shaping in the worst way. "I know we haven't gotten along all that well. I want to apologize for that, and to tell you I thought you were really brave."

She snorted. "What, for getting into that weenie's face? That's not what I'd call it."

"But you didn't have to. You could have just let him say whatever and moved on."

"Maybe. But Carly's had a little practice being in your position, and we got her through that. And you can tell when the person's innocent."

"Yeah?" I huffed a laugh. "How? Anyway, there's only two of us that think so."

"Three," Lissa said.

"Four," Carly added.

"Five, if you count Jeremy," Shani said. "I heard he and Travis had a major blowout on the basketball court this morning. A lot of shouting and bad language. Detentions all around."

"No kidding," I said. "I'd like to have seen that. Travis deserves to have his butt kicked for knuckling under to Lucas and spitting up all those lies."

"Jeremy felt the same, I guess." Shani gazed at me, one corner of her mouth quirked up. "You really don't have a clue, do you?"

I guess I must have looked it. "Huh?"

She shook her head and grinned at the others. "Miss Ninety-eighth Percentile. What are you gonna do?"

"What?" I looked from one to the other of them. "Hello?"

Now Carly was smiling. "Jeremy, *idiota*. He's totally crushing on you and you have no idea."

I goggled at her. "The Jeremy who's madly in love with Shani? That Jeremy?"

Shani hooted and actually slapped her knee. I didn't think people did that outside of books. "He's not madly in love with me, you goofball. He hangs with me because he doesn't have the guts to ask you out. Misery loves company, I guess."

I got my mouth working. "But that day on Angel Island. The two of you took off to be alone."

"We took off, yeah. After you and Lucas went on your little hike. I had to spend the next hour listening to him moaning the blues about it and talking about you incessantly."

I let out a breath, completely flummoxed. Jeremy Clay. Who knew?

Of course, it was completely impossible. Flattering, but impossible. "I am so done with guys," I said. "I made a decision. No dating until after graduation."

Carly's eyebrows disappeared into her wispy bangs. "That's a long time away."

"Exactly. So far, the whole concept has been a disaster."

"How can you say that?" Lissa wanted to know. "Lucas was a disaster. Jeremy's a completely different guy."

"And relatively normal, as far as I can tell," Shani added. "No weird control issues. No pretending to be something he's not.

And to my knowledge, he's never sent anyone flowers, especially not white ones."

They thought it was funny, but I was serious. "I mean it, you guys. It's nice that he likes me and everything, but I can't think about a guy that way. Not for a long time. I am so messed up over this, you wouldn't believe it. Besides, I'll be out of here by the weekend, according to Vanessa Talbot."

Now it was Lissa making the snorting noise. Nai-Nai would not approve of my rude friends, not one bit.

"If Vanessa had her way, the student body would be males only—with her the only girl after all the others got expelled. Don't listen to what she says."

"I think there's something going on with her and Lucas," I told them. "She was at his table at lunch today, looking all slinky."

"Now, there's a match made in heaven," Carly said. "Ew."

"Beauty and the beast," Shani agreed.

"Beauty and the brain."

"The beast and the brain."

We cracked up, and as I looked around at them, these girls who were so loyal even when it wasn't smart for them to be, who hung out with me and made me feel better just being with them . . . well, it was almost enough to make a girl cry.

Or pray.

Thank You, Father, for giving me friends like this. Thank You for Carly, and for giving her the heart to forgive me. I even thank You for Jeremy, who could maybe be a friend if I can figure out how that works.

Be with me now, Lord, and bring the truth to light. I know it's all in Your hands, but I sure hope I don't have to go home to New York in disgrace. If that's part of Your plan, though, help me to be willing for it.

Maybe it was some kind of loophole in the rules, but nobody seemed to care if "house arrest" included having your friends in the room or going down to supper with them. I had to eat in the room, but at least it wasn't like lunch, where I had to walk into the dining room by myself. With my friends around me, I could almost fool myself that everything was normal.

Almost.

As soon as we walked through the big double doors, the tension rose up and smacked us in the face. Rory Stapleton, flushed and shaking, stood next to the popular kids' table. Callum McCloud was eating like his life depended on it. Vanessa lounged against the end of a neighboring table where Lucas sat, watching Rory as though he were auditioning for *American Idol*. And DeLayne Geary and Brett Loyola were watching him, too, as they slowly edged their way toward the door, leaving their food abandoned next to Callum, where they'd been sitting.

"Who are you?" Rory demanded of the room in general, circling, his hands flung out ready to grab. "Come on, Source10, be a man and show yourself. Take some responsibility!"

"Rory, give it a rest," Brett called. "Source10 is that Chang chick. Everybody knows that."

"No, it isn't, you dope. She's on lockdown with no fricking phone or computer and I got an IM from the guy this morning!"

The students looked at one another, and Rory saw it.

"She could have used the computer lab," someone said.

"Didn't you hear me say *lockdown*?" Rory's face was getting redder. I wondered if anybody knew First Aid. "I want to know who Source10 is. I want him to face me. And I want my grand back— I'm not paying for his lousy product."

Lissa looked at me. So did Carly. Both of them telegraphed "What are you going to do?" with their eyes.

I had nothing to lose. Not one single thing.

"Source10 is Lucas Hayes," I said clearly, taking three steps into the center of the dining room and projecting all the way into the kitchen. Thank you, freshman theater. "I didn't plant those exam sheets in his backpack. I *found* them in there."

Lucas turned with a huge smirk on his face. "And what were you doing in my room in the first place, Gillian? Missing me?"

"No," I said steadily. "You wouldn't give me back my property, so I went to get it myself." I held up my arm so he could see the bracelet.

"Thief," he said. "Burglar. What are you doing here, anyway? Curzon put you under house arrest because you're the guilty one."

I glanced at Rory, who was staring at Lucas, all the color drained out of his face. "Oh, I'm sure you'll be talking to Curzon," I said pleasantly. "If there's anything left once Rory gets done with you."

"Is it true?" Rory said to me. "It's him?"

I nodded. "Think about all the computer classes he's taken. Hacking into the server is a piece of cake for him."

"Or for you," Lucas said. "Nice smoke screen for your own hidden talents, Gillian."

"I can hack my brothers' laptops," I told him. "Not a secure server. That would be *your* talent."

"I want my money back, too." DeLayne Geary had almost reached the door, but she turned back, her eyes snapping with rage. "What'd you do with it?"

Lucas turned his palms up. "Why don't you ask Gillian?"

"Because I'm asking you."

"Then you won't get an answer, because I don't have one."

Lissa began circling to the left. I don't think anyone but me noticed—Carly and Shani were too busy getting ready to body-check anyone who tried to come after me, and everyone else was riveted on the drama.

"What about the PayPal account?" somebody shouted from the back. "Grab him and force him to open it up."

"What PayPal account?" Lucas sounded exasperated. "What is the matter with you g—"

Splat. A ripe Bosc pear from one of the fruit bowls on each table clocked him on the side of the head.

"Hey!" he howled, and grabbed a plum. He whipped it in the direction the pear had come from—narrowly missing Vanessa Talbot as she sashayed toward Callum McCloud, right through the empty space in the middle where Lucas and Rory and I were facing off.

"Watch it!" Callum grabbed a granola bar and overhanded it at him, but Lucas smacked it out of the air and with a fast redirect, sent it into Rory's chest. Who said geeks were bad at sports? His reflexes were as fast as any I'd ever seen.

Another plum whistled past my ear and splatted on Lucas's shoulder, making a round reddish-purple stain on his white shirt. Okay, this was going to get ugly. I grabbed Shani's and Carly's wrists and backed up until I could feel the edge of a table against my legs, then got it between me and him.

Which put his aim off just enough so that the full carton of milk he'd aimed at my head went sailing over my right shoulder instead, cartwheeling off some poor freshman and showering her in two-percent.

As if someone had flipped a switch of boiling tension, the dining room erupted in shrieks and yells as kids grabbed whatever they could lay their hands on and took sides. The Science Club abandoned their leader and ran for their lives, their hands over their heads as bits of tomato and mozzarella on focaccia rained all over them.

The whole junior class must have picked this moment to be in the dining room, and they made the most of it.

"Come on!" Shani tried to drag me to the door. "They'll hear this in the staff lounge. If the teachers catch you in here, you're dead."

"Wait—we can't go without Lissa!"

We both whirled and tried to find her in the melee. "There she is, under the table!" Carly screamed. "Lissa!"

Lissa crawled out from under the abandoned Science Club table with a backpack.

A very familiar silver-and-black backpack.

I gasped. "What is she doing?"

She ripped it open, rummaged around inside, and yanked out a single sheet of paper. A huge grin spread across her face, and she tracked the room with her gaze until she found me. Then she gave me a victory thumbs-up.

"Oh, my gosh." I squared two and two with lightning speed. "It's the Bio final she bought."

I leaped onto the nearest table and put two fingers in my mouth. I don't have three brothers for nothing. My whistle could shatter glass.

"Look!" I shouted. "Proof! Lissa's got proof!"

She climbed onto the nearest table, too, holding Lucas's backpack up like a sport fisherman displaying a record weight swordfish. "Look what I just found in his backpack," she yelled. "The answer sheet I bought from him last night—the one he chickened out on this morning because he knew we were onto him!"

"Liar!" Lucas screamed, apple juice dripping from his chin. "You planted it!"

"Oh, come on, Lucas," I called. "That story's not going to work twice."

And that was all I got a chance to say, because Rory tackled him from behind. Two more juniors jumped into the fray—one of them the beefy chick who had spit on me that morning—and Lucas disappeared, still screaming, under a sea of angry bodies.

A huge crash made us all jump, and the double doors bounced off the walls to reveal Mr. Milsom in full combat mode. "WHAT IS THE MEANING OF THIS?"

Ms. Tobin and Dr. Arnzen pelted in close on his heels—and the first thing they saw was me, standing on the table.

"Miss Chang, get down from there at once and go to your room!" With both arms, Ms. Tobin grabbed me around the waist and half-dragged, half-swung me off it.

"Wait!" I panted. "Wait, Ms. Tobin. It's Lucas. He's the one. Lissa has proof, right there in her hand!"

On the other side of the room, surfing that dining table, Lissa screamed encouragement at the heap of people on top of Lucas. She looked like a California Valkyrie, the answer sheet in her hand waving like a flag.

"Miss Mansfield, get down *at once*." The headmistress was no slouch at projecting, either. In fact, you could have heard her in Tiburon as she strode in. "Stop that fighting and give me order or I'll suspend the lot of you!"

The last plum bounced wetly off a sophomore and fell to the ground. The students on top of Lucas untangled themselves and got to their feet. People at tables in the back looked at each other and began to edge toward the kitchen doors, which led into a secondary hallway and an outside fire door.

Lissa jumped down from her table and handed both backpack and answer sheet to Ms. Curzon. "Here it is, ma'am. The answer sheet that was supposed to be in Locker 254 this morning. I found it just now in Lucas's backpack. He's your criminal, not Gillian."

Ms. Curzon took both, and her glance flicked over the answer sheet. Then she turned to face Lucas, who was struggling to break Rory's grip. "Well, Hayes? What do you have to say for yourself?"

Hayes, huh? No more cozy first names for you, sunshine.

"Nothing," he snapped. "This is a setup engineered by an ex-girlfriend with an axe to grind."

"Is that so? Well, hopefully some time confined to your room will loosen up a few facts."

"You can talk to my dad's lawyer."

She raised her eyebrows in an amused smile. "Thank you so much. I didn't realize you expected us to accuse you of anything."

Lucas's shoulders sank as he realized the trap he'd just sprung for himself. "I—I meant—you—"

"That will be all, Hayes. Mr. Milsom, please escort him to his room. No class privileges. No dining room privileges. His room-mate may bring him a tray three times a day. And I want Security on his door until we get this sorted."

Lucas stalked out, Mr. Milsom attached to him like a ball and chain.

And still no one moved. They all looked like a movie audience, waiting for the Easter egg at the end of the credits. Ms. Tobin still gripped my wrist, but as Lucas passed us, she loosened her hold and then finally dropped it altogether as Ms. Curzon approached me.

"Miss Chang." She considered the tangle of spaghetti on the floor in front of my shoe, then lifted her gaze to mine. "Are you responsible for this astonishing display of epic bad manners?"

That was debatable. But hadn't I predicted there would be a riot when people figured out I was in here? "Yes, ma'am."

"Do you stand by your statement of last night?"

"Yes, ma'am."

"Are you prepared to testify to that effect in front of the school board?"

"Yes, ma'am."

"Then it seems I owe you an apology."

I stopped myself from saying "Yes, ma'am" just in time.

She raised her voice so the entire bedraggled and dripping student population could hear her. "Gillian Chang, I apologize for taking Lucas's part instead of listening and carefully weighing the evidence you had to offer. You are cleared of all suspicion, and the suspension will be expunged from your school record."

Wow. A public apology by the headmistress? That took guts. And honesty.

"Thank you, ma'am."

But she wasn't finished. "You are, however, still guilty of entering the boys' dormitory and a boy's room." At least she didn't say *consort* in front of everybody. "You will serve your detention this evening—immediately, in fact—by assisting the housekeeping staff in cleaning up this appalling mess."

As my mouth fell open in dismay, the kids around me began to laugh. And then someone started to clap. Hot tears of humiliation flooded my eyes as I realized that Shani was clapping. And Carly. And even Lissa, who I'd thought was my friend.

And then I actually looked at them. Really, honestly looked.

They weren't laughing *at* me. They were clapping *for* me. The sound of applause rolled over me in a wave and I began to laugh, too. Because really, we all looked completely goofy, covered in food, dripping on the floor . . . goofy and a little bit crazy, and a whole lot happy.

And even though it took me nearly three hours, I had to admit, as I scraped the remains of the Bosc pears up off the glossy hardwood floor, that there were worse ways to spend a detention than cleaning up the field where God and my friends had fought on my side—and savored the taste of victory.

It only goes to show that in the end, it's all about us, isn't it?

SPENCER ACADEMY

American Association of Physics Teachers
One Physics Ellipse
College Park, MD 20740

Re: Physics Olympiad

On behalf of Spencer Academy, I very much regret
to inform you that our student, Lucas Hayes, must
surrender his place among the semifinalists for this
year's Physics Olympiad.

Mr. Hayes has been caught in behavior of a damaging
and fraudulent nature, and we no longer consider him
an appropriate representative of our institution. In fact,
he is no longer enrolled here.

I wish each and every semifinalist the very best of luck
in the final round.

Sincerely yours,

Terence Arnzen, Ph.D.
Dean of Sciences
Spencer Academy

chapter 23

YOU'D THINK THE SOUND of the rain flinging itself against the common room's windows would be depressing, but the contrast between the storm outside and the snug comfort inside only made me happy. Of course, a lot of things were making me happy today, on the last day of term.

Lucas was expelled.

Beefy Chick came up to me this morning and apologized.

I got an Incomplete in my efforts with the personal trainer— but it was better than the F that I deserved, and it meant I never had to run one more lap of the track in my entire life.

I still didn't know how I'd done in AP Chem or English, but all in all, life was good.

Except for one thing. Okay, two things.

One, I was not looking forward to spending my entire spring break at home, being nitpicked by Nai-Nai and keeping my mom company during my dad's inevitable hours of overtime.

And two . . . "Have you guys seen Shani today?" I asked.

Lissa lounged in one of the overstuffed chairs, her legs hanging over the arm. I'd lent her Camy Tang's new chick-lit novel, and she was devouring it—along with the bowl of popcorn in her lap.

She looked up and popped a corn in her mouth. "I saw her in the gym this morning. Why?"

"I just wondered how she's doing, that's all."

"Doing how?" Carly, stretched out on one of the couches, opened her eyes and pulled her earphones out.

"Belief-wise," I said. "Has anyone talked with her about it lately?"

"Here you guys are. I've been looking all over."

The girl herself strolled into the common room, with Jeremy right behind her, carrying a six-pack of soda.

"Hey, Jeremy," I said brightly in a "just friends" kind of voice. You know.

"Hey, Gillian. They had one case of Weinhard's Orange Cream in the dining room, so I swiped it."

"Ooh, my favorite." Lissa swung her legs down and helped herself to cream soda, then offered what was left in her bowl to the newcomers. Fortunately she wasn't down to the unpopped kernels in the bottom yet.

"So," Shani said. "Who wants to talk to whom about what? What'd I miss?"

Carly and I glanced at each other. "I was just wondering about you," I said slowly. "Not talking behind your back or anything, but asking these guys if they knew how you were doing with—with your belief."

She smiled a little half smile. "Trust you to come right out with it."

"I do that," I said quietly.

She slumped in one corner of the couch and rubbed her thumb in the condensation on her bottle. "I don't know. I've been doing a lot of thinking."

"And some of us have been doing a lot of praying," Jeremy said.

She smiled at him, and I tilted my head. Was that a "just friends" smile? Had she changed her mind about him? And why did I care? I'd just given him a "just friends" hello, hadn't I?

"I don't know if praying works," she said. "It just seems to make things harder."

"You can say that again," Carly said.

Shani nodded. "You're sitting there going, hello God, can You help me out on this one, and how do you know if He's even listening?"

"He's listening," Lissa said with conviction. "He knows what you need before you even say it."

"So then how come I got a C+ in History?"

"Probably for the same reason I did." Lissa sighed. "Because I completely blanked on every date I ever knew."

"And because all of us were stressed out of our minds," I put in. "But God knew that. Maybe He didn't focus on our exams, but He made sure everything else all came out right. Believe me, Carly and I had the most to lose."

"Yeah, but you already believe. Who says He was listening to me?"

"He was," Jeremy said. "He knows everything. The fact that you were asking means that He was listening." I looked at him in surprise. That was pretty profound. "That's all we can do, right? Ask. Tell Him stuff. That's where belief comes in. Faith is when you leave the answer up to Him."

Whoa. Maybe I'd better rethink this "just friends" thing. Or was it already too late?

"And like Gillian said, He totally came through." Lissa hunted down the last kernels in the bottom of the bowl.

"Hm." Shani was quiet for a minute. "So, how do I get from asking Him stuff to having faith and all that?"

"Take it one step at a time," I said with a glance at Jeremy. *Lord, did You pull the two of us into this room with her right now for a reason? Help me out, here.* "All He wants to do is hear you asking Him. He loves that. If you do that, He'll take it from there."

"She's right." Jeremy grinned at her. "I know this is pretty personal, but we're all here for you."

"But I have to go back to Chicago in the morning," she said with a groan. "What if I need you guys during spring break? What if I get all messed up and I can't take it?"

"Give me your phone." Lissa held out a hand. "I'll program all our numbers into it. You can call any of us whenever you feel like it."

"How come you don't want to go home?" I asked. Maybe that was more personal than she wanted to get. But something in the set of her mouth, the unhappiness in her eyes, forced the words between my lips.

She lifted a shoulder. "It's just me and the staff and that big old house. Mom's in Florida with my grandparents and Dad's who knows where on business. They try to schedule it so they're both home when I am, but sometimes it doesn't work out." She pasted on a smile. "On the bright side, I get to watch anything I want. On every TV in every room in the house. Which comes to, like, eighteen."

"Why don't you come to New York with me?" I heard myself say, and then blinked in total surprise. Where had *that* come from?

She gawked at me, the chandelier earrings she wore with her sleek updo swinging. "What?"

"Good idea," Jeremy said immediately. "I'm in Connecticut. Two hours on the train and we can hang together."

"Go shopping," Lissa said dreamily.

"Or not," Jeremy retorted.

"Go to the Met," Carly said. "And Broadway and stuff."

"I have a huge room with a guest bed." I was warming up to this in a hurry. "You can protect me from my grandmother, and she'll feed you *shui jao* and pork buns until you explode."

"Okay, whatever *shui jao* is," Shani said. "I'm good with grandmothers."

"Steamed dumplings," Lissa explained. "Her mom sent us a bunch in a care package once. They're to die for."

"I'm in." Shani's gaze met mine, with surprise on both sides. "Thanks."

Lissa got up and tossed the last of the popcorn in the trash, then put her glass soda bottle in the recycling container by the door. "I've gotta go pack, you guys. We're heading down to Santa Barbara at nine or some horrible early hour. See you at breakfast."

Within a few minutes, Shani and Carly had melted away, too, leaving me alone on the couch with Jeremy and a couple of random kids on the other side of the room watching TV.

"That was nice of you," he said. "To invite her home with you."

"I had no idea I was going to until it just . . . popped out. I hope it turns out okay." I looked down at my hands. "We haven't exactly had a beautiful friendship up until now."

"You will."

"You sound pretty confident."

"She's nice. A little in-your-face, but so are you."

I smiled. "Thanks a lot."

"I meant that in a good way. You're honest. Most people know where they stand with you."

More honest with other people than with myself sometimes, but I didn't say that to him. Maybe being honest with yourself was something you had to learn. I was a work in progress.

He closed one hand inside the other, then switched them. "So . . . where do I stand?"

I blinked and focused on him. "What do you mean?"

"Come on, Gillian. Are you going to make me say it?"

"Say what?" What was he talking about?

His knuckles turned white. "That I think you're amazing, and it's taken me almost three months to get you alone to tell you?" The words fell out of him in a rush.

For the second time in a week, my mouth opened and nothing came out.

"I know you're probably still recovering from Lucas and everything, but if you think that maybe you'd like to do something together—not now," he said hastily, "but sometime—then I'd be . . . available."

I could feel the hot color creeping into my cheeks. In fact, my whole body temperature seemed to go up ten degrees and my heart began to pound.

"Would that be before or after the two hours on the train to come and see us?" I said carefully. "You promised, remember."

"That would be after. When we're back here. And just for your information," he added, the dimples deepening in his cheeks, "I always keep my promises."

When You yank two people into a room, Lord, You don't mess around, do You?

"You're not the only one," I said, and smiled at him.

Spring break—and maybe even next term—were definitely looking up.

about the author

Shelley Adina wrote her first teen novel when she was thirteen. It was rejected by the literary publisher to whom she sent it, but he did say she knew how to tell a story. That was enough to keep her going through the rest of her adolescence, a career, a move to another country, a B.A. in Literature, an M.A. in Writing Popular Fiction, and countless manuscript pages.

Shelley is a world traveler and pop culture junkie with an incurable addiction to designer handbags. She knows the value of a relationship with a gracious God and loving Christian friends and loves writing about fun and faith—with a side of glamour. Between books, Shelley loves traveling, listening to and making music, and watching all kinds of movies.

IF YOU LIKED

the fruit of my lipstick,

check out the third book in the All About Us series:

be strong and curvaceous

available January 2009

wherever books are sold

chapter 1

BE CAREFUL WHAT you wish for.

I used to think that was the dumbest saying ever. I mean, when you wish for something, by definition it's wonderful, right? Like buying a new dress for a party. Or getting a roommate as cool as Gillian Chang or Lissa Mansfield. Or having a guy notice you after six months of being invisible. Before last term, I used to think having wishes like that come true would be the best.

I don't anymore.

Let me back up a little. My name is Carolina Isabella Aragon Velasquez . . . but that doesn't fit on school admission forms, so when I started first grade it got shortened up to Carolina Aragon— Carly to my friends. Up until I was a sophomore, I lived with my mom and dad, my older sister, and little brother in a huge house in Monte Sereno, just south of Silicon Valley. My dad's company invented some kind of security software for stock exchanges, and he and everyone who worked for him got rich.

Then came what Dad calls Black Thursday and the stock market crash, and suddenly my mom was leaving him and going to live with her parents in Veracruz, Mexico, to be an artist and find herself. Alana finished college and moved to Austin. Antony and I stayed with Dad in a condo about the size of our old living room, and since he spends so much time on the road, where I've found myself since September is boarding school.

The spring term started in April, and as I got out of the limo Dad sends me back to Spencer Academy in every Sunday night even though I'm perfectly capable of taking the train, I couldn't help but feel a little bubble of optimism deep inside. Call me corny, but the news that Vanessa Talbot and Brett Loyola had broken up just before spring break had made my ten days off the happiest I'd had since my parents split up. Even flying to Veracruz and being introduced to my mother's boyfriend hadn't put a dent in it.

Ugh. Okay, I lied. *So* not going there.

Thinking about Brett now. Dark, romantic eyes. Curly dark hair, cut short because he's the captain of the rowing team. Broad shoulders. Fabulous clothes he wears as if he doesn't care where he got them.

Oh, yeah. Much better.

Lost in happy plans for how I'd finally get his attention (I was signing up to be a history tutor first thing because let's face it, he needs me), I unlocked the door to my room and staggered in with my duffel bags.

My hands loosened and I dropped everything with a thud.

There were Vuitton suitcases all over the room. Enough for an entire *family*. In fact, some of them were so big you could put a family *in* them—the kids, at least.

"Close the door, why don't you?" said a bored British voice with a barely noticeable roll on the *r*. A girl stepped out from behind the wardrobe door.

Red hair in an explosion of curls.

Fishnet stockings to *here* and glossy ankle boots.

Blue eyes that grabbed you and made you wonder why she was so . . . not interested in whether you took another breath.

Ever.

"Who are you?" How come no one had told me I was getting a roommate? And who could have prepared me for this anyway?

"Mac," she said, returning to the depths of the closet. Most people would have said, "What's your name?" She didn't.

"I'm Carly." Did I feel lame or what?

She looked around the door. "Pleasure. Looks like we're to be roommates." Then she went back to hanging things up.

There was no point in restating the obvious. I gathered my scattered brains and tried to remember what a good hostess was supposed to do. "Did someone show you where the dining room is? Supper is between five and six-thirty and I usually—"

"Carrie. I expected my own room," she said, as if I hadn't been talking. "Who do I talk to?"

"It's *Carly*. And Ms. Tobin's the dorm mistress for this floor."

"Fine. What were you saying about dinner?"

I took a breath and remembered that one of us was what my brother calls *couth*. As opposed to *un*. "You're welcome to come with me and my friends if you want."

Pop went the latches on one of the trunks. She threw up the lid and looked at me over the top of it, her reddish eyebrows lifting in amusement.

What was so funny?

"Thanks so much. But I'll pass."

Okay, even I have my limits. I picked up my duffel, dropped it on the end of my bed, and left her to it. Maybe by the time I got back from dinner, she'd have convinced Ms. Tobin to give her a room in another dorm.

The way things were going, she'd probably demand the head-mistress's suite.

"WHAT A *MO guai nuer*," Gillian said over her tortellini and asparagus. "I can't believe she snubbed you like that."

"You of all people," Lissa said. "Who wouldn't hurt someone's feelings for anything."

"I wanted to," I confessed. "If I could have come up with something scathing. But you know how you freeze when you realize you've just been cut off at the knees?"

"What happened to your knees?" Jeremy Clay put his plate of linguine down and slid in next to Gillian. They traded a smile that made me feel sort of hollow inside—not the way I'd felt after Mac's little setdown, but like I was missing out on something. Like they had a secret and weren't telling.

You know what? Feeling sorry for yourself is not the way to start off a term. I smiled at Jeremy. "Nothing. How was your break? Did you get to New York?"

He glanced at Gillian again. "Yeah, I did."

Argh. Men. Never ask them a yes/no question. "And? Did you guys have fun? Shani said she had a blast after the initial shock."

Gillian grinned at me. "That's a nice way of saying my grandmother scared the stilettos off her. At first. But then Nai-Nai realized Shani could eat even my brothers under the table no matter what she put in front of her, so after that they were best friends."

"My grandmother's like that, too," I said, nodding in sympathy. "She thinks I'm too thin so she's always making pots of mole and stuff. Little does she know."

It's a fact that I have way too much junk in my trunk. Part of the reason I'm majoring in history with a minor in fashion design is that when I make my own clothes, I can drape and cut to accentuate the positive and make people forget that big old negative following me around.

"You aren't too thin or too fat." Lissa is a perfect six. She's also the most loyal friend in the world. "You're just right."

Time to change the subject. The last thing I wanted to do was talk about my body in front of a guy, even if he belonged to someone else. "So did you guys get to see *Pride and Prejudice: The Musical*? Shani said you were bribing someone to get tickets."

"Close," Gillian said. "My mom is on the orchestra's board so we got seats in the first circle. You'd have loved it. Costume heaven."

"I would have." I sighed. "Why did I have to go to Veracruz for spring break? How come I couldn't have gone to New York, too?"

I hoped I sounded rhetorical. The truth was, I didn't have any money for things like trips to New York to see the hottest musical on Broadway with my friends. Or for the clothes to wear once I got there—unless I made them myself.

"That's it, then." Gillian waved a miniature tomato on the end of her fork. "Next break you and Lissa are coming to see me. Not in the summer—no one in their right mind stays in the city in July. But at Christmas."

"Maybe we'll go to Veracruz," Lissa suggested. "Or you guys can come to Santa Barbara and I'll teach you to surf."

"That sounds perfect," I said. Either of Lissa's options wouldn't cost very much. New York, on the other hand, would. "I like warm places for my winter holidays."

"Good point," Gillian conceded. "So do I."

"Notice how getting through the last term of junior year isn't even on your radar?" Jeremy asked no one in particular. "It's all about the vacations with you guys."

"Vacations are our reward," Gillian informed him. "You have to have something to get you through finals."

"Right, like you have to worry," he scoffed.

"She does," Lissa said. "She has to get *me* through finals."

While everyone laughed, I got up and walked over to the dessert bar. *Crème brulée,* berry parfaits, and German chocolate cake. You know you're depressed when even Dining Services' *crème brulée*—which puts a dreamy look in the eyes of just about everyone who goes here—doesn't get you excited.

I had to snap out of it. Thinking about all the things I didn't have and all the things I couldn't do would get me precisely nowhere. I had to focus on the good things.

My friends.

How lucky I was to have won the scholarship that got me into Spencer.

And how much luckier I was that in two terms, no one had figured out I was a scholarship kid.

Come on, Carly. Just because you can't flit off to New York to catch a show or order up the latest designs from Fashion Week doesn't mean your life is trash. Get ahold of your sense of proportion.

I took a berry parfait—blueberries have lots of antioxidants—and turned back to the table just as the dining room doors opened. They seemed to pause in their arc, giving my new roommate plenty of time to stroll through before they swung shut behind her. She'd changed out of the fishnets into a simple leaf-green dress with a black sweater and heels that absolutely screamed Paris—Rue de la Paix, to be exact. Number 11, to be even more exact. Gaultier.

My knees nearly buckled with envy.

"Is *that* your roommate?" Lissa asked.

Mac seemed completely unaware that everyone in the dining room was watching her as she floated across the floor like a runway model, collected a plate of Portobello mushroom ravioli and salad, and sat at the empty table next to the big window that faced out onto the quad.

Lissa was still gazing at her, puzzled. "I know I've seen her before."

I hardly heard her.

Because not only had the redhead cut into line ahead of Vanessa Talbot, Dani Lavigne, and Emily Overton, she'd also invaded their prime real estate. No one sat at that table unless they'd sacrificed a freshman at midnight or whatever it was that people had to do to be friends with them.

When Vanessa turned with her plate, I swear I could hear the collective intake of breath as her gaze locked on the stunning interloper sitting with her back to the window, calmly cutting her ravioli with the edge of her fork.

"Uh oh," Gillian murmured. "Let the games begin."

chapter 2

VANESSA, DANI, and Emily formed a fighting V and strolled to the table with their plates.

"Excuse me, do we know you?" Dani asked politely.

"Poor thing," Mac said. "I'm so sorry about the short-term memory loss. No, we haven't met."

Dani's mouth worked while she tried to figure out whether or not she'd just been insulted.

"My name is Vanessa Talbot."

"Pleasure. Mac."

"Mac?" Emily repeated. "What kind of a name is that?"

Vanessa ignored her. "And you're sitting in my seat."

Mac looked at the empty table, which could seat eight. "Really?"

"Really. I suggest you move. My friends and I sit here. Everyone knows that except clueless noobs."

Mac's face dimpled with laughter, as if Vanessa had told her a real knee-slapper. "I'd say you were the clueless one, if you think *that's* any reason to move. Sit where you like, darling. I'm eating." And she went back to her pasta.

Vanessa's face set as though it had been cast in porcelain. "This is the last time I'll ask you nicely. After that . . ."

Mac glanced at her. "What? You'll turn me into a ferret?"

Even from where I stood, I could see the color burn its way into Vanessa's cheeks. When was the last time anyone had stood up to her? Certainly not this year.

Well, except for Gillian and Lissa, our first term here.

"You wish," Vanessa said. "Try a social outcast."

"From your society?" Mac drawled. "What a terrible loss."

"Do you have any idea who she is?" Dani hissed. "You big, red-headed loser."

"Vanessa Talbot. Hmm." Mac consulted an imaginary PDA in her head. "Daughter of a former U.N. Secretary and Eurotrash." She rolled her eyes. "Such a bore."

"At least you've done your research," Vanessa snapped. "Unfortunately, I can't say the same about you. You don't seem to be anyone."

"No one you'd know, and I'd prefer to keep it that way." Mac looked the three of them over. "Are you staying or going?"

I tried to keep my grin under control as a ripple of something that was almost laughter sighed through the room. This was the best thing that had happened since the infamous food fight last term, but nobody dared to laugh outright. The truth was, Vanessa was stuck. If she stalked off to another table, she and her posse would lose their territory. If she didn't, she'd have to let Mac sit with them—and that might imply she'd accepted her.

Can you say *lose/lose*?

Mac smiled—not a victorious or malicious smile, but the sweet kind. Like frosting that comes in a can—close enough to fool you into thinking it's the real thing. With a huff of impatience, as though she didn't have any more time to waste on Mac while her food got cold, Vanessa slid into a seat.

I finally got my feet moving and took my blueberries back to our table, where Gillian and Lissa telegraphed "Did you see that?" and "What's going to happen now?" to me with their eyes.

It didn't take long for us to find out. Vanessa was not the kind of girl who let anything go unresolved—especially a power struggle. I think I'd only been here a week or two when I learned that. She was so used to winning that it never occurred to her there could be any other outcome.

She made a show of picking at her lunch, then reached for her drink. Dani said something to her, and whoops! Her soda went flying . . . all over Mac's lime-green Chanel dress.

I would have screamed and burst into tears.

Mac stood slowly, looking down at her lap, where a brown stain spread. Coke dripped slowly from the hem to the floor.

"Oh, I'm so sorry," Vanessa said, while Dani made tsking noises and Emily offered a handful of napkins. "I hope it's washable."

Every female in the room knew it wasn't. Every one of us knew Vanessa had just done the equivalent of painting a mustache on the Mona Lisa.

"Eurotrash." Mac finally sighed. Lifting her head, she gave it a slow, regretful shake. "What a pity a person can't overcome their DNA."

And she floated out of the room as effortlessly as she'd come in, leaving Vanessa fuming behind her.

Vanessa 1. Mac 1.

I wondered when round two would begin—and what kind of fallout there would be. At the moment I couldn't see any positives about being Mac's roommate.

None at all.

AFTER DINNER, LISSA and Gillian came back to my room to talk over the excitement.

"It's like the Slayer," Lissa said. "In every generation there can only be one, you know?"

"You are such a dork." Gillian flopped down on my bed. "But you're right. I can't see this going on for very long. One of them is going to kill the other or get her expelled by the end of the week. And it's only Tuesday." She blinked. "Is all this stuff hers?"

"Yep." I sank into my desk chair, leaving the other end of my bed for Lissa. "I left all my Vuittons at home." Not.

"Wow. And I thought I had a lot of stuff."

"I just don't know where she—"

The door opened and Mac stepped in. "Company?" she inquired pleasantly. "Lovely."

Turning her back on us, she shrugged off the black sweater and unzipped the dress, tossing it in a corner. Completely unconcerned that there were two people she'd never met in the room and she was in her underwear—oh my, La Perla, too—she kicked off her shoes and pulled on a pair of jeans and a T-shirt.

"Will—will you be able to do something about the dress?" I asked, hoping I sounded concerned. There was no hope of being friends, of course, but a catastrophe like this deserved some mourning over the body, at least.

She glanced at it. "Oh, I don't know. Haven't the faintest idea where to get it seen to. I'll probably just order another one."

From Chanel Couture. In Paris. *Sure, I'll take two.*

"It's still a shame. Vanessa is such a—" Gillian stopped herself, then crossed the carpet and held out a hand. "I'm Gillian Chang. Carly says you're called Mac. Is that short for something?"

Mac ran a glance over her—tennies, jeans, cashmere sweater, face—and shook hands. "Hello. It's short for MacPhail."

Lissa got up, too. "I'm Lissa Mansfield. It's a pleasure to meet anyone with the spine to stand up to Vanessa. What's your first name?"

She got the same once-over before Mac spoke. "I prefer Mac."

O-o-kay. I took a tiny bit of comfort from the fact that she was an equal-opportunity snubber.

But unlike me, Lissa didn't go away quietly. "You know, I could swear we've met before. Your face is familiar for some reason."

"I don't see how." Mac picked up a brush and ran it through her unruly curls. "I've never been to California in my life."

"What about New York? Montreal? Vancouver?"

Mac shook her head, twisting her hair up and securing it with a clip.

"MacPhail. Are you from the U.K.? Scotland?"

"Originally. I go to school in London, of course. We have to do one term of cultural exchange. That's how I ended up here." She made it sound as though she were researching pygmies in Borneo—against her will.

"What was your first choice?" I meant it as a joke, but she didn't take it that way.

"New Zealand."

Oh. Never mind. Was it possible to have thirty seconds of conversation with this girl without being flattened? Did she do this to everybody, or was I the only lucky one?

"Well, I'm glad you came here," Gillian said. "Vanessa needs a little humility."

"Oh? What have you got against her?"

Whoa. Was she switching sides? Did money and European connections stick together, no matter what?

"Me? Nothing. Except that she tried to steal my boyfriend last term. And she set Lissa up—"

"I don't think Mac would be very interested in that," Lissa interrupted. "Come on, Gillian. Carly, are you coming to prayer circle? It's Tuesday."

"Absolutely. Just let me change my blouse. I got pesto on this one."

Mac looked from them waiting by the door to me tearing off

the babydoll top I had on and reaching for a tailored blouse that made my waist look half an inch smaller. "Prayer circle?" she said in the same tone some people would say, "Head lice?"

"Sure." Gillian smiled at her. "Tuesday nights, seven o'clock. Everyone's welcome."

"Term always starts on a Wednesday," Lissa put in. "It kicks it off on a good note, I think."

"Is that, like, a Christian thing?" Mac asked.

Lissa nodded. I finished buttoning up the blouse and gave it a final tug. *Jump right in.* "Want to come?"

Mac actually shuddered. "I'm going out. Where do you lot party around here?"

We exchanged a look. "You'd have to ask someone like Vanessa about that. She probably knows where the underage clubs are."

"The what?"

"Underage clubs," I repeated. "You're sixteen, right?"

"Do you seriously think I'd waste my time with children?"

"Let me rephrase. You'd have to ask Vanessa about that. She probably knows where you can get a fake I.D."

"What has that got to do with clubbing? Do you know or not?"

I gave up. "I don't. Sorry." I grabbed Lissa and Carly by the arms and hustled them out the door. "Have fun."

We were halfway to room 216 before anyone spoke. "I know what I'm praying about tonight," Lissa said.

"No kidding." My voice sounded grim, even to me. "And while you're at it, pray that Tobin finds her another room."